AT ANY
COST

AT ANY
COST

Mandy Baxter

ZEBRA BOOKS
KENSINGTON PUBLISHING CORP.
http://www.kensingtonbooks.com

ZEBRA BOOKS are published by

Kensington Publishing Corp.
119 West 40th Street
New York, NY 10018

First Printing: June 2016
ISBN-13: 978-1-4201-4105-4
ISBN-10: 1-4201-4105-8

eISBN-13: 978-1-4201-4106-1
eISBN-10: 1-4201-4106-6

10 9 8 7 6 5 4 3 2 1

Printed in the United States of America

Chapter One

"What in the hell am I going to do with you, Brady?"

Deputy U.S. Marshal Nick Brady worked his jaw as he stared at his chief deputy, Doug Metcalf. Not even three months on the job and already he was being reprimanded. A new record. It had taken his SWAT captain a full year before he'd put Nick's ass in a sling. Obviously he was getting better at pissing off his superior officers.

"Well?" Oh, he was actually looking for an answer? Metcalf passed his hand over what was left of his hair and fixed Nick with a stern eye.

"I suppose you could say, keep up the good work, Brady. Keep taking those fuckers down."

Metcalf snorted. "You'd like that, wouldn't you? Hooking and hauling is what you're supposed to be doing for the next six months. Warrants are off-limits until your probation is over. You've had that badge for all of sixty days and you already think you're some sort of badass fugitive hunter. Shit." The chief looked away, disgusted. "You're lucky your brains haven't been splattered all over some poor son of a bitch's wall by now!"

It wasn't for lack of trying. Nick had joined the USMS for one reason and one reason only: fugitive recovery. Hooking and hauling—babysitting sorry bastards as he transported them to and from court and trying to stay awake while their lawyers attempted to save their law-breaking asses—wasn't what he'd had in mind when he applied for the job. Six months of courts duty would be the death of him, so he did what any ambitious cop would do, he went out and found the action on his own.

"I'm working courts now. So what does it matter what I do with my free time?"

"Yeah, *now.* You were working with the warrants squad for a damned month before anyone realized you weren't with that division! I'll give it to you, Brady, you know how to work the system. How in the hell did you make it past the entrance interviews?" Metcalf asked with disbelief. "You're a smart-assed, insubordinate pain in my ass. I'm starting to think that SWAT gave you a glowing recommendation because they wanted to get rid of you."

Nick had earned every word of that glowing recommendation. He was a *stellar* cop. That's not to say that his coworkers weren't anxious to see him go. They didn't buy into Nick's Wild West mentality. The way he saw it, the only way to catch a criminal was to step a toe over the line that separated him from them. If that meant bending a rule or two, so be it. And if it resulted in one less murdering son of a bitch on the street, even better. Which was why he'd snuck into warrants his first day on the job, rather than reporting to courts like he was supposed to. He didn't want to escort criminals who'd already been caught. He wanted to do the catching.

Man hunters.

That's what they called the marshals on the warrants squads. They were relentless. Like dogs after a bone, they hunted down the most violent and notorious criminals in the U.S.—hell, the *world*. They kicked down doors knowing that once they walked inside a room, they might not ever walk out. And they did it to make the world a better place. To protect innocent people from evil bastards who wanted nothing more than to do harm. Those men were the reason Nick joined the USMS, and they were the reason he wouldn't ever be satisfied playing babysitter to some piece of shit while he had his day in court.

"There's not a man in this district who wants to work with you right now." Nick had never been much of a team player, but that stung. "You're stubborn, cranky, and goddamned bossy. You need to remember something right now: You're the new guy. You don't pay your dues just like every other man out there."—Metcalf stabbed a finger toward the cubicles beyond his door—"not a damned one of them is going to respect you no matter how many fugitives you haul in. This is a brotherhood, Nick. Believe me, you're going to need them as much as they need you."

Nick wasn't opposed to paying his dues. He simply wanted to pay them out in the field. He got brotherhood. It came with the badge. He wasn't trying to alienate anyone. He needed the opportunity to prove himself. "I've made five arrests in two months. That has to count for something."

"Case files that you stole from other deputies' desks."

Okay, so that probably didn't do much for him in the brotherhood department. "I *borrowed* them," Nick stressed. "Put them right back where I found them and even filed the paperwork when I was done."

"Well," Metcalf said dryly. "Wasn't that big of you?"

Nick slumped back in his chair. "Why am I being penalized for doing what we're trained for? Isn't it better for everybody if there's one less bad guy on the streets?"

The chief deputy sighed. "Jesus Christ, Brady. Do you always gotta swim upstream?"

Yeah, he guessed he did. Especially if it was the only way to get shit done. "Warrants are what I want to do. But since I've been reassigned to courts, I haven't missed a day."

Metcalf rested his forehead in his palm. "True, you haven't. But every night, weekend, and hour you're not on shift, you're out hunting fugitives. Nick, you've got to slow down. You're going to burn out and you're not going to be any good to anyone. You put your life in those men's hands and they put theirs in yours. If they can't trust you, they won't work with you. You won't last a year here."

"Fine." Nick let out a gust of breath and raked his fingers through his hair. "What do you want me to do?"

"I want you to take a month off." Nick sat up straight and opened his mouth to protest, but Metcalf cut him off. "This isn't negotiable. Take a month, think about this job, why you want it, and what it's going to take to be successful at it. *Then*, when you come back, you show up when you're supposed to, do your six months of court duty, without any after-hours fugitive hunts. If you can do that, I'll consider taking you off of probation and assigning you to a warrants squad for a full-time rotation. Deal?"

"Do I have a choice?" Nick couldn't do anything about the sourness in his tone.

The chief deputy leveled his gaze. "No. You don't."

"I guess my ass is taking a month off, then."

Without another word, Nick pushed himself out of the chair. This was absolute, utter bullshit. As he made his way down the hallway toward his cubicle, other deputies averted their gazes. No doubt every last one of them knew about the ass chewing he'd just endured. Perfect. His temper mounted with every step he took and it wouldn't be long before Nick lost it entirely. *A month?* Four fucking weeks of suspension—because there was no way this was a vacation—for going out there and arresting slimy bastards who ought to be in jail in the first place. Fan-fucking-tastic.

Nick threw himself down in his chair and swiveled around toward his computer screen. A file folder peeked out from the top desk drawer and he leaned back to look up the hall and down to see if anyone was watching. He pulled the file out and flipped it open to a picture of one of those slimy assholes who'd avoided a jail cell for far too long. Joel Meecum. Supposed *ex*-president of the Black Death motorcycle club and a lying, raping, murdering, gunrunning piece of shit. He'd been on the run for the past four years and hit the top of the USMS's Top 15 Most Wanted list at the beginning of the year. Nick flipped through the file at the notes he'd scribbled down. There was a promising lead in the case. One that everyone else had overlooked. A woman. A rumored ex-girlfriend to be exact. An informant had mentioned to the Oakland PD that Joel put the word out that he'd been looking for his ex, a woman by the name of Kari Hanson, and was willing to pay a healthy reward to anyone who might know where she was. The informant knew someone who knew someone who knew someone and so on, who thought Meecum's old lady was hiding out in Idaho somewhere. A small town in the mountains.

All they knew about Meecum's mysterious ex was that she had a tattoo on the inside of her right wrist. When the guys in Oakland ran her name, nothing had come up, which meant that Hanson might have been an alias. Without much to go on, the lead had gone cold. Something about it had stuck with Nick, though. Meecum never would have gone to the lengths he'd gone to find her if she was inconsequential. He was certain that Kari Hanson was the key to finding Meecum.

Nick looked over his shoulder, feeling a lot like a kid with his dad's *Playboy*. He could make the drive in about nine or ten hours. It wouldn't hurt to check out the lead. It's not like he was hunting a fugitive, per se. Just . . . the ex-old lady of a fugitive.

He opened a search engine on his computer and typed in *McCall, Idaho*. A road trip didn't sound like a bad idea. Besides, there were worse ways to spend a month off.

Livy Gallagher triple-checked the deadbolt on her front door, the locks on the windows that lined the tiny living room, and the ones beside the dining room table. She'd already checked the back door, kitchen windows, and upstairs windows. This had been her nightly routine for almost four full years. One thousand, three hundred and seventy days of checking, double-checking, and triple-checking every lock in the house before she went to bed.

When she did the math, it seemed so much more depressing. She went to sleep every night afraid. Woke up every morning afraid. Went to work, put in her eight hours, drove home, and the entire time, she looked over her shoulder. She'd been running scared for so long, she couldn't remember what it felt like to not be afraid.

With a long sigh she stared through the old warped glass of the antique windows at the snow falling gently outside. A chill danced over her skin, reminding Livy that she'd better rekindle the fire before she went upstairs or she'd be huddled under the electric blanket before midnight. The old house was quaint, in a this-is-where-Norman Bates-lives sort of way. She snorted. Okay, maybe it wasn't that bad, but it didn't scream *welcome*! It had been built around 1912 and along with the modest cabin next door, was one of few remaining houses on

Payette Lake that hadn't been mowed down and replaced with a six-plus-million dollar "cabin" that the owners stayed in maybe once or twice a year. Either way, she'd scored with this old place because it fit her needs to a T. Out of the way and cheap. But it didn't exactly sport the type of modern insulation that retained heat or was even marginally energy efficient. And since there was a snowball's chance in hell that she'd ever have a man to keep her warm in bed, she left it up to her furry tabby cat and electric blanket to get the job done.

Livy let out a groan. She was living the life of a ninety-year-old woman. If not for the athleticism necessary for her winter job, she would have been convinced she was a twenty-five-year-old nonogenarian. She should have been living her life, damn it! Partying, club hopping, sleeping around and making shitty decisions that she'd regret well into her thirties. She should have fallen in love at least three times by now and had her heart broken at least twice. Instead, she was afraid of her own shadow, only talked to people when it was absolutely necessary, and stuck to routines that made people with OCD seem chill.

Livy missed *life*! She hadn't lived in a long damned time and it wasn't fair. She couldn't even remember what it felt like to be carefree. "Shit on a stick!" Her voice carried throughout the quiet house. And now, she was talking to herself. Great.

Livy grabbed her cell from one of the end tables and turned it over in her hand. She rarely used the prepaid phone, and in a few months, she'd recycle it and buy a new one with a new number. Who knew if it would help to protect her? With technology the way it was, she doubted anyone could stay completely hidden for long. Like the phone she'd eventually trade out, she'd put this town behind her soon as well. Four years was a long time. She couldn't allow herself to put down roots.

With a sigh, Livy swiped her finger across the screen and opened the phone app. She dialed her mom's number and left the pad of her finger to hover over the send button. Snow slid from the roof with a scrape against the tin before it landed on the other side of the porch. Livy's heart leaped up into her throat and she stifled a scream. "It's just snow, you moron. Chill the hell out." Her heart hammered against her rib cage and a burst of adrenaline caused her limbs to quake. "Way to rock that tough-girl vibe." Talking to herself *and* freaking out over a snow slide. She was one step away from a padded room.

She cleared the call from the display. She only called her mom once every three months. Still a month to go. Frequent calls were easy to track. At least, that's what she'd learned from watching cop shows. A call every few months wouldn't be as noticeable as one every few weeks. It was safer for the both of them if she kept her distance, no matter how damned lonely she might be.

"Come on, Simon. Let's go to bed." The large tabby gave a forlorn meow as he hopped down from the hearth. "You're such a baby," Livy said. "I'll turn on the electric blanket."

He swished his tail from side to side, obviously pleased. It probably would have been better to own a rottweiler or a nice, loyal pit bull. Simon didn't mind being cooped up, though. A dog—especially a large breed—would have gone stir-crazy shut up in the cabin all the time. Besides, she didn't own Simon for protection. She owned him for company. For a warm body to curl up with when she felt as though the loneliness were sucking the air from her lungs. He was a poor substitute for human companionship, but he was a sweetheart. And unlike a boyfriend, at least Simon would never leave the toilet seat up.

She scooped him up into her arms as she turned off the lamp and headed for the stairs. "Let's get a move on, buddy. It's thank-you notes night on Fallon." Simon purred in her grasp. "I know, right? We're livin' on the razor's edge."

Chapter Two

Nick stared out the window, through the steady fall of snow outside, at the woman he'd spent months researching and the past week tracking down. Sometimes, the key to following even the vaguest lead was simply being too stubborn to let it go. Lucky for Nick, stubborn was the only way he knew to be. A fairly reliable USMS informant had been picked up for petty theft. In order to get out from under a probation violation, he'd offered up info on Meecum's ex. According to the informant, he'd been passing through McCall, Idaho, with a group of buddies for a concert. Among the waitstaff at the venue was a woman who fit the description of Kari Hanson. He'd told the investigating marshal that her nametag read "Livy." The USMS, unable to confirm the intel, assumed the guy had made up the story to get out of being charged.

But not Nick. He'd researched the small town for over a month prior to his mandatory vacation and it had seemed like a promising location for someone to hide out from law enforcement. The town's population barely broke thirty-five hundred. He'd searched DMV records for any vehicles registered to women named Livy. He'd come up empty-handed, but had found two cars registered to women named Olivia. His options had been easy to narrow down from there. One of the Olivias was a seventy-five-year-old retired teacher. Definitely not Meecum's ex. The other had only lived in the county for about four years and other than that, Nick hadn't been able to find anything else out about her. It was like she'd appeared out of thin air, which had only further convinced him that she was, in fact, the woman Joel Meecum had been searching for.

She might be going by Olivia Gallagher now, but that didn't matter. He was on the money. The kitchen of the rented cabin provided the perfect vantage point with a direct view of her driveway, and he watched her talk to her shovel as she moved scoop after scoop of snow. Her grumbles, spoken between bouts of profanity that could be heard even through his kitchen window, had woken him from a deep sleep. Pretty much what he'd expect from a woman who hung out with bikers. Those words would make a sailor proud.

She'd done a damned good job of flying below the radar, but not good enough. No one could simply vanish. Sporting a new name and Social Security number wasn't enough. Living in an obscure town in the middle of BFE wasn't enough. Nick had only set up shop in the cabin across from hers yesterday afternoon. Not even twelve hours in McCall and he had eyes on his target.

She wasn't quite what he'd expected.

She continued to shovel, but struggled as the snow stuck to the metal scoop. With every new shovelful, she was forced to knock the snow out before she could clear another section of it away. Labor intensive, and obviously frustrating as evidenced by the constant string of profanity.

"Frank, you piece of shit! How could you do this to me?"

Nick's lips quirked as Olivia continued on with her tirade, loud enough to wake up everyone on the lane. Well, it would have if anyone else had been living on the lane. He grabbed a notebook from the kitchen counter and scribbled the name Frank with a question mark beside it. According to his research, she lived alone. Maybe Frank was her snowplow guy. Or an ex-boyfriend. That wouldn't make Joel Meecum very happy, would it?

A tingle of excitement raced from the base of Nick's neck down his spine, sending a killer rush of adrenaline through his system. Who needed coffee for a morning jolt when he could live off the excitement he felt every time a lead panned out. He'd hit the jackpot with Olivia. Pure solid gold. He watched as she continued to struggle in the fresh snow, wading through a drift that had to have been pushing three feet as she made her way to the back of the car. In the dull red glow of the taillights of the still-running vehicle, he could barely make out her profile. Two long braids on either side of her head trailed down from a large, slouchy beanie that she pushed back up on her forehead. She was decked out in snow gear: ski pants, coat, gloves. Nick watched as she plopped down on the ground to check something out under the car. Hell, she looked like a little kid whose mom had gotten her dressed for the trek to the bus stop.

Where was she going this early in the morning, anyway? Nick hadn't been there long enough to determine any patterns in her comings and goings yet. This could be part of her daily routine for all he knew. He noted the time in his notebook as he flipped on the light in the kitchen. She straightened, her head turning in his direction. Now was as good a time as any to introduce himself. From the rage-fest going on outside, he already knew that Olivia Gallagher had a bit of a temper. What would a conversation with her reveal?

She continued to wrestle with the snow and Nick left her to it as he headed for the bedroom to get dressed. Her car was buried to the hood in the deep drift; she wasn't leaving anytime soon. And for that matter, neither was he.

The sleepy town in the heart of Idaho had to have taken her some time to get used to after living in Southern California where Meecum was rumored to be hiding out. He wondered how she'd come to the decision to move here. Had she closed her eyes and stabbed her finger down on a map? Motorcycle-club life was a far cry from the picturesque tourist town she'd settled in. He'd have to ask around, shake the bushes and see what fell out. People loved to gossip in tiny places like this. Someone had to be willing to talk. Was Olivia an upstanding member of the community? Did she pass bad checks? Hang out at the local bars? When you knew the right questions to ask and how to ask them, people could be pretty damned informative without even knowing they were being questioned.

Nick had yet to unpack his shit. He tossed his duffel onto the bed and dug out a pair of jeans, T-shirt, and a sweater. He searched around in the bottom of the bag and found a pair of wool socks that he added to the pile. His boots were in the mudroom along with his coat, gloves, and hat. Probably should have brought long underwear or some shit. Another angry shout came from outside and spurred Nick into action as he threw on his clothes.

He didn't have a snow shovel, damn it.

Hell, he didn't have much of anything. No groceries and a little over a week's worth of clothes. Was it wishful thinking that he'd get the job done and be out of there in less than a week? Probably. Which meant if he was planning on sticking around Ski Town, USA, then he should probably get his ass in gear and load up on some shit. It might not be a bad idea to get his hands on a snowblower if he had any intention of making it up the lane to the city street. He had four-wheel drive and good tires, but still. This was some serious fucking snow on the ground.

Good Lord, it took less time to get outfitted in his vest and tactical gear to go out in the field. Once he got his boots laced, Nick headed out onto the porch. Olivia stood beside her car, digging snow out from underneath it as best she could with the snow shovel's scoop, which was way too big and awkward for the job she was trying to use it for. But since Nick didn't have even a piece-of-shit shovel like hers to help her out with, he supposed they'd have to make do.

She kept her back turned to him, completely oblivious to his presence. It was a vulnerable position, one that left her exposed to all sorts of danger. He found himself wanting to chide her, but why? No doubt Joel Meecum's old lady could take care of herself. Meek and weak didn't cut it when you rolled with bikers. He waded through the knee-deep snow, closer. Olivia straightened to lean on the shovel and pushed her slouchy hat up on her forehead. A frustrated shriek sent a cloud of steam billowing up into the air above her. "Son of a bitch!"

This snowstorm was absolute, fucking *bullshit*.

Fingers of trepidation speared Livy's chest as she tried to focus on the task at hand and not the lights that had sprung to life at the neighboring house. This time of year, most of the cabins along the lake went uninhabited or rented to vacationers, like the cabin that faced hers from across the narrow lane. She hadn't met her new neighbors yet and she didn't plan on it. Livy kept to herself and she couldn't help but be a little annoyed that her peaceful, deserted haven had gained another resident. No matter how temporary.

That light flicking on—a simple, everyday act that probably had nothing to do with her—was a sore reminder that not a fake identity nor a life a million miles from anywhere in all directions was enough to make her feel safe.

She continued to dig, but with every scoop of snow she moved, it seemed that twice as much sloughed from the drift to take its place. "Stupid, fucking, powdery pain in my ass!" Snow might be pure and white, it might be fun to plow through on her skis, but this morning, with her car hood-deep in it, the snow was surely a device of the devil. Five months and counting till spring . . .

After what felt like a year's worth of shoveling, Livy got in the car and put it in gear. The Caliber's wheels continued to spin and the engine growled as she punched down the accelerator. "Come *on,* you Dodge piece of shit! Move!"

From the corner of her eye, she glanced at the cabin next door. No doubt she'd given her neighbor a lovely six A.M. wake-up call with her revving engine and swear-fest. The Toyota pickup parked in the driveway looked like it had the clearance to maneuver through the accumulated snow with little effort.

Maybe they had a tow strap? *No.* Livy banished the thought from her mind. She had no idea who had rented the cabin. It could be anyone. And she'd managed to stay hidden the past four years by *not* taking chances.

A frustrated growl grated in Livy's throat as she threw the car into park and got out. She scooped several more shovelfuls of snow out from under the car, her breath coming in quick pants. Was twenty-five too young for a heart attack? Because she was pretty sure she felt one coming on. Her back ached as she straightened and leaned on the shovel handle. Damn it, she needed to take a breather. The wood splintered under her weight and broke in two. "Are you fucking kidding me?" she shouted as she held the splintered remains of her snow shovel. The damned thing was beyond ancient, and she'd needed a new one about two winters ago. But when forty dollars could be better spent on groceries, she'd decided to live dangerously and work the poor thing to death.

"Well, Frank, I wish I could say it was fun while it lasted."

Frank totally sounded like the sort of name a snow shovel would have. Utilitarian. All business. Frank didn't take any shit. He plowed through the accumulated feet of powdered evil and made that snow his bitch. Sort of.

The scoop was bent and the sharp metal dug grooves into the wood of her deck and stairs every time she tried to clear the snow away. Wet snow—like the shit currently piled in her driveway—stuck to the scoop and refused to let go. Tough to make any progress. She might as well be trying to shovel peanut butter. Like her life, Frank was useless and pathetic, hiding out in the shed when he wasn't being put to use. For the hundredth time she wondered how she hadn't died from the excitement.

Commercials always made you think that an all-wheel drive vehicle could go anywhere and do anything. But after a winter storm dumps a few feet of snow overnight, even the most stalwart of cars is going to have some trouble. High-centered in a snowdrift, and now no shovel to dig out with. She wasn't going anywhere.

"Goddamn it!"

Livy pulled her gloves up tighter on her hands and went to her knees with the scoop end of the broken shovel. If she could clear some of the snow out from under the car, she might have a chance of getting unstuck. She was already late for work, and since her paycheck was dependent on the number of students she had, she couldn't afford to miss a half day getting her car out of the driveway.

Nope, she wasn't going to ask for help. She'd gotten by this long on her own.

She kicked at the back bumper and her boot slipped against the slick plastic. Her legs went out from under her and she landed in the snow squarely on her ass. "Fuck!" Her voice echoed in the quiet of snowfall. "Fuck, fuck, *fuck*!"

She took the broken handle and wedged it underneath one of the back wheels of her car for traction and went to her knees. The cold soaked through her heavy ski pants. Ass up in the air, toes anchoring her to the ground, she continued to shovel the packed snow out from under her car. Who needed to go to the gym for a workout? With every scoop of snow, the calories melted away. . . .

"You stuck?"

The rumble of a deep voice behind her sent Livy's heart up into her throat. She could practically feel the icy barrel of a gun pressing into the exposed skin at the back of her neck. A shiver of trepidation traveled down her spine and Livy's brain went absolutely blank. Her mouth went dry. She froze; one half of Frank's severed body clutched in her fists.

Slowly, Livy rose up to her knees. The fact that she wasn't dead yet was a good sign. Either that, or she'd grown so paranoid that she couldn't even carry on a simple conversation with another human being in fear that he might be one of Joel's thugs sent to get her. With the shovel clutched close to her chest, Livy stood. Took a deep breath, and turned to face the source of that deep voice.

She brought her gaze up, up, *up* to the face of the man standing just to the left of her headlights. His features were indistinguishable in the dark, making him look sinister and strangely alluring all at once. Livy's heart raced and she swallowed the lump of fear that rose in her throat.

"H-high centered," she rasped just before clearing her throat. "The road's drifted shut. The snowplow hasn't been by yet."

He tilted his head to one side as though studying her. She could make out the outline of a strong jaw, and his lips curved as though in amusement as he turned his attention to her car. His profile displayed strong, sharp features and a shock of hair poked out from beneath his beanie, brushing his brows. "You're trying to go forward when you should be backing up." He jerked his head toward the driver's-side door. "Get in. I'll push."

Livy regarded him for a moment. *Bossy neighbor is bossy.* But his voice wasn't at all as threatening as her first impression had led her to believe. Instead, it was decadent and warm, like a bubble bath on a cold night. It eased the tension that caused her muscles to ache and filled her with a sense of calm. Holy shit. If he could bottle his voice, he'd make a fortune. It had been a long damned time since she'd felt comfortable in the presence of a stranger. Anyone, really. That didn't mean she was going to let her guard down, though. "Okay. Thanks."

Her tongue stuck to the roof of her mouth and she was suddenly painfully aware that she was decked out in five layers of clothes and a slouchy hat that she had to keep pushing up on her forehead. If he was there to kill her, he'd have no problem catching her. She looked like that kid from *A Christmas Story*, and if she fell down, Livy was pretty sure she wasn't getting back up.

She knocked the snow from her boots on the partially exposed front tire before getting in the car. With her teeth, she pulled her gloves from her hands as her neighbor waded through the deepest part of the drift and rounded the car. Livy shifted into reverse and braced both hands against the wheel. He stepped into the glare of her headlights and brought his head up to look at her through the windshield.

Dear God.

Livy's breath left her lungs in a rush. There might as well have been a cape waving in the breeze behind him. Those chiseled features weren't simply a play of shadow. And the warmth of his voice was nothing compared to his deep brown eyes. The dark hair that brushed his brow curled just a bit at the ends. He smiled, showcasing a row of straight white teeth, and Livy thought her ovaries might explode right then and there. *Ka-boom!* It would totally be just her luck that her assassin would show up with killer good looks to match his profession.

"Straighten out the wheel. Then give it a little gas and let off. We'll see if we can rock you out." Oh, he could rock her out all right. His rugged features had to be an illusion. Like a reverse mirage brought on by the predawn dark, cold, and snow. Livy's jaw went slack as she continued to stare. One brow arched curiously over his eye. "Ready?"

Huh? Ready for what? If it wouldn't have made her look insane, she'd have given herself a solid slap across the face. "Oh yeah. Right." She hit the button on her armrest and lowered her window a crack. "I'm ready. Just say when."

"Okay." He braced his arms on the hood of the car. "Now."

It took a moment for her brain to kick into gear. He was Atlas, and Livy knew that under the layers of clothes, there was a body that could easily shoulder the weight of the world. Why did it have to be the dead of winter when a hot guy rented the cabin next door? Mid-August would have been *soooo* much better. He paused and looked up, quirking a brow. *Shit!* Her boot slipped in her haste to hit the gas and the engine revved. "Sorry! I'm ready now."

"Okay." His eyes locked with hers and Livy's insides went molten. She put the car into reverse, hit the gas, and the car rocked backward. "Again."

He gave the car a solid shove and she eased down her foot on the accelerator. The snow gave way under the car and moved a few feet back before rocking forward.

"One more and I think we've got it!"

He put all of his weight into the action and Livy stomped her foot down on the pedal. The car gained traction and backed out of the drift with little effort. Free of the deepest snow, she put the car in park and opened the door. "Thank you so much. I would have been screwed if you hadn't come out to help. I owe you. Big-time."

"Big-time, huh?" Good Lord, that smile should've been illegal. "What do you have in mind?"

I owe you? Jesus, Livy, have you lost it completely? She was trying to keep people away, not draw them closer. But as she took a second glance at her new neighbor, part of her wanted to throw caution to the wind. Just this once.

Chapter Three

Olivia stared at him, jaw slack. She couldn't have been older than twenty-six, which would have made her barely old enough to legally buy a drink when she'd been with Joel. Nick's stomach turned. What a fucking scumbag. He couldn't help but wonder how she'd wound up with him. Had her parents been in the life? Maybe she'd been a runaway and Joel had given her a place to stay. Nick refused to let his thoughts wander any further than that. There were too many unsavory scenarios to consider and the woman standing in front of him now seemed much too soft for the hard motorcycle-club life.

Maybe his intel had been wrong?

"I uh, well. That is . . . I guess I could . . ."

She was sort of adorable in an awkward way. An introvert with a potty mouth. Again, totally not what Nick had expected. "I'd settle for a coffee. I haven't had a chance to buy groceries yet."

Olivia looked back at her house and then to Nick. Fear flickered over her features. She checked the driveway and the lane beyond as though trying to assess a viable escape route. Obviously on guard.

"I'm Nick, by the way." Metcalf had said that Nick's attitude wasn't conducive to trust. And if he hoped to get any information out of her, he needed to gain Olivia's. His usual dog-with-a-bone attitude wasn't going to cut it with her. This was going to take some finesse. "Nick Brady."

"Hi, Nick Brady." Olivia stretched her arm out, hesitating as she looked at their gloved hands. "I'm Livy."

Instead of trying to shake her hand in the bulky gloves, Nick reached out and lightly pounded his fist against hers. Her brow puckered as she fought a smile and something caught in his chest. "Just Livy?" he asked. "Like Madonna?"

"Just Livy," she quietly responded. "I'm going to be late for work, so maybe a rain check on the coffee?"

Nick canted his head to the side. "You must think I'm Superman."

That same unsure smile flirted with her lips. "What do you mean?"

"If you think I can push your car all the way to the street." Her smile grew a fraction. *Finesse.* "Sorry to say, but you're not going anywhere until a plow comes." Nick hadn't had much time to think about a cover story. Duplicity wasn't really his thing. When he approached witnesses or even persons of interest, he was a straight shooter. And a hell of a lot more growly. Her earlier trepidation reappeared on her expression and Nick decided to go with his gut. "As an officer of the law, I can't in good conscience let you out on the roads until the plows come through."

Her lips thinned almost imperceptibly. "You're a cop?"

Livy kept her skeptical tone but her response wasn't as nervous or scared as Nick expected it to be. A person hiding from law enforcement would have been more on edge. "Yup."

Her eyes narrowed as she studied him. "Local?"

"No. I've got a month off and my friend's cousin said I could use his cabin."

"Where do you live?"

"Washington. Bellevue."

Her shoulders relaxed but she kept him in her line of sight. "You're probably right about the roads. I might as well call the mountain and let them know I'll be late. Come on, I'll make some coffee. It's the least I can do for waking you up and letting you push me out of a drift."

Excellent. Who said Nick couldn't be a team player? He'd just used teamwork to get his neighbor out of a snowdrift while simultaneously making contact with the best lead on Meecum they'd had in years. Metcalf would be so proud.

Nick waited while Livy moved her car back into the parking space and killed the engine. He hadn't been entirely truthful with her, but he had a tendency to favor that lovely gray area between fact and fiction. He'd been a cop, a sniper on Seattle's SWAT team, before he'd joined the Marshals Service. The job had been satisfying enough but it hadn't offered the kind of gratification he was after.

Livy stomped her feet as she climbed the steps up onto the front porch. "The place is sort of a mess." She stuck her key in the lock. "And it might be a little chilly because I let the fire die."

"As long as the coffee's hot, I'm good," Nick replied.

Inside the entry was a little alcove with a wooden bench lined with cubes for shoes, and hooks above for coats. Nick followed Livy's lead and kicked off his boots and shucked his coat. "I'm pretty sure that you and I have way different definitions for what constitutes a mess."

The place was tastefully though not richly decorated. In the low light he made out a cream microfiber couch and two worn leather recliners that faced a modest brick fireplace. The walls of the cabin were rough-hewn wood that she'd decorated with black-and-white and color photos of landscapes and wildlife scenes. There were no personal photos anywhere in the living room. In fact, the entire house was fairly generic, as though it had been staged to look quaint and comfortable.

Livy hung up her coat and gave him a sheepish smile. She reached up to snatch the hat off her head at the same time she flipped on a light. "Okay, it's a mess for *me*."

Nick's breath stalled in his chest. The house could have looked like something out of *Hoarders* and he wouldn't have given a single shit. He was too preoccupied with Livy to care about anything else. Golden-brown braids hung down past her shoulders, the tasseled ends just barely brushing the tips of her breasts. Her eyes were bright hazel, greener than they were brown, and her lips were dark pink and full. A little on the pouty side. She wasn't wearing any makeup but her face was fresh and dewy. She was like a delicate pale rosebud poking up through the snow. Even prettier in full light than she'd appeared in the dark of dawn outside.

In a flock of black sheep like the Black Death MC, her fleece must have been as white as the snow falling outside. How in the hell had someone like her ended up with Meecum and his crew? Again, nothing seemed to add up.

Don't forget, looks can be deceiving.

"Go ahead and sit wherever. I'll get some water going."

For the first time since he'd left Seattle, Nick needed to remind himself that he was on the job. Sort of. It would be his ass if anyone at the Eastern Washington district found out that instead of taking the mandatory vacation his chief deputy had insisted on, he was hunting down a lead on Joel Meecum. The U.S. Marshals Service didn't look kindly on deputies who didn't follow direct orders. Then again, they were all a little wild. Crazy. Prone to making reckless and life-threatening decisions. Hell, the agency was founded on Wild West cowboy shit. And Nick wasn't any different than any of the rest of those crazy bastards. He'd be forgiven, but only after he slapped the cuffs on that lowlife son of a bitch and crossed his name from their Top 15 Most Wanted list.

Rather than sit down, Nick ventured into the

kitchen. Livy was scooping coffee grounds into a weird glass pot. "Do you want cream and sugar?"

"Yeah, thanks." He leaned against the opposite counter, careful to keep his stance relaxed. "Is Frank late this morning, or were you leaving early?"

Livy's brow puckered. "Huh?"

"Frank?" Nick repeated. The best way to get information out of someone was to simply engage them in conversation. People often let things slip in a casual back and forth that they'd be more guarded about during an interview or interrogation. "You were yelling at him when you were digging your car out."

Livy's face screwed up into a grimace and she let out a groan. Her voice was light and soft, feathers caressing his skin. "I was yelling at my shovel." She glanced at him from the corner of her eye as though gauging his reaction as she crossed to the fridge and grabbed a container of half-and-half.

"You call your shovel Frank?" Uncharacteristic laughter bubbled in Nick's chest. He didn't have much of a sense of humor, but he'd never met anyone who named their snow shovel before.

"Yeah, and he's a dirty, rotten jerk, too." She set the cream on the counter along with the sugar. "I gave him some of the best years of my life and when I needed him the most, he snapped. I mean, where's the loyalty?"

Soft and shy with a sense of humor and a mouth that would make a sailor blush. Nick liked to think that he could read people fairly well. He'd been trained to. But Olivia Gallagher was a mystery. Was it a part she played? Maybe a new persona to match her new identity? Nick couldn't let his guard down around her. He knew the type of people she'd kept company with. Joel Meecum was a piece-of-shit murderer and that was only one of his more unsavory traits. For all he knew, Livy was simply playing a part. Though admittedly, she played it well.

"Does the coffeepot have a name? Let me guess . . . Carl the Coffeemaker?"

"No," Livy answered with a snort. "That would be weird."

Nick cocked a challenging brow but she met him with a wry smile that tugged at his chest. Damn it. Reminding himself of who she really was and why he was here might be harder than he'd thought.

A cop! Of course, he could've been lying. Or even crooked. She'd heard Joel brag more than once that he had cops on his payroll. For all she knew, Nick Brady was waiting for the chance to put a bullet in her head and take the evidence of her death back to Joel. *God, Livy, morbid much?* The kettle whistled and she poured the boiling water over the grounds in the French press. From the corner of her eye, she studied Nick. It couldn't hurt to further vet him. Hell, he might even be a decent guy.

Her earlier assessment had been correct. Under his heavy coat was a body packed with bulky muscle. He towered over her by at least a foot and his jaw seemed to be perpetually squared as though always on the cusp of anger. Dark stubble roughened his face, adding to his hard edge. His lips weren't too full or too thin. Perfect in Livy's opinion. He could easily have been a gun for hire, or even one of the members of the Black Death. Imagining him atop a Harley, decked out in leather, wasn't much of a stretch.

But his eyes . . . *Wow.* The brown depths told another story. One that Livy was curious to hear. On the outside, Nick was a rock. But beneath his tough exterior, she sensed something deeper. Further vetting was *definitely* in order. He could have lied about being a cop, but maybe he really was who he said he was. Having a cop next door could be a good thing. Being from Washington, he couldn't possibly know who Joel Meecum was and Livy might feel a little safer having him next door. It would be nice to come home from work and not have to deal with the tension that perpetually pulled her shoulders taut.

Shit. Work.

Livy put the lid on the carafe and depressed the plunger. She technically didn't need to be there until the lifts opened at nine, but she'd figured that the lift operators might've needed help clearing last night's snow from the loading areas. She didn't mind getting up early or doing extra work. Anything was better than sitting home alone, worrying.

She poured two cups and slid one over toward Nick. "I need to call the mountain. Be right back."

"The mountain?" Nick's voice called after her and Livy dug her phone out of her coat pocket. "One of Frank's distant cousins?"

"Uh, Brundage Mountain," Livy said with a laugh. "I'm a ski instructor."

"So basically, you get paid to hang out at a ski resort all day? Sounds like a sweet gig."

As though she was some sort of lodge bunny? Livy dialed the lift supervisor's cell but only got his voice mail. "Hey, Tim. I'm snowed in so I won't make it up until around nine. Sorry I can't help you guys out this morning. I'll see you in a couple of hours."

Livy clutched her cell tight in her hand and looked around her living room, at the pictures hanging on the walls. Photos she went out and shot in order to keep her mind off the gnawing loneliness that ate away at her. Nick was officially the first person to step inside her house in four years. The first to see the pictures. To have a cup of coffee. The first to have a conversation with her that didn't revolve around her job. A knot of emotion lodged in her chest, but Livy forced herself to swallow it down. Lonely was better than dead. It had become her mantra, the single thing that kept her going day after day. Offering Nick a cup of coffee to thank him for pushing her out of a snowdrift didn't change anything.

"You okay out there?"

The rumble of Nick's deep voice broke her from her reverie. She never should have invited him in. Wasn't he only here for a month, though? What could it hurt to share a cup of coffee or two? This was about her safety, too. She had to know that he was trustworthy. That he wasn't one of Joel's goons come to get her. If he checked out, he'd be gone soon enough, and Livy would go back to her relatively isolated existence.

"Oh. Yeah." Nick appeared at the archway that led from the kitchen, a steaming mug in each hand. "I left a message. I'm sure everyone is digging out right now. It really came down last night."

Livy took a cup from his outstretched hand. "I wasn't sure what you wanted in it, so I took a wild guess."

She savored the creamy goodness as it rolled over her tongue. Not too sweet, and just dark enough to taste the kick of the rich roast. A cop *and* he could make a great cup of coffee? Nick Brady really did need a cape. "Are you cold? I can turn up the heat. It just doesn't make sense to rekindle the fire when I'm going to be leaving in a couple of hours."

"Nah, I'm all right." Nick walked past her and made himself at home on one of the recliners that faced the fireplace. She wondered if he made it a habit to hang out in strangers' houses. He seemed comfortable enough in hers. "Are you a good ski instructor?"

Comfortable and up front. Was it a cop thing that even the most innocent of conversations made you feel like you were being interrogated? "I guess. I haven't had any complaints yet."

Nick studied her with an intensity that Livy couldn't help but find both unnerving and a little exciting. As though he were trying to climb right into her mind and dissect every single one of her thoughts. Her stomach tightened as a pleasant rush jolted through her bloodstream.

"Maybe I'll come up and take a lesson. I haven't skied since I was a kid. I could probably use a refresher."

Livy grinned. "I'm sure you'd be right at home with the group of four to six year olds that I usually teach."

"Yeah, in that case, I think I'll stick to motor sports."

She could totally picture him as a motorhead. He was probably one of those guys who did hill climbs and took their sleds into avalanche country because that's where the best powder was. "I didn't see a snowmobile in your driveway. Is that why you decided to vacation here?"

"I don't own a snowmobile," he said. "And I came here because the cabin was free and my supervisor told me to get the fuck out of the office before he threw me out."

"Suspended?" Livy sipped from her cup to keep her hands from shaking. This was why it was important to get know him. The last person she needed as a neighbor was a morally ambiguous cop who might not be opposed to bending—or breaking—the law.

"Not exactly. I'm a little . . . intense. It gets me into trouble sometimes."

Livy didn't doubt that for a second. The set of Nick's jaw, the deep focus of his dark eyes, his brow that seemed set in a permanent scowl all indicated a personality that swung toward type A and obsessive. But how was he *intense*? "Do you shake down grandmas and coerce confessions from teenage shoplifters?" She was only half kidding.

"I like to ruffle feathers," he said without breaking eye contact. "And I don't quit until I get what I want."

Livy's stomach wrung into a tight twist and released. The dark edge to his words shouldn't have excited her. She didn't know anything about him, for shit's sake! There was a certain appeal to a man who knew what he wanted and went after it, though. Then again, men like that were usually trouble with a capital *T*. "Do people typically do what you tell them to? No questions asked."

He answered without a hint of humor. "Yes."

A rush of heat spread from Livy's belly, outward between her thighs. "So"—she cleared her throat to keep her voice from quavering—"I take it you're a loner?"

"Yeah. Always have been."

Livy stared into her cup. "Me too."

A forlorn meow came from the staircase to the left. Livy turned to find Simon perched on the post of the banister. Nick's lips quirked. "Not entirely a loner."

Simon leaped in a graceful arch and landed on the back of Nick's recliner. The large tabby stretched out, looking curiously at their guest before leaning in to boop Nick's forehead with his own. He froze, as though unfamiliar with even base affection and Livy's heart stuttered in her chest. "You're not allergic, are you?"

"No. I'm not much of a pet person."

"Don't tell Simon that," Livy remarked. "It'll break his heart."

As though this hulking, stern-faced man was no more harmful that his favorite squeaky mouse toy, Simon continued to rub against Nick. And whereas Nick barely tolerated the affection, the cat reveled in it, evidenced by his loud, rumbling purrs. Simon licked the top of Nick's head and his eyes widened a fraction of an inch as one brow arched curiously.

"Okay, buddy, I'm pretty sure Nick doesn't need a bath. You're so needy first thing in the morning, aren't you?"

Livy set her cup down on the end table and reached over to retrieve Simon. He let out a yowl in protest as she relocated him to the couch. "Sorry. He doesn't get out much."

"Do you?"

The question left the opportunity for too many answers. Answers Livy didn't want to give. Before she could respond, the loud growl of an engine followed by the scrape of a blade echoed from down the lane. "Plow's here," she said. "Looks like I'm going to work after all."

Nick's expression fell but he quickly recovered the stern countenance that Livy assumed was his "relaxed face." She'd hate to see what he looked like when he was truly angry, because he could be considered threatening while exchanging polite conversation.

Nick stood and handed Livy his cup. "Thanks for the coffee, Livy, and be careful out on the roads today."

She wondered at the way he stressed her name

and a shiver danced down her spine. "It's always the other guy you've gotta watch out for, isn't it?"

"True." Nick gave her a tight smile that didn't quite reach his eyes as he headed for the tiny foyer, put on his boots and coat, and grabbed his gloves. "See ya around?"

Did she want to see more of him? His gaze locked with hers, warm and so intense that it sucked the air right out of Livy's lungs. Heat swamped her. Yes, she definitely wanted to see more of him. "Sure," she said with a tentative smile. "See ya around."

Chapter Four

Nick stuffed a potato chip in his mouth as he studied the case file on Joel Meecum and the Black Death motorcycle club. Several notebooks were scattered across the table, his own notes that he'd taken over the past few months. Some guys hiked, fished, went to concerts in their spare time. Nick investigated fugitives.

Outside, snow was coming down steadily. The second wave of winter storms that were supposed to be hitting the area over the next couple of weeks. Payette Lake beyond his dining room window stretched on for a couple of miles, the water hidden by a layer of ice and snow that painted a pretty damned serene picture.

But he hadn't come here for the view.

Nick's phone buzzed, the vibration sending the device crawling across the table toward him. He checked the caller ID and swore under his breath. He could let it go to voice mail. He was on *vacation*, after all. Against his better judgment, he grabbed the cell and swiped his finger across the screen. "Brady."

"Hey. It's Morgan."

Ethan Morgan worked the warrants squad and had several arrests under his belt, all of them from past and current Top Fifteens. Nick also suspected that he was the one who suggested to their chief deputy that Nick take some time off. He was a good guy, really. If Nick would have been better about forming any kind of relationship with one or two of his coworkers, the dude might've been cool to hang out with.

Nick's disinterest in camaraderie was only one of the reasons he'd been forced to take a break. "What's up?" It's not like Morgan was calling to see how his vacay was going. Might as well get down to business.

"I'm missing a case file. Meccum. Have you seen it?"

Shit. Nick knew that it would only be a matter of time before Morgan noticed that the file wasn't in the stack on his desk anymore, but he'd been hoping that it would be after he had Meecum in cuffs. "I haven't been there for a week. How would I know where it is?"

"Come on, Brady. You've had a hard-on for Meecum ever since you came on. And it's not like you haven't *borrowed* case files from other desks before."

"Maybe you misplaced it. Getting forgetful in your old age?"

"Fuck you, Brady." Morgan was annoyed, but even so his words were spoken with a certain amount of humor. As bristly as Nick was, the Marshals Service was still a tight-knit group. As the new guy, he expected a little shade to be thrown his way. "Where the hell is my case file?"

"Check with Courtney. He could have it."

"Nope."

"Why do you even need a case file? This is the digital age. Everything you need is right at your fingertips. In fact, why do we even still use hard copies? Seems like a waste of trees to me."

"You're a stubborn son of bitch, you know that?"

Nick had been called worse. Aggressive, antagonistic, dumb motherfucker. Stubborn was a compliment in comparison. "How long have you been working warrants, Morgan?"

"Few years."

"You feel like working courts again anytime soon?" On the marshals' list of duties, hooking and hauling was the most tedious. According to veterans, if you shut up and paid attention, you'd learn a lot about the job by listening to what went down in trials. All Nick found was that it bored him out of his freaking mind.

"I still work courts," Morgan replied. "Everyone does. It's part of the job. And you've got to pay your dues, Brady. Six months. That's all you have to put in and you can work a rotation on the warrants squad full-time. You're good at it. Probably too damned good. That ambition is either going to burn you out or get you killed, though. All I'm saying is, you need to slow the hell down, which is why you're on va-ca-tion. Now, where is my case file?"

Yeah, on a scale of one to dickhead, Morgan

wasn't too bad. That didn't mean Nick was going to show his hand. "I wish I could help you out." The sound of a vehicle coming down the lane drew Nick's attention. He craned his neck and looked out the kitchen window to see Livy's blue Dodge Caliber pulling into her driveway. "But if it turns up, let me know."

"Yeah, whatever," Morgan replied. "You're a pain in the ass, you know that?"

"Yup." He watched as Livy struggled with several bags of groceries. "Later."

He ended the call without giving Morgan a chance to respond. He wouldn't have said anything Nick would want to hear anyway. It only took a second to slip his Sorrels on and he didn't bother to tie the laces as he headed out the door. He hadn't found any opportunities to talk to Livy since the morning she'd made him coffee and the clock was ticking. Three weeks to find Meecum and counting.

"Is there something wrong with making more than one trip?" He hadn't meant to bark at her. Residual annoyance from his conversation with Morgan.

Livy jumped at the sound of his voice, dropping three of the green reusable bags onto the snow. "Holy fucking shit!" Even filthy words sounded sweet coming from her mouth. "You scared the hell out of me!"

Over the past few days he'd bided his time. Watched her come and go like clockwork. When she hadn't come home at five this evening, he'd grown anxious. Pacing a lap from the kitchen to the living room until he'd forced himself to sit his ass down and go over Meecum's case file for the hundredth time. Now that she was home a sense of relief washed over him. What the hell? Yeah, he wanted the win and getting Meecum had become not only his number-one work priority, but also his top priority in life. But this was different. Had he actually been worried about her?

"It's no wonder you didn't hear me walk over. You're obviously more interested in impersonating a pack mule than watching out for sneak attacks."

Livy whipped around to face him. Her hazel eyes flickered with fear and a deep flush rose to her cheeks. She hadn't been exaggerating. He'd straight-up scared her. She didn't exactly live her life like someone who was hiding out from the authorities. The reason the marshals were so good at finding fugitives was because they always made mistakes. Loved ones—parents, children, lovers—always drew fugitives to them. No one could completely isolate themselves, even shitbag scums of the earth. And more times than not, criminals were too arrogant for their own good. They sometimes flaunted their presence as a middle finger to the men who hunted them. Nick had gotten the finger before some bastard bailed out of a window to evade capture enough times to know. Livy, on the other hand, seemed to have closed herself off completely. Not as though she was lying low to avoid questioning. No, she behaved as if she hid from the entire world.

"If Frank were still alive, he'd never let you get away with calling me a mule."

Nick's lips quirked in a dubious half smile. He

didn't know what to make of her. She was either halfway to crazy or had the weirdest sense of humor of anyone he'd ever met. He scooped up the bags she'd dropped and grabbed two more from the back of the car. "Are you suggesting that if your shovel weren't broken you'd hit me with it?"

Livy took the remaining two bags and closed the hatchback. "Hey, all I'm sayin' is, you sneak up on a girl, you never know how she's going to react."

Nick chuckled. "Fair enough."

"How goes the vacation?" Livy wrangled her bags with one hand as she unlocked the door. "Doing anything vacation-y?"

Did poring over case files count? Nick couldn't think of anything else he'd rather do on his downtime. "Not really. Hanging out. Watching TV. Watching the snowfall." *Watching you.*

"If you want, I could get you a comp pass at the mountain."

"Yeah, somehow I don't think skiing is like riding a bike. I'm not interested in wearing a full-body cast."

"Want a refresher?"

He might have a better chance of learning more about her if he talked to the people she worked with. Though, if Livy was teaching little kids how to ski, he doubted the intel would be very reliable. "Do I look like I'd be comfortable in skis?"

"Honestly, you look like the pro-wrestler type to me," Livy teased. She looked him over from head to toe, her hazel eyes burning with an intensity that Nick felt right in the center of his gut. "Maybe not.

But definitely the football type. I don't think winter sports are your thing."

"No," he admitted. "They aren't."

Her lids became hooded and she averted her gaze. "So, Nick Brady, what is your thing?"

Livy was as hard up as a Catholic schoolgirl on prom night. Not a day of the past week had gone by without her thinking of Nick. Maybe more than once. Fine, under fifteen but more than ten. This wasn't a good idea. She wasn't even sure she could trust him yet. She absolutely *shouldn't* be flirting with him. But since she was on the subject, was it working?

She chanced a glance at him from beneath lowered lashes. She'd never met a man who could look so delicious and so damned gruff at the same time. He was hard in the way that Joel and some of his guys were hard—as though he'd seen some truly horrible shit. His expression wasn't hollow or empty. More . . . determined. A fire burned bright in Nick Brady's soul. Too hot to quench. Did he love with the same determination and ferocity? A shiver raced across Livy's heated flesh.

"What's my thing?" He cupped the back of his neck, showcasing the corded muscles of his forearms and Livy fought the urge to bite down on her bottom lip. He was *killing* her with his unassuming sexy act. *Act* because there was no way in hell Nick didn't know that he was smoking hot. "Unsolved mysteries."

"Like the TV show?"

"Sure. I like puzzles. Figuring things out." He stopped abruptly and Livy suspected that there was more to it than the answer he gave her. "I go to work, I go home. Hit the gym so I don't fail the physical agility tests. That's about it. Try not to die from the excitement that is my life."

Livy started to unload the groceries in an effort to keep from taking him to the floor in a full body tackle. Because picturing Nick as he lifted weights was making *her* sweat. "You've been here a week. Have you seen me throwing any ragers? At least you go to the gym. My life is so routine, it's a wonder my car can't get me from here to work on autopilot."

She reached up on her tiptoes to stow the box of Kashi GOLEAN Crunch on a high shelf. Nick plucked the box from her grasp and set the box on the shelf with ease. The man was a freaking redwood! She really needed to keep someone with a little height on the payroll. She wondered if Nick might be interested in the position. . . .

"There's nothing wrong with living simply."

Or simply living. She pursed her lips and met his gaze. "Says the *cop.*"

"What's that supposed to mean?"

Nick must have had a tendency to frighten people. Without trying, even a simple question came off with a hard edge. But rather than scare her, it drew Livy to him. Crazy, considering she was afraid of her own shadow.

"Nothing." She reached past him to put a package of linguini in the cupboard. Her hand brushed the unyielding muscle of his bicep and her eyes drifted shut for the barest moment. Could she be more of a loser? Going all weak-kneed because her fingers made contact with bare skin. She wanted to call him crazy for wearing a short-sleeved shirt in the middle of a snowstorm, but now, Livy considered sneaking into his closet with a pair of scissors. "I meant that for someone whose job is twenty-four-seven excitement, I doubt you know much about what it's like to lead a dull, uneventful life."

"Police work isn't always exciting." He gave her a lopsided grin that she was pretty sure triggered her body into instant ovulation. *Bam!* "There are all kinds of paperwork and admin duties that are totally mind-numbing."

"And that accounts for, what, ten percent of your workweek?"

"Sometimes more, sometimes less. It just depends on what's going on." Nick reached out his hand and Livy handed him a half gallon of milk that he put in the fridge. "The thing is, you go to work and you pretty much know how your day is going to go. I go to work and anything can happen. I have to be ready for that. Some days are fucked-up. And those are the days that I don't want to do anything but go home and not think about a god-damned thing."

Livy hadn't trusted the cops to help her when she'd needed them. Especially when half of the local authorities were getting kickbacks from Joel. Instead of going to someone for help, she'd run. Now, she was starting to think that her decision hadn't been fair to the people like Nick who took their jobs seriously. Maybe not everyone was on the take.

"What do you do to decompress?" From the looks of him, Nick hadn't hit the release valve in a *long* time. His jaw was practically welded shut, the muscle at his cheek ticking perpetually.

He shrugged a sheepish shoulder. God, she wanted to bite him there. Just sink her teeth into his flesh. *Whoa. Slow your roll, sister.* "I play *Call of Duty.*"

"You're kidding, right?" Livy deadpanned. "After a day of chasing bad guys and shooting at people, you go home and virtually chase bad guys and shoot at people?"

"When you put it that way . . ."

The glare of headlights shown through the kitchen window and the familiar and unwelcome rush of adrenaline dumped into Livy's system. Paralyzed by fear, her brain went completely blank and she couldn't force herself to take a breath, let alone move. Her cabin and the one Nick rented sat at the end of the lane, so it wasn't like anyone could simply be driving by. Who was it? What were they doing here? *Shit!*

Livy leaned over the counter, craning her neck to watch the progress of the car. Her breathing kicked into gear at the exact moment her heart began to hammer in her rib cage. Fingers curled around the porcelain of the sink, she watched as the vehicle pulled into her driveway, backed up, and drove out the way it came.

"Livy?"

Panic seized her and she fought for the self-control to not let Nick see how freaked out she was. Inside, though, she was falling apart. Whoever it was could have gotten lost. A lot of the lanes around the lake looked similar and weren't marked clearly. It's not like she'd never had turnaround traffic in her driveway before. But what if the person who'd pulled into her driveway had known exactly where they were going?

"Livy, are you okay?"

"What? Oh, yeah." She tried to play it off, but she was having trouble prying her hands loose from the sink. "I'm fine." She needed to move away from McCall sooner rather than later. *Alone is better than dead. Alone is better than dead.*

Nick reached over and covered her fingers with his. Warmth enveloped her as his hands swallowed hers. "You're not fine." He eased her hands away from the sink but didn't let go. "You're shaking. What's going on?"

She turned to face him, knowing that her eyes were likely wide, her lips thinned, and face flushed. "Living alone," she said with a nervous laugh. "Makes a girl paranoid. Especially when you're off the beaten path."

Though she tried to pull away, he kept her fingers firmly in his grasp. It felt so *good*. The simple act filled her with a sense of security she hadn't felt in years. This was dangerous ground to tread. She couldn't allow herself to feel anything when she was with Nick. He'd be gone in a few weeks and Livy would have to start all over again, building up her courage day by day.

Nick let go of her hands and reached up to smooth a strand of hair away from her forehead. "You can talk to me, you know. About anything."

Anything? Once again, Livy was struck with the notion that Nick's knowledge of her went beyond the superficial. Probably because he was a cop. They were trained to relate to people, to put them at ease when the situation called for it. "I'm fine. Really. I blame Frank. Without him around to bash unsuspecting house invaders and post-grocery-run ambushers, I'm totally defenseless. I think it's time to quit mourning and go out and buy a new shovel."

Nick's lips formed a hard line as he regarded her. She couldn't put anything past him. He saw right through her lame attempt to deflect with humor. Either that or she wasn't close to as funny as she gave herself credit for.

His brown eyes bore straight through her, burning with a heat that made her heart smolder in her chest. A rush of delicious warmth spread from her stomach outward and settled low in her abdomen. It seemed not even the fear of being dismembered and buried in a shallow grave could tame her sudden lust for this man. "Have you eaten? I could order a pizza? And I promise not to freak out when the delivery car comes down the driveway."

Nick's gaze narrowed. He still wasn't buying it. Well, too damned bad. He'd have to accept her explanation and get over it because she wasn't going to be confiding in him anytime soon. "All right," he said after a moment. He continued to stare down at her and Livy fought the urge to go up on her tiptoes. Touch her lips to his. *Alone is better than dead.* "In exchange for feeding me, I'll check around the house for anything that might invite solicitors, missionaries, or home invaders to try something shady."

"You forgot post-grocery-run ambushers."

Nick grinned. She couldn't remember ever seeing a better-looking man in her life. "I'll personally take care of any ambushers. Sound good?"

Good? "Better than good." Nick Brady was too good to be true. "Chop some wood for me and I'll throw in a hard cider with the pizza."

He smiled. "I'm sure we can work something out."

Her insides melted every time he smiled. The simple expression lit his features until it was almost painful to look at him. Like staring up at an exposed bulb. *Damn it.* Out of all the empty cabins ringing the lake, why did he have to rent the one next door to hers?

Chapter Five

"Mendoza's shipment will be coming through on Tuesday. You ready for it?"

Joel Meecum's lip curled at the doubt in Sawyer's tone. The SoCal Charter of the Black Death had been working more closely with the cartel for the past few years and it was a barb that stuck in Joel's craw. It had been Joel and the Oakland Charter that had formed the relationship with Chico Mendoza and the cartel. But it was Sawyer's crew that was distributing their heroin throughout California now.

And it was absolute fucking bullshit.

"Apparently you forgot who taught you how to distribute Mendoza's shit." Joel spat to his right as he cut Shorty Dodds, the club's VP, a look.

Sawyer smirked and Joel wanted to wipe that expression off his face with a forty-caliber bullet. "We're closer to the border. Closer to his tunnels." A pregnant pause followed and Sawyer cleared his throat. "And there are rumors goin' around that are making Mendoza nervous."

Joel's gut clenched and his jaw locked down. Shorty took a tentative step forward and said the words Joel couldn't manage to push past his clenched teeth. "What sort of rumors?"

Sawyer shrugged. "There's a lot of heat on you," he said. "You've been laying low for a long goddamned time, man. You don't think Mendoza notices that shit?"

It was true Joel had been dodging federal warrants for the past four years. None of which had a damned thing to do with the club's business with the cartel. "That's a load of bullshit, Sawyer. I've got feds on the payroll and Mendoza knows that. My business is tight."

"Is it?" Sawyer countered. Shorty took a lunging step forward and Joel held up a hand to stop him.

"Spit it the fuck out or quit wasting my time, Sawyer. Just what the hell is it that you think has Mendoza nervous?"

"You do a lot of business with a lot of important players," Sawyer remarked. "When you've got your hands in so many cookie jars, records gotta be kept. Accounts managed. Mendoza doesn't want to see any of his information wind up in the wrong hands. It's the digital age, man. Ain't nobody's shit private anymore."

That Sawyer knew anything about what worried Mendoza rankled. Further proof that Joel needed to tie up his loose ends and get his club—and his business—back on track. "My shit's private," Joel quipped. Digital age? Shit. Joel didn't even own a fucking smartphone. He made sure all of his burners were basic. "Mendoza knows I don't fuck around with computers."

"True," Sawyer agreed. "But paper trails can be followed too."

Joel regarded Sawyer with a caustic eye. Just what did the SoCal president know? Or worse, what had he heard? "Not mine," he replied. "Not ever."

Sawyer's brows shot up into his graying hairline. His dark blue eyes narrowed and he took a slow drag from his cigarette before expelling the smoke. "That's not what I heard."

Joel's fingers caressed the butt of the revolver tucked into his waistband. Sawyer was pressing his luck and if he didn't watch his fucking mouth, he'd be eating a bullet. "Yeah?" Joel challenged. "Just what did you hear, motherfucker?"

The bastard had the good sense to pull back on his cocky attitude. He flicked the butt of his cigarette to the ground. "It's not me that's talkin'," Sawyer said with a nervous wobble to the words. "It's not even anyone in the MC. Some cocky shit who slings for one of Mendoza's distributors said he heard you were lookin' for your old lady. That maybe she has something you want. Maybe something she took. You know how rumors spread."

Joel did know how rumors spread. He'd counted on word of mouth to find Kari. What he hadn't counted on was the speculation that hit too close to home for his peace of fucking mind. Which meant that someone in his own club might have been flapping their lips when they shouldn't have. When Joel figured out who the sorry bastard was, he'd kill him with his bare hands. "Well, whoever the hell he is, he's *wrong.*"

"She must be some piece of ass for you to go to so much trouble to get her back," Sawyer pointed out. "Plenty of pussy around that you don't have to chase after if you know what I mean."

Joel fixed Sawyer with a caustic stare. He took a nervous step backward, and then another. Joel's temper got the better of him more times than not. And violence went hand in hand with his hot-headed nature. Sawyer was wise to keep his distance. One more word, and Joel was going to beat the ever-living fuck out of him.

"Who I want and why I want her is none of your—or anyone else's—fucking business," Joel barked. "So unless you know where she is and are looking for that five-k reward, keep your goddamned mouth shut about her. Feel me?"

Sawyer gave a stiff nod of his head. He raked his fingers through his graying hair and let out a slow breath. "It's not me you've gotta worry about, man. It's Mendoza."

And didn't he fucking know it.

"As soon as the heat from the feds is off of me, I'm outta here," Joel said. "I'll be across the border and taking care of Mendoza's operation from the other side."

Sawyer didn't miss the inflection in Joel's tone. *That's right, motherfucker, as soon as I'm set up in Mexico, you won't be shit with the cartel.* "No one's trying to step on your toes," he replied. "We're all the same club. What's good for one charter is good for another."

Sawyer could take all of that brotherhood bull-shit and shove it up his ass. Joel was in it for the money, plain and simple. And he wanted as much of it as he could get his hands on.

"Let Mendoza know that we're ready for the ship-ment," Joel said. "And tell him I'll be in touch soon."

Sawyer took the cue that their conversation was over. He straddled his bike and the engine roared to life. "I'll let him know," Sawyer called over the rumble of the pipes. "In the meantime, if anyone gets a bead on your old lady, we'll let you know."

He gave Joel a knowing look as he pulled out of the turnout and back onto the highway. Cowardly piece of shit. He wouldn't have dared to bring Kari up again if he hadn't been about to drive off.

"He's bound to cause trouble if he doesn't shut his mouth," Shorty said from behind him.

For the most part, the VP had kept quiet during their meeting. One of the reasons he was Joel's right hand. "He thinks he can run Mendoza's dis-tribution operation," Joel replied without turning to face the other man. "Heat's on me, so he's tryin' to move in."

"Won't be for long, though." Shorty's bike creaked with his weight.

Joel sure as hell hoped so. He'd been looking for Kari for a long damned time. She was the key to reclaiming his freedom. Finding her would secure his future. Without her, his life would be shit and he wasn't willing to live another day like he had over the past four years.

"Maybe." Joel wasn't as optimistic as Shorty. Especially since the bitch had become a ghost. Not a damned trace of her anywhere. And the bounty he'd put on her wasn't a small one. Five thousand dollars was a lot of money just for information. If anybody connected to any of the MCs on the West Coast had seen her, he'd know about it by now. Had she moved to Siberia or some shit? The South fucking Pole? With every passing day, Joel grew more anxious about finding her. As the weeks turned to months, his temper mounted. The longer she stayed in hiding, the worse it would be for her.

When Joel found her, she was going to pay for every single day of it.

The drive to Brundage Mountain Ski Area was a harrowing one. The narrow, winding, snow-covered road went on for about ten endless miles before dumping Nick at the base of the mountain and a gaping parking lot. After last night, his surveillance of Livy made Nick feel dirty. As though he was no longer keeping tabs on her in a professional capacity. After you've shared a pizza and casual conversation with a lead, it felt more like stalking than surveillance. Especially when the lead was drop-dead gorgeous, quirky, funny, and made his stomach tie up into an unyielding knot.

Something didn't add up. He'd known it from the moment he laid eyes on her. Joel Meecum was forty-eight and about as rough as a backcountry dirt road. The man was a violent sociopath and likewise, he associated with the sort of people who fit the bill. Livy didn't strike Nick as the type of woman who'd be caught in the same room with a bunch of violent bikers, let alone one who'd date one.

Could their intel have been wrong?

So far, Livy had given away nothing that might indicate she had anything to hide. She followed a strict routine, though. Left for work and came home at almost the exact same time every day. She'd spent her days off at her house. In fact, aside from work and the grocery store, Nick had yet to see her venture out. He'd been in her house three more times in the past week and her cell hadn't rung once. Not even a text message. Her guarded behavior and lack of any friends, family, or other personal interactions threw up a red flag.

She had secrets and Nick wouldn't stop digging until he uncovered them.

He drove past the lower parking lot at the base of the mountain and headed farther up the road to park closer to the lodge. He killed the engine of the Tacoma and stuffed his cell in his pocket before he pulled a knit beanie over his head. He might not be packing skis around, but at least he looked the part. Besides, he wasn't planning to be anywhere near the slopes—where he assumed Livy would be—he just wanted to get a bead on her.

The mountain seemed pretty busy for a Friday. Nick figured that when you lived in a resort community, there was always an influx of vacationers no matter the day of the week or time of year, though. He made his way up the flights of stairs, past the first and second levels, to the third floor of the lodge. Nick took stock of the people around him, decked out in ski gear that had to cost upward of a thousand dollars and that didn't even include the actual skis.

Joel or any of his crew would stand out in this crowd. And with the ground being covered in snow for four months out of the year, the chances of the town gaining the attention of an MC would be slim. Really, Livy had chosen the perfect place to hide out.

Nick found a quiet table in the lodge next to a large picture window that faced the ski lifts and several steep runs. From his vantage point, he could watch the skiers and snowboarders speed down the hill on their way to the lifts as well as the people filtering out of the lodge. This far away, it would be tough to discern Livy in the group, especially with all of her snow gear on. But that's not why he was there. He wanted to know if she kept to herself at work as much as she did at home.

The question that burned like a cinder in Nick's gut was more than likely the one he wouldn't find an answer to, however. What in the hell had Livy's relationship with Joel been and why was she hiding out in a small Idaho town?

A single fugitive was harder to track than a pair. If she'd still been with Joel when he went on the run, he would've instructed Livy to take off and he would have met up with her later. The informant's story had painted a very different picture of Livy and Joel's relationship.

Joel wants her back. Bad. She took off on him a few years back and he never got over it. Been looking for her ever since. Put the word out that he'd pay five large to whoever found her.

Livy was gorgeous enough to prompt any man to do whatever it took to keep her. Nick's heart rate kicked into gear just thinking about her warm complexion, long golden hair, and bright smile. There had to be more to it than unrequited love. Guys like Joel Meecum didn't pine over women. Especially when they were busy dodging a federal warrant.

"Mind if I sit?"

Nick looked up to find a woman smiling down at him. She wore the same black ski pants and blue coat with the Brundage Mountain logo that Livy wore along with an employee badge dangling from the zipper. The lodge had gotten busy since Nick had sat down and he was surprised to see that his was one of the only tables with a free chair left. It couldn't have worked out more perfectly. He smiled and held out a welcoming hand. "Go ahead."

The woman shucked her coat and hung it from the back of the chair. She set down a steaming paper cup of coffee and a blueberry muffin. "Spectating this morning? You should get out there, the powder is killer."

"Oh, I'm not skiing," Nick said with a laugh. "I'm waiting. My daughter has a lesson this morning. With um . . ." He paused as though trying to remember. "Livy, I think."

"Great," the woman—Nick checked her badge, Cori—said. "She's getting ready to take her group down the run one last time before they're done for the day. If you look over there"—she pointed to a smaller chair lift to the south—"you can see them getting off the lift for Easy Street."

"Easy Street," he said. "That's cute."

"There's not much of a slope," Cori said. "It's perfect for the little guys. And Livy is great with beginners."

"Yeah," Nick said. "She seems really nice. I guess she hasn't lived here long?"

"I'm not sure," Cori said. "She's worked here longer than I have, though."

"You guys probably see a lot of turnaround." So far, Nick wasn't having much luck. If he could keep the conversation rolling though, he might glean some small bit of insight into Livy from her coworker.

"Oh yeah," Cori replied. "I think the only person who's been here longer than Livy is Jane down in customer service. Not a lot of people have what it takes to get through one of our winters." She laughed. "Are you here on vacation or do you live here?"

"Vacation," Nick said. "My wife stayed in town and I volunteered to drive our daughter up."

Cori turned her attention to the mountain as she sipped from her cup and broke off a chunk from her muffin. Nick erred on the side of caution and didn't push for conversation. After a few more minutes, she dug her phone out of her coat pocket and checked the time. "I have a private lesson in ten minutes so I'd better get going. It was nice talking to you."

"You too," Nick said. "Have a good one."

Cori might have been a dead end but she'd given Nick a good lead. He waited until he saw Cori emerge from the lodge. She retrieved a pair of skis from a rack and locked her boots into the bindings and took off toward a small building near the lift. Nick pushed out from the table and headed out of the lodge to the ground floor and the customer service office.

He took the stairs slowly as he thought of a cover story. Under any other circumstances, he would have simply flashed his badge and gotten right down to business. He couldn't be so forthright now. He couldn't let Livy know he was investigating her. If she happened to be tipped off that someone was asking around about her, she could get spooked and run again. If that happened, Nick would be back at square one and no closer to bringing Meecum in.

The customer service office was tucked away at the back end of the ground floor behind the ticket windows. Nick held open the door before going inside for a trio of kids who examined their shiny new season passes as they exited. A long counter spanned the small office space and a woman with short blond hair and bright blue eyes greeted him with a smile.

"Hi! What can I help you with?"

"Hi, I was wondering if I could get some information on a youth lesson package. I was told to ask for Jane."

"I'm Jane," she said with a wide grin. "What would you like to know?"

Everything you know about Livy, for starters. "A friend of mine said his daughter took lessons from Livy last year and loved her. Does she still work here?"

"Oh sure," Jane replied. "Livy's great. The kids really respond to her and she's super patient."

"That's great," Nick said. "Is she local?" Jane gave him a strange look and he added, "I heard you guys have a high turnaround and I just want to make sure she'll still be here at the end of February."

"Livy's been here for about four years," Jane said. "I doubt she'll be leaving anytime soon."

"That's good to know." So far, he hadn't learned anything more than what Cori had told him. Damn it, getting information was so much easier when he showed up with a gun on his hip and his badge on his belt. "Do you mind if I ask what her level of experience is?"

"Not at all." Apparently Jane regularly dealt with parents concerned for their child's ski instructor's credentials. "She's an expert-level skier. Raced at the junior level, if I remember correctly."

Finally, something Nick could use. There was a chance she'd fabricated her ski experience in order to get a job but there was always a little bit of truth to every lie. "That's impressive."

"She trained in Tahoe when she was younger, I'm pretty sure. Anyway, you won't have to worry about her on the slopes. Your . . . ?" Jane trailed off.

"Uh, daughter," Nick said.

Jane smiled. "Your daughter will be in good hands."

"Great."

She reached under the counter and produced a

brochure that she slid toward him. "Would you like to book the lessons today?"

"I'll let you know after I show this to my wife. Thanks for the information, though."

"Anytime," Jane said. "Just give us a call when you're ready to schedule."

It might have been a tiny kernel of insight into Livy's life, but even a tiny kernel could produce a plant. Nick headed out of the office and down a long boardwalk toward the stairs, a hell of a lot more confident than he'd been this morning.

"Nick?" He turned to find Livy heading toward him, her steps awkward and clunky from her ski boots. "What are you doing up here?"

Shit.

Chapter Six

Nick looked a little like a kid with his hand in the cookie jar, but he recovered his calm resolve quickly enough to make Livy hope she'd imagined it. Fear trickled into her bloodstream but she forced the sensation away. Nick had every right in the world to be up here and it didn't mean that it had anything to do with her. She needed to cut the paranoia and try to act like a normal human being for a change. The problem was, Livy had been looking over her shoulder for so long, she had no idea how to do that anymore.

"Hey." His easy smile as he walked toward her relaxed the unwelcome tension that pulled her muscles taut. "I was looking for you, actually."

"Me?" He'd only been her neighbor for a week but in that time, Livy felt like she'd gotten to know him a little bit. He wasn't a skier, so if he was looking for her it wasn't because he wanted a lesson. "Why?"

He gave a sheepish grin that did traitorous things to Livy's body. Did Nick have any idea how good-looking he was? He seemed to wield his charm like a weapon. At least, it felt that way to Livy. A simple grin stabbed her through the heart. "Honestly?" He looked away as though embarrassed. "I'm going stir-crazy in the house. I drove around town but that took all of about ten minutes. You talk about the ski hill so much, I got curious. So I went for a drive. I figured since I was up here, I'd see if you wanted to get some lunch."

His story wasn't too farfetched. She still couldn't understand what in the hell he was doing on vacation in a place that had nothing to offer him, free house or not. That familiar suspicion crept up on Livy. Her equal measure of comfort and discomfort in Nick's presence was another reminder that she needed to pull up camp and move on. *He's only here for a few more weeks. What would it hurt to let yourself enjoy a little human contact?* "I've got about forty-five minutes until my next lesson. I could grab a bite."

Nick smiled and she swore if her ski boots weren't holding her up, her legs would've given out. The fear that had kept her going for the past four years scratched at the back of Livy's mind, warning her that getting close to anyone—even a guy who wouldn't be around for much longer—was a bad idea.

"This is your wheelhouse," he said. "Lead the way."

Her stomach leaped into her throat and floated back down in a not altogether unpleasant way. Yep. Letting Nick get close was definitely a bad idea.

Livy paused and hiked up the legs of her ski pants to unbuckle her boots before they headed up the stairs to the third floor of the lodge and the restaurant. She usually didn't mind walking around in her cumbersome ski gear but she suddenly felt like an elephant walking beside a sleek tiger.

"Try to ignore the fact that I look like a goose waddling around on land," she remarked as they climbed the stairs.

Nick chuckled. The deep timbre rippled through her like rings on a pond and she suppressed a shiver. "I bet when you're on the slopes you're as graceful as one in the water."

The compliment, whether intentional or not, caused a rush of heat to flood Livy's body. Thank God the telltale signs of a blush were hidden beneath the chill that painted her cheeks and nose. "I try," she said with a laugh.

"How long have you been skiing?"

Nick held open the door and followed Livy inside the crowded lodge. Finding a table might be problematic, but they'd squeeze in somewhere. She contemplated his question as she headed for the cafeteria area. She'd made the mistake of answering personal questions when she'd first moved here. Livy Gallagher didn't have a history and it needed to stay that way. "Oh, you know, a while," she said. She pointed toward the end of the food line where a stack of plastic trays rested on the counter and smiled. Smiles always put people at ease. Curt responses, frowns, those made people suspicious. "Grab a tray and follow me."

"A while, huh?" Nick placed his tray next to hers on the counter and stepped up to the grill to order a burger and fries. He cast a questioning glance Livy's way.

"Oh, I'll take the black bean chicken quesadilla and mango salsa," she said to Craig who was manning the grill today.

"Are you like, Olympics good?"

His question caused anxious nerves to rear their ugly little heads. The question was innocent enough she supposed, but it also made her feel as though Nick might know more about her than he let on. *Danger, Will Robinson!* "Not really," she remarked as she accepted the plate with her quesadilla from Craig. She set it on her tray and continued down the bar after Nick got his burger. "I can handle the black diamond runs, though."

Livy grabbed a bottle of water out of the cooler and Nick swiped an iced tea. He pulled his wallet out of his jeans as they approached the register but she stopped him.

"It's on me."

Nick cocked a brow. A half smile flirted with his mouth and Livy fought the urge to sigh. The man was too good-looking for words. "I'm the one who invited you, remember."

"True. But I'm the one with the employee discount."

"All right. You can get this one," he said as though he did her a huge favor, "but next time is on me." The thought that there'd be a next time filled her with equal parts anticipation and fear. "You paid for pizza the other night too. You're going to put me to shame."

They found a table tucked away in a far corner

and close to the windows. The lodge was always so busy it was tough to have a conversation without shouting. Livy tended to avoid the third floor because the press of people made her nervous. Too many bodies crammed together and not enough space between her and the nearest exit. Sitting here with Nick made her feel more at ease than she had in a long time, though. Was it because he was a cop or because his sheer size and imposing presence made her feel as though nothing could touch her?

Did it really matter?

"You dug me out of a snowbank, packed in my groceries, and chopped firewood. I should be feeding you every night." Nick's brow furrowed and a smile played on his lips. A warm glow settled in her belly and Livy's pulse skittered in her veins. Rather than try to smooth over her own embarrassment, she turned her attention on the quesadilla. "The food here is really good."

The great thing about Nick was that he didn't press her. They ate and talked, but he didn't ask her any more personal questions or grill her about her past. One of the reasons Livy kept herself from forming any relationships was because people were naturally curious and the more time she spent with someone, the more they wanted to know about her. Where had she lived before she moved to McCall? What had she done for work? Did she go to college? What about her parents? Where did they live? Did she have any brothers or sisters? Livy hated to lie and so rather than make up stories about a life she hadn't lived, she opted to simply refrain from making friends. Sure it was lonely. But lonely was better than dead.

"Most people ski on their days off." Nick put his lips to the bottle of iced tea and took a long pull. Livy tried not to be jealous of an inanimate object, but she suddenly found herself wishing she'd been born a bottle of Lipton. His mouth looked absolutely delicious. "Since you ski at work, I doubt you're anxious to spend your free time here."

Truth be told, there wasn't much else that Livy did. She felt relatively safe here. There was only one road in or out and the slope of Brundage Mountain gave her the perfect vantage point to keep an eye on the parking lot. Not that she expected a horde of loud, growling motorcycles to climb the steep, winding mountain road in the dead of winter, but she'd take a false sense of security over the crippling fear any day of the week.

"I come up on my days off sometimes," she said. "The kids I teach are always beginners. They never graduate from Easy Street. Sometimes I like to take the big girl runs, you know?"

Nick smiled. The expression was as blinding and brilliant as the sun. Did he employ his charm often, she wondered? Did he realize how much it made her want to lean in closer? Maybe close enough to touch. He smelled like winter: clean and crisp. Livy snapped back in her chair as she realized she'd unintentionally angled her body toward his. It had been so long since she'd gone on a date, let alone kissed a guy. She was starved for the contact. The reminder of her isolated existence opened up a giant hole in her chest. She had Joel to thank for that feeling and she hated him for it.

"Hey. Everything okay?"

Livy brought her gaze up to find Nick studying her. His expression was full of concern and she wondered what she'd let slip as she lost herself to her own stupid thoughts. "Oh, sorry. Did I zone out? I um, was thinking about Simon. I forgot to put food in his bowl before I left for work this morning."

Nick gave her a dubious look but he didn't call her bullshit. A gorgeous, easygoing guy who didn't pry. Too good to be true. The thought sent a shiver of warning through her. She needed to remain mindful of that very thing. When something was too good to be true, it usually was. Despite the fact that Nick made her feel safe, Livy needed to stay on guard.

Lonely was better than dead.

Livy obviously had a lot of practice at deflecting. She gave noncommittal answers, was careful to keep the topics of conversation light, steering it where she wanted it to go. More than once during their lunch, Nick had watched as her concentration flagged and her mind wandered. The sadness that came over her features was enough to steal his breath.

She hadn't been thinking about her cat. Her overly cautious and distracted behavior was just another telltale sign that he was on the money. Livy Gallagher was Kari Hanson. He might not have the solid evidence to prove it but he trusted his gut. It didn't answer the one burning question, though: Why did Joel really want her and why had she gone into hiding?

She pulled the knit beanie from her head and smoothed a hand self-consciously over her hair. Her braids had kept it neat and Nick wondered what the golden strands would look like if she ever let them hang loose about her shoulders. Her cheeks were flushed from the cold; even her lips were darker pink and inviting, making her skin seem even more creamy and fair. *Jesus, snap the hell out of it!* She was a person of interest, not a date. It didn't matter what she looked like. Even unofficially, Nick was still on the job.

A few moments of companionable silence followed, each of them lost in their own thoughts. The connection between Livy and Joel was the ultimate puzzle, one with too many pieces for him to easily put it back together. The informant had been adamant that Joel was looking for his ex, a woman he hadn't been able to get out of his head. He wanted her back at any cost and had put the word out to MCs across the country to keep an eye out for her.

Currently, there were multiple federal warrants out for Joel's arrest. Every law enforcement agency in the country was looking for him. A smart man—one with Joel's extensive local and international connections—wouldn't have wasted any time finding someone to smuggle him into Mexico. He had dealings with the cartel; it would have been relatively easy for him to slip over the border undetected. But according to their informant, Joel wasn't going anywhere until he got his old lady back.

Why? Why was Joel's safety and freedom less important that getting his hands on Livy? She was beautiful, intelligent, funny. . . . It would have been enough to keep Nick by her side. Was it enough for Joel Meecum as well?

"Looks like I'm not the only one zoning out today," Livy remarked. "And you don't even have a cat at home who's more than likely plotting your demise because you forgot to feed him."

The comment tumbled from her lips with such ease. Nick wondered how long it had taken Livy to buy into her own lies and this life she'd fabricated for herself. "I think the cold weather is freezing my brain."

Livy laughed. The sound washed over him, warmed him from the inside out. Nick chided himself for allowing her to affect him in any way. He was investigating her, for shit's sake. This wasn't a date.

"Winter is the price we pay for amazing summers." Livy's tone changed, no longer playful, but sad. "The summers in McCall are spectacular. Not too hot, not cold. The lake is amazing. I kayak, paddleboard, swim. I bet even you could get into those types of activities," she added with a wry grin. "It's a great place to live."

Goddamn it. She was getting ready to run.

Livy spoke about the town as though in mourning. Regret shone in her eyes and tugged her mouth downward. The gears cranked in Nick's brain and he fought to keep his expression impassive, the conversation light, when what he really wanted to do was grab her by the shoulders and shake some sense into her. Running wouldn't solve anything. It would only make matters worse. "It sucks that I won't get a chance to see it. Maybe I'll have to drive up for a week in July or something."

She averted her gaze. Livy wouldn't be here in July. "That would be great. You'd probably have a lot of fun. There's more to do here in the summer anyway."

"Livy—" Nick snapped his jaw shut before he said something he'd regret. It was too soon to show his hand. She was as spooked as a rabbit caught in a snare and he still didn't know her history with Joel. Livy appeared soft and innocent but looks could be deceiving. If he backed her into a corner, pushed her, she might show her teeth. He couldn't afford to lose the one lead they'd had on Meecum in over a year.

"What?" Her wide hazel eyes drank him in. Nick swallowed past the lump that rose in his throat. God, she was beautiful.

"Why don't I feed Simon for you?" It was an excuse to get into her house while she wasn't home. She'd all but put the suggestion out there when she'd used her cat as the reason for her wandering thoughts.

"Oh, um, yeah." She drew her full bottom lip between her teeth and looked to her right. She rolled her shoulders as though trying to coax away some tension. "The doors are locked, though."

Her expression became pinched as though she waged some internal battle. Nick waited patiently. If he pushed her on the matter, she'd be suspicious.

He was just making a friendly offer, being a good neighbor. He wanted her to trust him. Part of him needed her to.

"If you think he'll be okay until you get home, it's fine," Nick said. "I'm not doing anything but sitting in the house, so I thought I'd offer."

"I'm sure he'll be okay," Livy said after a moment. "He ate last night before bed, so it's not like he'll starve to death."

"No worries." *Shit.* Nick hid his disappointment as he took a pull from the bottle of iced tea. The cold chill almost numbed his throat on the way down, better than the sting he felt at not being able to earn a small amount of Livy's trust.

Livy fidgeted in her seat, glanced toward the parking lot, over her shoulder, and again to her right. She leaned back to check the large clock that hung from the far wall. "I've got a group lesson in about fifteen minutes. I'd probably better go get ready."

It wasn't a brush-off per se, but Nick's offer to go into her house had made Livy nervous. She reached for her tray at the same time Nick did and their hands touched. The contact was electric and sent a rush of heat through his bloodstream that settled and pooled in his gut. Their eyes met and Livy's full pink lips parted. How could a man spend any amount of time with her and not think about kissing her? Nick found himself thinking about it more and more and that was a huge fucking problem. "I'll get your tray." The words came out much rougher than he'd hoped. He cleared his throat. "You've got a lot more gear to get on than I do."

Livy pulled the knit beanie back on and pushed it up over her forehead before situating her goggles over the hat. Nick stood and gathered up their empty plates and stacked their trays but he watched from the corner of his eye as she put on her coat. Everything she did drew Nick's undivided attention.

"Thanks for having lunch with me." She reached down and fiddled with her ski boot before turning toward the exit.

Nick stood there, holding their lunch trays, mouth slack like some sort of idiot. "How about dinner tonight?" The words left his mouth before he could think better of it. Nothing like coming on too strong to earn a woman's trust.

A frown marred her brow for the barest second. That sadness and regret, no matter how fleeting, tore a hole in Nick's chest every time he saw it. She paused and a smile tugged at one corner of her mouth. "My place or yours?"

"How about we go out?" he suggested. "You could show me the town."

She worried her lip, unsure. Was Livy so afraid that besides work and the grocery store she never left her house? "All right," she said after a moment. "I get off at four. How 'bout we eat around six thirty?"

"I'll be ready," Nick replied. "Have fun on the slopes."

Her smile brightened. "Always. See you tonight."

This was research, Nick reminded himself. Nothing more. His interest in Livy didn't go beyond how she could get him closer to Joel Meecum. And maybe if he kept telling himself that, like Livy, he'd start to believe his own lies.

Chapter Seven

Livy checked her reflection in the full-length mirror one last time. On a scale of one to ten of bad ideas, going out on a date with Nick ranked somewhere around a fifty. She'd always been able to justify her decision to live like a hermit. Fear could be a hell of a motivator. And likewise, she didn't date for the same reason that she kept her interpersonal interactions to a minimum at work: Livy hated lying. Always had. And a relationship founded on lies was doomed no matter her reasons for doing it.

She shouldn't have accepted Nick's offer for dinner tonight. She shouldn't have eaten lunch with him this afternoon. Hell, she never should have let him pack in her groceries or push her out of the snowdrift in the first place. She never should have exchanged even a single word with him. Common sense took a permanent hiatus from her brain when he was near, though. Her thought process stalled and all she wanted was one minute more with him. When their hands had touched earlier today, it sparked something inside of Livy. A desire so hot and thick that she'd nearly choked on it. God, it was embarrassing how hard up she was. An innocent touch from a good-looking guy and she was on fire. Just one more reason going out to dinner with him tonight was a bad idea. Her tongue would be lolling out of her mouth before dessert. Totes sexy.

Ugh. Could she be more of a loser?

The knock at her front door startled Livy and she lost her hold on the tube of lipstick she held in her grasp. She took several even breaths to slow her racing heart and cast a sidelong glance at Simon who narrowed his eyes at her in judgment.

"We can't all be as cool as you are, Simon."

The cat gave her a forlorn meow before he jumped down from the bed and headed out of the room. Livy retrieved the tube of lipstick and smoothed some on her lips before following Simon down the stairs. Through the glass pane of the door, she caught sight of Nick waiting on the front porch, something clutched in his grip. Curiosity piqued, Livy hustled down the last few stairs and opened the door.

"Hey. I'm almost ready, just have to grab my coat."

Nick held the snow shovel aloft, a wide smile curving his lips. Prince Charming had nothing on Nick. His smile literally weakened her knees. Livy expected a glint of light followed by a high-pitched *ping!* every time he grinned at her. His smile was by far Nick's greatest asset and his most powerful weapon. She clutched the doorknob a little tighter to help keep her upright.

"He's no Frank, but hopefully he'll get the job done."

Livy's heart soared. What kind of woman was moved by a fucking snow shovel? This one, that's who. A dozen roses wouldn't have meant more to her than the plastic snow shovel Nick offered her.

She took the shovel from his outstretched hand. "This is probably the best present anyone has ever given me. Thank you so much!"

Nick's brows came together and his lips formed a hard line. "If that's the best present anyone has ever given you, I'd say I need to have a talk with the gift givers in your life."

Heat rose to Livy's cheeks. She'd forgone birthday and Christmas presents when she was a kid in lieu of skis and coaching fees. Money had been tight and as a single parent, her mom worked two jobs not only to make ends meet but to make sure that she could continue to ski. Her mom was the only family she had, and in four years, Livy had talked to her all of fifteen times. So yeah, a stupid shovel meant so much to her that it caused tears to prick at her eyes.

"I think I'll call him Frank Junior." It was easier to change the subject than to try to fabricate a reason why Livy didn't have anyone in her life who might want to give her a gift. "I only hope he can live up to his father's legacy."

Nick gave her a look as though he knew she was deflecting, but he let it slide. Again she was struck by how great it was to be with someone who didn't try to pry and simply spent time with her. Sadness threatened to swallow her as Livy thought about moving away from the place she'd called home for four years. Knowing Nick would be leaving in three short weeks didn't contribute to her melancholy, either. Not at all.

"So, where are you taking me?" Nick waited on the porch as Livy threw on her coat and locked up the house. "And dinner's on me so don't let that influence your decision at all."

She checked the deadbolt once, twice, and again. If he noticed her obsessiveness, he didn't say anything. Though, what would he say? *So . . . I see you like to lock doors. What's up with that?* She wanted to knock her head against a wall.

Livy gave him a sidelong glance as she wrapped a scarf around her neck. "So are you saying I shouldn't feel guilty about choosing somewhere very high-end?"

"I encourage it," Nick said. "I want the best."

"Oh my God!" Livy gasped with feigned shock, and Nick cast a suspicious glance her way. "Are you a . . . *foodie?*" His charming half smile sent her into a frenzied state where she pictured her ovaries perking up and panting like happy little puppies. The man was so fucking gorgeous it wouldn't surprise her that the mere sight of him made her as fertile as the Nile.

Darkness swallowed them as they stepped beyond the stretch of the porch light toward Nick's truck. Livy had always loved winter—the cold and piles of snow didn't bother her—but the seemingly perpetual darkness got to be a bit of a downer after a while. Summer nights in McCall were amazing. Sunsets were gorgeous until almost ten o'clock and the cool air from the lake wafted in through the upstairs window to cool the house from the heat of the day. It sucked that she wouldn't be here for another summer. She'd miss living here.

"Livy?"

Nick stood at the passenger side of the truck, the door held open for her. Good-looking and a gentleman? Jesus. He really was Prince Charming. Her sex drive wasn't simply yipping like an excited puppy anymore, it was full-on howling.

"Sorry." She hoofed it through the snow and hopped in the truck. "I, uh, couldn't remember if I locked the door or not." *Oh dear Lord. Livy, are you insane?* Like he didn't notice her lock and unlock her door a hundred freaking times. Her excuses for getting lost in her own stupid thoughts were becoming less believable by the second.

Nick gave her a wry look. "I'm pretty sure you're good to go." Her stomach did a backflip as his eyes met hers for a moment before he closed the door and rounded the truck to the driver's side.

"Okay, where are we going?" Nick asked as he climbed in and started the truck.

"No price restrictions, huh, foodie?" Livy teased.

"I want my credit card to weep at the end of dinner."

Laughter bubbled in Livy's chest. "All right, you asked for it. Let's go to The Narrows at Shore Lodge," she said. "I promise, your Visa will *sob.*"

"Perfect."

Perfect. That one word described Nick to a T. Livy

was starting to wonder if he had a fatal flaw. Guys like Nick weren't usually what Livy went for. Way too far out of her league to even have a chance. Nick made her feel like she could be a different person, though. One who deserved better than a user or abuser. She just hoped that he wouldn't eventually prove that wild theory wrong.

The Narrows wasn't far from the house. Situated in the swanky Shore Lodge on Payette Lake, the place boasted a world-class chef and the cuisine to go along with their rustic décor. The hotel itself was gorgeous and looked out over the lake. Nick felt cheated of the view in the dark of night. Maybe he'd bring Livy back for breakfast or brunch on her next day off.

Jesus. He gave himself a mental shake. He wasn't in McCall to date Livy. Why did it seem as though he had to remind himself of that fact more and more? This was about slapping cuffs on Meecum, bringing a violent criminal to justice, and claiming the bragging rights of being the marshal who brought him in. He peeked over the top of the menu at Livy. He'd quit thinking of her as Kari Hanson the minute he'd introduced himself to her that morning in the snowstorm. That was part of the problem. Like her, he'd bought into the persona she'd created. He didn't want her to know anything about Meecum. He didn't want her to be a person of interest.

Scratch that. She was a person of interest all right, but Nick's interest in her was starting to become more personal by the day. If he'd been officially on the job, he'd be working this case with a partner. They would have introduced themselves to Livy, flashed their badges, and thrown their weight around from the get-go. They wouldn't have wasted any time in calling her out on her fake identity. Nick would have personally shaken her down and demanded that she turn on her ex or face jail time for conspiracy and obstruction. As a united front, they would have pushed her, scared her, thrown out a few thinly veiled legal threats. They might've even played good cop, bad cop with her and ultimately offered her protection if she flipped on Meecum and told them everything she knew.

Instead, Nick was practically dating her. He was a real credit to his badge.

Livy studied the menu with wide eyes. The delight so obvious in her expression transformed her, made her even more beautiful and soft. "Everything on the menu looks delicious," she said with a wide grin. "I haven't eaten anything like this since—" A look of pure shock chased over her features and she reached out to take a nervous sip from her water glass.

She'd been on the verge of letting something slip. "Since what?" Nick asked, hoping to edge her closer to finally divulging something about herself that was real. Something personal that he could use in his research of her.

She studied him for a moment. The quiet intensity of it unnerved him. Livy looked straight into his eyes, inside of him, through him as though she could somehow test his worthiness of whatever she'd been about to say. They balanced at the cusp of something huge. Trust. Nick wanted her to trust him, he practically *willed* it. *Come on, Livy. I can help you. Let me.*

"Not since I won the junior division slalom title when I was seventeen and my mom took me out to celebrate."

Yes! Warm emotion swelled in Nick's chest. Livy was a tough nut to crack but he'd managed to create the tiniest fissure. The knowledge that she'd given him some small bit of truth felt like a gift. Something precious and invaluable that had been entrusted into his safekeeping. And damn it, it felt *good.*

Nick lowered his menu to give her his full attention. "You must be a much better skier than you let on. Not really Olympic level? I'd say you were being modest. That's amazing, Livy."

Color rose to her cheeks and Nick's breath hitched. She glanced away as though embarrassed. *No.* She was angry with herself for letting a personal truth slip. Her lips thinned before she let out a slow breath. "It's not a big deal," she murmured. "It was a long time ago."

"You're what . . . twenty-five, twenty-six?" Nick ventured. "It couldn't have been that long ago."

"Twenty-five," she said with a wry grin. "It feels like forever ago." The sadness in her tone gutted him. "I'm practically a grandma."

Oftentimes, the marshals caught fugitives simply because they grew tired of hiding out. Even lowlife violent criminals couldn't survive in isolation for long. It was a wonder Meecum had made it this far, though the Marshals Service had always surmised that it had been easier for him to evade capture because of the network of members in the Black Death MC that helped him. Livy hadn't been so lucky. One of the reasons it had been hard to track her down was because they literally hadn't been able to find any information on Kari Hanson that would help lead them to her. No family, no work history, nothing. They'd assumed that Kari was another alias and that she'd been a fugitive when she'd hooked up with Joel. That theory had been shot to shit the moment Nick laid eyes on her. There wasn't a single scenario he could conjure in his mind that made her a criminal or put her in any sort of relationship with Joel Meecum, romantic or otherwise.

"Why'd you quit racing?"

Livy traced the pad of her finger around the lip of her water glass. Nick's gaze was drawn to the motion and he couldn't help but wonder what it would feel like to have that digit trace a similar pattern on his skin. A tingle of sensation raced down his spine and settled at the base of his cock. He needed to get his shit together and focus on why he was here before he did something stupid. Because with every passing second in her company, stupid gained more and more appeal.

"Ran out of money," she said with a shrug. She tried to play it off as no big deal but Nick didn't buy it. "Ski racing is a super-expensive sport. I had a couple of sponsorship offers but they weren't enough. In juniors, there's a lot of travel. Private schooling to accommodate training schedules, that sort of thing. It adds up."

"Damn." Nick could only imagine how crushing it had been for her to quit. "That's rough. I'm sorry, Livy."

"It is what it is." She took a sip from her glass. "It could have been worse. I could have been forced to quit because of an injury. At least I'm fit and can still ski for fun. That's what's important."

"And that you have no regrets," Nick added.

Her expression darkened. Livy obviously had a few regrets. He just wished he knew what they were. "Right," she said, low.

Their conversation was interrupted when the server came back around to take their order. "Remember," Nick said with a grin, "I want my credit card to weep."

She cast a sidelong glance at their server who wore an ear-to-ear grin. No doubt he expected everyone at the table—including himself—to be pleased with the outcome of tonight's meals. Nick found himself wanting to spend money on Livy. To buy her things she needed or simply wanted. To wine and dine her, to make her feel lavished with attention. Had anyone ever spoiled her? Had Joel? Or had he simply hurt her? Done something so horrible to her that she'd had no choice but to run and hide.

The thought sent Nick's temper into a sudden and unexpected tailspin.

"And for you . . . ?"

Nick looked up into the expectant face of their server as though he'd only realized the guy was standing there. "Oh, um, I'll have the Elk chop with purple potatoes."

"That's one of my favorites," he said. "Totally a local specialty." Nick had a feeling that he'd missed more than one question from their server while he'd been lost in his thoughts. He raised his brows in question and he added, "Did you want to start off with any appetizers, or just the entrees?"

He had said he wanted his credit card to cry. Obviously their server felt as though they'd barely made it break a sweat. Nick took a quick glance over the menu. "We'll start with the steamed mussels and the duck meatballs."

"Great!" He perked up with every item added to their ticket. "I'll get the apps started and I'll be back to refresh your drinks in a bit."

"What did you order?" Nick couldn't believe that he'd lost himself so completely in his thoughts. Finding Meecum had become his obsession, but now that he knew the one woman who could lead him to the bastard, his focus had slowly begun to shift. He needed to get his damned head back in the game.

"The lobster linguine," Livy said with chagrin. "I hope that's okay."

Nick had been so preoccupied with the woman seated across from him that he hadn't even bothered for more than a cursory glance at the menu. "Of course it's okay," he replied. He'd come to the conclusion that Livy didn't appreciate people spending money on her. Why? "I told you we were going all out tonight. I want the full culinary experience."

"You're gonna get it," she said with a laugh. "Elk chops?"

He smiled. "You heard our server, it's a local specialty."

Nick tried to steer their conversation back to Livy's life. Not only because he was looking for something to get him closer to Meecum, but because he found himself greedy for every little detail. He wanted to know *everything* about her. Every tiny nuance. Livy wasn't having it.

"Nope. Enough about me." She'd slipped once tonight and it became apparent that it wasn't going to happen again. She didn't waste any time in shutting him down. "I want to know more about you. What's it like to take down the bad guys every day?"

Her tone showed genuine interest. Not exactly what you'd expect from someone who kept company with assholes who harbored nothing but disdain for law enforcement.

"It's amazing," Nick said. He wanted Livy to trust him. To be honest with him. It was going to take more than a one-sided exchange of personal details to get it done. He looked away and raked a hand through his hair. "Sometimes I take it a little too personally."

"Why?"

Nick couldn't bring himself to meet Livy's gaze. The softly spoken word made his gut knot up tight. His mind was at war with his emotions and he wasn't sure which he wanted to win.

"My sister was assaulted when she was in high school." Nick wanted to open up to Livy, but he couldn't go deeper than that. Despite the time that had passed, even thinking about what had happened to Lindsey sent him into a rage. "It was pretty bad. I want to make sure that never happens on my watch. Somebody does wrong, I'm going to do *everything* in my power to make sure they stand accountable for it."

Livy's expression softened with a deep sadness. Her wide hazel eyes drank him in and when he allowed himself to meet her gaze, his breath stalled in his lungs. Her lips parted on a sigh and Nick gripped the edge of the table to keep from reaching out and brushing his thumb against her petal-soft bottom lip.

"You're not what I expected, Nick."

Neither are you. Maybe they'd both gotten more than they'd bargained for.

Chapter Eight

Dinner passed in a blur. Livy had resisted the urge more than once to poke herself with her fork, just to make sure she wasn't dreaming. Four years. One thousand, four hundred and sixty days of loneliness. Of being afraid. Of looking over her shoulder. Of being so goddamned tense that her muscles never stopped aching. One evening with Nick erased all of it. Almost made her feel . . . *normal.*

Now that their evening was winding down, Livy's shoulders no longer felt as though they crept toward her ears. She hadn't obsessively checked behind her once. Not a passing thought had been given to her house and whether or not she'd remembered to lock all of the windows and doors. She could have stayed at the restaurant all night. Sitting with Nick, talking about nothing and everything, sipping wine and simply enjoying his company. She couldn't remember the last time she'd felt so comfortable with another person. Especially with a man.

Nick wasn't a dirty cop. He wasn't on the take. He didn't have an agenda. He was a good guy. Honorable. With every minute spent in his company, Livy became more convinced that he was someone she could trust. Maybe even someone who could help her. It was dangerous to let her guard down like that, but she couldn't help herself. Nick made her want to trust. To finally let someone in. She wanted him despite her own self-imposed rules and safeguards.

But Livy knew better. She couldn't allow herself to want anything or anyone. Nick made her forget the very real danger in her life and the *very* dangerous man who would never stop looking for her. She'd gotten a glimpse of what a normal life could be and it further strengthened her resolve to pack up and find a new place to settle down.

Alone is better than dead.

Livy clutched the cardboard box that contained the rest of her cheesecake close to her body as Nick rounded the front of his truck. She caught his profile in the glow of the headlights and a rush of delicious heat raced through her veins. The food had been too good, the dessert too decadent, and the wine too heady. It left Livy feeling a little too brazen. She wanted to do something irresponsible for a change. She wanted to be reckless.

With Nick.

The dome light came on when he opened her door. Cold flooded the cab of the truck and she shivered, but Livy wasn't sure if her reaction was from the winter wind or the man who stood in the open space beside her, close enough to touch.

"Are you a nice guy, Nick?" The question left her lips, unbidden. Too late to suck them back in, Livy gauged his reaction from the furrow of his brow to the set of his jaw.

"No." He didn't bullshit her though, and that earned him a few points no matter the tremor of fear that settled in her belly. "Not really. Do you want to know why I'm on vacation, Livy?"

Did she? Despite the cold that soaked through her coat and permeated her skin, Livy stayed put. "Why?"

"Because I don't follow orders well." The dark timbre of his voice heated Livy from the inside out. "My coworkers think I'm a reckless, pigheaded pain in the ass. My chief told me to take a month off, to think about what I wanted and to come back with a clear head, ready to follow orders. And you know what? Nothing's going to change. I'm going to go back and continue to be the same disagreeable asshole I was before he kicked me out of his office. Because I have to be. Because those violent sons of bitches out on the streets aren't going to change. I'll keep going, until I put as many of those bastards in cuffs as I can and I'll do whatever it takes to get it done."

A knot lodged in Livy's chest. "That doesn't make you a bad guy, Nick."

"Maybe not," he said with a derisive snort. "But it probably doesn't make me a good cop."

He thought he was a bad cop? Livy wanted to laugh out loud. It seemed strange to be having this conversation while they sat out in the cold, but somehow it was easier for Livy to talk to him in the low light that shadowed his handsome face. "Have you ever taken a bribe, Nick? Planted or tampered with evidence? Blackmailed someone?" She swallowed down the fear that coated her throat. "Threatened someone?"

His lips thinned. "No."

"Then you're *not* a bad cop."

Nick leveled his gaze and Livy found herself helpless to look away. "What do you know about bad cops?"

His tone wasn't angry or even accusing. More concerned. It cut through her. "I . . ." But it didn't mean she was ready to put her full trust in him either. "Nothing. I mean, that's how bad cops are on TV. They're not interested in taking down the bad guy, just serving their own interests."

Nick's shoulders slumped almost imperceptibly as though he'd expected a different answer. That couldn't have been the case, though. Nick couldn't possibly know anything about her. She'd made damned sure that no one would. Olivia Gallagher was a ghost. And when she left McCall—which would be soon—Livy would stay behind and some other woman would take her place. Strange, but she almost mourned the imposing "death" of a person who didn't exist. She liked Livy. Livy wasn't bitter. Or disappointed. Livy's dreams hadn't been squashed before they'd even had a chance to take flight. Livy didn't have expectations and enjoyed her simple life. Livy went on dates with gorgeous cops and ate lobster and cheesecake.

Nick reached out and took her hand. They'd been out in the cold for a good fifteen minutes but his skin was warm as it covered hers. A comfort that caused her heart to race and butterflies to take flight in her stomach.

Maybe it was the wine or the euphoria of their dinner date that caused her brain to buzz and her body to hum. Or maybe it was simply Nick. His overwhelming presence was more effective at getting her drunk than an entire bottle of too expensive wine.

"You're shivering." His voice was a warm caress. It wasn't the cold that made her tremble. "Let's get you inside."

Livy couldn't form the words to respond so she merely nodded.

He didn't let go of her hand after he helped her out of the truck. Instead, Nick held on tighter as though afraid she'd pull away. Not a chance. She wanted his warmth, the sense of security he lent her without even trying. The reassurance of his presence. They walked up the snowy steps in silence and Livy reached into her pocket to retrieve her keys. For the first time in four years, she unlocked the deadbolt without checking first to make sure it was still locked.

Livy opened the door and glanced up at Nick from beneath lowered lashes. She worried the inside of her cheek as she battled the indecision that caused her stomach to churn. It's not like he'd never been in her house before. But this was different. She was different. In just over a week, Nick had managed to change her. He'd made her want more than what she'd settled for. What did it matter if she reached out and took it just this once? Nick would be headed back to Bellevue in a few weeks and Livy would be moving soon. What would it hurt this once to give in and allow herself some small comfort?

"You're not a bad guy, Nick," Livy said, low. "You're one of the good ones."

He reached up with his free hand and brushed his fingertips along her temple. Livy broke out into delicious chills that hardened her nipples and heated her blood. Her breath quickened as he closed the distance between them. His chest brushed hers and she had to angle her head upward to look at him. Nick's brows drew down sharply over his dark eyes and his jaw squared. "You think I'm a good guy, Livy?"

"I know you are."

His expression grew even darker. "Don't be so sure."

Nick's mouth descended on hers in a crushing kiss. Livy's world spun out of control and if not for the arm he wrapped around her waist, her legs might have slipped out from under her. His intensity stole her breath as he pulled her hard against his body and slanted his mouth over hers to deepen the kiss. His tongue thrust past her lips, a command that she part for him, one that Livy couldn't resist. She wanted him with a desperation that caused her to tremble in his embrace.

Livy's free arm wound around Nick's neck. He urged her backward and she took one slow step after another. The sound of the door closing behind them barely registered as he guided her into the living room. He tugged at her coat and

Livy let go of him to set her left over cheesecake down and shrug out of her coat. It fell to the floor and a moment later, his landed beside it. When he took her in his arms once again, the heat of his body met hers and Livy sighed. It had been so long since she'd had this kind of contact and it brought tears to her eyes. If she let this go any further, it might break her.

And yet, she did nothing to stop it.

Nick cupped the back of her neck with one large palm. His fingers threaded through her hair as he claimed her mouth once again. He kissed her with all of the desperation and hunger that Livy felt and then some. She'd never realized this sort of searing heat existed. Livy knew it would consume her but she didn't care. She welcomed the lick of flames that Nick ignited within her. She wanted more, wanted to *burn*.

Alone is better than dead. For once, she didn't buy into her own lies.

A good man wouldn't be doing what Nick was right now. If Livy thought he was anything other than a sorry bastard, she was kidding herself. He was on the job, for shit's sake. Whether officially or not, he was a marshal investigating a lead. Investigating Livy. And rather than keep a respectable— professional—distance, he'd given in to his own damned selfish wants.

He wanted Livy. Had wanted her since the first time he'd laid eyes on her.

Her hair slipped through his fingers like strands

of silk. A hint of wine lingered on her lips and Nick deepened their kiss so he could taste the sweetness of her mouth. Her tongue wound with his in a warm, wet glide that hardened his cock to stone behind his fly. Livy was soft, sweet, and at the same time strong and full of fire. Beautiful. He wanted to be inside of her so badly that he hurt.

Nick urged her toward the couch and eased her down to the cushions. Never breaking their kiss, he followed her down and settled between her thighs. He brushed against her core and the not-so-innocent contact set him on fire. His cock throbbed hot and hard and his gut knotted up. As though he had no control over his own body, his hips gave a gentle thrust. Livy's answering moan only served to encourage him and he thrust again, harder.

She nipped at his bottom lip before drawing it into her mouth and sucking. A tingle of sensation raced down his spine and settled in his sac. He wanted the heat of her mouth and those petal-soft lips wrapped around the head of his cock. The last remaining shred of Nick's common sense tugged at the back of his mind, urging him to take a minute to think about what the fuck he was doing. Career suicide wasn't on his to-do list, but he'd already disobeyed a direct order by using his mandatory time off to hunt Joel Meecum. He was already damned, what would one more sin matter?

Nick abandoned Livy's mouth and let his lips wander the path along her jawline to her ear. His tongue flicked out at the lobe and she arched into him. The press of her breasts against his chest was torture. There were far too many clothes between them, a problem Nick planned to remedy ASAP.

"Livy." His voice rasped in his throat. "Are you sure about this?"

He hoped that she'd tell him to stop. That she'd change her mind and ask for a little space. Anything to keep him from taking what he wanted and at the same time violating every code of conduct he'd ever laid out for himself. Livy made him want to douse all of his stubborn convictions with gasoline and light a match. He was counting on her to be the voice of reason because his had gone silent the moment his lips met hers.

"No." Her voice quavered on the word. "But that's what makes it so perfect."

He felt the same way. It was the impetuousness of the moment, the sudden bright fire of passion that made it so great. Not knowing what would happen next and not caring was what Nick lived for. It quickened his blood, just like the woman in his arms. He was addicted to the thrill of the chase, of the capture. Being with Livy was no different. He wouldn't be satisfied until she was his.

Nick kissed her temple, down her jawline, the pulse point below her ear. He scraped his teeth over the delicate skin at her throat and flicked out at her fragrant skin with his tongue. He wanted to take his time, savor Livy. Enjoy every moment with her in case he came to his senses and tonight was all they'd have together. He could be Nick, a guy on vacation, and she could be Livy, a small-town ski instructor. Tonight, he'd let himself believe the lie because tomorrow, he'd have to face the harsh reality of their truths once again.

Hungry for bare flesh, Nick let his hand wander down Livy's torso. He dragged the hem of her shirt up before his hand ducked beneath the fabric. Livy let out a slow sigh that ended on a whimper as his palm met her heated skin. He kissed her collarbone and the swell of one breast that rose above the low cut of her shirt. Little pants of breath escaped from between Livy's parted lips as Nick dragged his palm slowly up her torso. She was so warm, so soft, and everywhere their skin met little sparks of electricity ignited.

"That feels so good, Nick." The husky words sent a rush of adrenaline through his body. "It's been so long—" She bit the word off and he paused as a seed of common sense took root in his brain. She was a fugitive for all he knew, an associate of one of the most violent criminals Nick had ever investigated. Livy changed course, the words so quiet he had to strain to hear them. "I feel safe with you. I haven't felt safe in a long time."

His resolve crumbled under the onslaught of emotion that rose in his chest. He put his mouth to hers. A slow, gentle kiss that was nothing more than a glance of his lips against hers. Livy arched up to meet him. The muscles in her abdomen twitched and flexed as his palm continued its unhurried path up her torso. He cupped her breast through the fabric of her bra, brushing the pad of his thumb over her nipple. It hardened to a tight bead beneath the fabric and Nick brushed it again.

Livy drew in a sharp breath that was half pleasure

and half shock. How long had it been since a man touched her? The entire four years she'd been in hiding? Nick's cock throbbed harder at the prospect of being the one to reawaken her body after so long.

Her hips rolled up to meet his and he answered the motion with a gentle thrust. Through the fabric of her bra, Nick continued to circle the tight bead of her nipple until her quick breaths transformed into low, desperate moans. He continued to kiss her, his mouth parted just enough to taste her. Her tongue flicked out at his lips and he pulled away. Nick didn't usually get off on teasing a woman in this way. He was more of a down and dirty, get to business sort of guy. But Livy was different. Drawing out her pleasure and driving her to the point of mindless abandon became more important than simply satisfying his own lusts.

He wanted to make her beg.

Her long-sleeved shirt covered far too much of her body. Nick eased away and Livy came up from the couch, following his mouth as though she couldn't bear for him to stop kissing her. Nick smiled against her lips before he pushed himself upright and grabbed the hem of her shirt. He paused for the barest moment and took in the sight of her.

Livy's hazel eyes burned with a heat that seared every inch of his skin. Her chest rose and fell with quick little breaths and her cheeks were flushed. Her lips, full and dark pink, formed into an almost-pout that made him want to nip at the tender flesh with his teeth. Nick pushed her shirt up her torso and Livy raised her arms so he could remove it the rest of the way.

Seeing her fully clothed was enough to cause Nick's libido to take notice. But the more of her naked skin he revealed, the harder his cock became. By the time he got her pants off, it wouldn't be Livy who was begging, that was for damned sure.

She wore a sexy little red lace bra, the cups barely concealing her nipples from his view. The dusky half-moon of her areolas peeked out from the fabric and Nick swallowed down a groan. He was the one being teased, and it was goddamned cruel at that.

"Holy shit, Livy."

Nick scrubbed a hand over his mouth. A slow smile curved her decadent lips and it was all he could do not to take her down in a tackle. He shed his own shirt, desperate for the skin-on-skin contact, and lowered himself over her. She stretched her arms high above her head and her nipples sprang free from the low-cut cups of her bra. Nick groaned and he enjoyed the erotic sight for a moment before he brought his mouth to one stiff peak.

Livy's back arched off the couch and the barest whimper left her lips. He swirled his tongue over her nipple before sucking deeply. Livy's hips rolled up to meet his and she reached up to take his forearm in her grasp, the blunt tips of her short nails digging into the skin. Nick groaned as he grazed his teeth over the delicate flesh. Livy's muscles twitched and she let out an almost surprised gasp that filled Nick with smug satisfaction.

As though she'd been shocked at the pleasure she felt.

Had no one ever made Livy feel so good with such a seemingly innocent touch? Taking her breast in his mouth was virginal compared to what he wanted to do to her. Nick continued to tongue her nipple while he reached out to roll her other nipple gently between his thumb and forefinger. Livy squirmed beneath him, her hips thrusting up to his. Her gasps of pleasure became low moans that made his cock throb.

He'd make her feel so damned good she'd never think of another man again. Especially that bastard Meecum.

Chapter Nine

Livy couldn't be bothered to feel embarrassed by her reaction to Nick's touch. She hadn't so much as flirted with a man in four years and before that she'd only had a couple of not-so-serious boyfriends before she'd focused her attention on taking care of her mom. The whole of her sexual experiences could be summed up in a word: *uneventful.* That is, until now.

Holy effing crap!

Nick had barely touched her and Livy's body came alive. Every nerve ending on her body sparked with sensation. Her skin heated and her blood pumped hard and fast through her veins. The moment his mouth sealed over her nipple, Livy's world spiraled out of control. And when his teeth teased the aching peak, her pussy clenched as a renewed rush of wetness spread between her thighs.

You'd think a man had never touched her like that before. Of course, no man she'd ever known could compare to Nick Brady.

He jerked down the cup of her bra and captured her other nipple between his fingers. Livy's nerve endings fired, her muscles twitched, and a contented moan rose up in her throat as she writhed beneath him. The hard length of Nick's erection brushed between her legs and even through the barrier of their clothes, Livy thought she might come if the delicious friction continued for only a little longer.

"Nick. Oh my God, Nick." She was lust-addled, drunk on pleasure, and want, and the man tucked between her thighs. She was past the point of coherent thought, unable to make a rational decision. The years of self-imposed isolation and loneliness melted away with every touch. Emotion swelled in her chest and tears stung at Livy's eyes. She didn't know how Nick felt about this moment but for her it was *everything*.

Nick switched to her other breast. He kissed, licked, sucked, nibbled at the pearled peak until Livy's breath came in desperate pants. He lavished her with passionate attention for what felt like hours. And still, he didn't show any signs of stopping.

"I love your nipples." Nick's heated murmur brushed the swell of her breast and Livy shuddered. He grazed the pad of his thumb over one and Livy's back came up off the couch and her eyes drifted shut. The sound of Nick's deep voice was a full-body caress. It touched every part of her and stoked the flames of her passion to a near inferno.

"You do?" Livy had always been a little self-conscious about her athletic build. She was lean and hard without the lush curves and full breasts that she thought made a woman attractive. Nick's words, the heat in his tone, made her feel desirable and it banished any niggling doubts left in her mind.

"Oh yeah."

He latched his mouth over the other nipple to emphasize his point and sucked. A jolt of sensation rushed through Livy's center that caused her clit to throb. She kept herself from crying out but even so, a whimper escaped from between her lips.

Nick stilled above her and silence stretched between them. Livy peeked through one eye and then opened the other to find him looking at her, his dark eyes blazing with intensity. He held her gaze as he covered the tip of her nipple with the pad of his forefinger. "These are perfect." He brought his fingertip to the sensitive skin of her areola and traced a circular pattern that spiraled outward. "I love the color, the shape. You're so soft here." His touch became lighter and Livy shivered. "You fit perfectly in my mouth and when I suck"—he lowered his mouth and sucked her nipple briefly into his mouth—"your nipple gets hard against my tongue. Do you like when I do that, Livy?"

She nodded. Words refused to form on her tongue. It was as though she'd forgotten how to speak, how to think in Nick's presence. All she could do was *feel*.

He took her into his mouth and sucked again, this time nibbling the tight peak before pulling away. "How about that?"

She was like an eager puppy, nodding her head in anticipation of another scratch.

His voice went lower. Dark and demanding. "Tell me. I want to hear you say it."

Dear God. Livy thought she might burst into flames at any second. "I like it," she said on a breath.

He repeated the action on her other breast. "How much?"

"So much that I'm pretty sure I've forgotten my own name."

His brows came down over his eyes and something that Livy couldn't identify passed over his expression.

He swirled his tongue over one nipple. Livy sucked in a breath, her own curiosity over Nick's furrowed brow forgotten under the onslaught of pleasure.

Nick kissed the tip of her nipple, around it, over the shallow swell of her breast, across her collarbone, and up her throat. He dragged his teeth up her neck before placing a hot, openmouthed kiss just below her ear.

"I want my mouth on your pussy," he murmured. Livy sucked in a breath. No one had ever spoken to her the way he did and it set her on *fire*. "I can't wait to taste you, Livy."

She wanted him there too. So much so that she reached between them to unbutton her pants and work the zipper down. Nick didn't move, though. He kept his mouth by her ear while he continued to fondle her breast with his left hand. He stroked her thoroughly, lewdly, covering her entire breast with his large palm before bringing his fingers together to pluck at the pearled nipple.

"I'm going to lick you until you come on my tongue. I want my fingers inside of you, your clit in my mouth. I'm going to lap up every drop of you. Would you like that? Would you like to come against my tongue?"

"Yes," she said on an anxious breath.

It was a miracle Livy's own tongue wasn't lolling out of her mouth. If he kept up with the dirty talk, his mouth wouldn't need to be anywhere near her clit to bring her to orgasm. Nick gave a gentle thrust of his hips and Livy let out a whimper. If he didn't get her—and himself—naked soon, she was pretty sure she'd burst into flames.

"I bet you taste like honey."

Holy shit.

"Is your pussy wet, Livy? Is it dripping with all that sweetness for me?"

Her underwear had been damp since the moment he'd kissed her. Wet was an understatement. She was embarrassingly ready for him, every inch of her begging for it. Nick took her earlobe between his teeth.

"If I slipped my hand into your underwear, would you be wet?"

"Uh-huh."

She felt him smile against her throat.

"I want to fuck you." Nick inhaled a deep breath and let it all out on a rush. "God, I've wanted to fuck you since the moment we met."

He had? The admission made Livy want to purr.

"I think about what it's going to feel like to be inside of you and it makes me so damned hard it hurts. I want to fuck you slowly. Hard and deep. I want to fuck until we're too exhausted to move. I want to make you moan, Livy. I want you to scream. I want to hear you say my name when you come. Would you do that? Would you scream my name?"

In Livy's mind, she'd already experienced at least a dozen orgasms. Nick painted a vivid picture with his words, colored in shades of raw, vibrant passion that nearly blinded her with its brilliance.

He wanted her to scream his name? Already, she was prepared to do or say any damn thing he wanted.

"I'll scream whatever the hell you want me to Nick, as long as you don't stop."

Her breathy reply tickled Nick's ear and tingled down his spine. His cock throbbed and his sac ached and if he didn't bury himself to the hilt in her slick heat soon, he was going to fucking explode.

Admitting all of the hot, dirty things he wanted to do to Livy felt like absolution somehow. As though he'd made his confession and with every agreement from her lips, she'd forgiven him. For what? For wanting to fuck her until neither of them could form a coherent thought?

Nick didn't like to beat around the bush. He called it like he saw it, never shied away from what he wanted and never felt bad about how he went about getting it. Now, though, he felt the slightest twinge of regret tug at his chest. He might've been straight with Livy about all of the lewd things he wanted to do to her, but Livy thought Nick was someone he wasn't. Sort of.

Wasn't she playing the same game, though? Technically, they were on level ground. So really, he had no reason to feel even an ounce of regret. Right?

God, she smelled good.

Nick nuzzled Livy's neck. She was so soft, so responsive, so goddamned desirable that he could hardly control himself. He wanted to strip her bare. Bury his face between her thighs. Lick, suck, and bite until she couldn't form a single word to save her life. He wanted to fuck her so hard and so deep that he lost all sense of where his body ended and hers began. Nick wanted to lose himself to Livy.

He was already halfway there.

"Tell me you want my mouth on your pussy."

He wanted to hear it from her lips in her sweet, seductive voice. Wanted her to twine his hair through her fingers and shove him between her legs. He wanted to feel her thighs quiver against his face, wanted to hear her cries. Nick wanted all Livy could give him. *All of her.* But was it because he truly wanted to make her his or because he was hell-bent on taking something that Joel Meecum wanted?

Nick's obsessions bled together until he couldn't distinguish between them anymore. And maybe he didn't want to.

"I want your mouth on me, Nick." The desperation in Livy's tone tested his control. "I don't think I can wait anymore."

Part of him wanted to make her wait. To continue to talk to her. To tease her until Livy begged him to take her. Common sense threatened to spoil the moment as Nick's sense of honor scratched at the back of his mind. He could stop. He could end this before he crossed a line and did something he might regret. Nick pulled away to find Livy's head tilted back, her eyes closed. His gaze wandered over her pale, delicate breasts that swelled over the cups of her bra and any resolve he might have had shattered.

Not even his own goddamned morality could stop him now.

Nick leaned back on his knees. The couch wasn't exactly the most comfortable spot for what he wanted to do but he wasn't going to waste another second getting Livy naked. The couch, the floor, the recliner . . . he didn't care. He'd take her on the front porch in a foot of snow if that was his only option.

Livy's eyes came open. The hazel depths burned with molten heat and Nick kept his gaze locked with hers as he finished what she'd started and unzipped her jeans the rest of the way. Careful not to drag her underwear down with the denim, he eased them over her thighs and Livy obligingly brought her legs up between them so he could pull them the rest of the way off. He discarded the jeans behind him but kept hold of her ankles. The half-moons of her ass peeked out from the legs of her underwear that looked more like tiny shorts and served to whet his appetite for her.

The light blue fabric was darker where it covered her pussy, soaked with her arousal just like she promised him it was. With the pad of his thumb, Nick stroked her there, softly, and she moaned.

"Does that feel good?" He stroked her again.

"Yes," Livy said on another moan.

He spread her legs and stroked her once more. He teased himself as much as he did her. When he finally took her, they'd both be mindless. Urgent. Starved. Nick could hardly wait.

From the kitchen the sound of glass shattering on the tile floor sliced through the quiet. Livy sat up with a start, nearly knocking her head against Nick's. Her eyes were wide with fear and her brows pinched. She struggled to free herself from their tangle of limbs as she disengaged from his hold. She scrambled to her feet and snatched her shirt from the floor, pulling it over her head in a flash of turquoise blue. He'd seen that look of panic before—the fight-or-flight reflex that couldn't be controlled—and it wrenched his heart. Her gaze darted from the kitchen to the front door and back. "Oh my God, what was that?"

Nick tried to calm her but she'd nearly steam-rolled him in her haste to get off the couch. He reached out and caught her wrist as he stood from the couch and hauled her against him. Violent tremors rocked her body and her eyes glistened as though with unshed tears. Her expression rocketed

Nick into his past, trying to calm his own sister after her fear and anxiety had gotten the better of her.

"It's okay, Livy. I've got you."

She glanced toward the kitchen as though what he said didn't even register. "Was that the window? Did someone break the window?"

It didn't sound like it, but Nick knew that Livy wouldn't be convinced unless she knew for sure. "I don't think so, but I'll go check, okay?"

He tried to let go of her but she kept an iron grip on his forearm. Her fear vibrated through her limbs into his and Nick clenched his jaw. He didn't want Livy to be afraid. Couldn't stand her fear. It damned near crippled him. He'd do whatever it took to make sure she didn't feel that way ever again.

"Come on, Livy. Let's go see what's up in the kitchen."

Nick's gut knotted up as they rounded the corner. Her anxiety rubbed off on him and he half expected a crew of leather-clad bikers waiting to drill a bullet into both their heads. Instead, he found a very smug-looking Simon perched on the countertop. Below him on the floor was a shattered glass. Nick eased Livy to his side though she resisted. He wrapped his arm around her shoulder and tucked her against his body.

"I think someone was jealous he wasn't getting all of the attention."

Livy relaxed against him and Nick had a feeling that if he wasn't holding her upright she would've fallen square on her ass. "Simon!" The relief in her tone allowed Nick's muscles to loosen. "You're a bad boy!"

The cat blinked slowly at her before he brought one paw up to his mouth to lick. The little bastard had effectively ruined Nick's night and he seemed pretty goddamned pleased about it, too. No way would Nick be able to salvage it, not with Livy as shaken up as she was.

She might've settled down, but she was hardly at ease. Nick put his lips to the top of her head as though it was the most natural thing to do. "Want me to check outside, make sure all of the windows are locked?"

She nodded.

"Why don't you take Simon upstairs? I'll come up when I'm done."

Another nod answered him. Livy's steps were mechanical as she walked to the counter—careful to avoid the shards of glass—and scooped Simon up in her arms. She cast Nick a nervous glance as she walked past him, through the dining room and up the stairs to her bedroom.

If any of Livy's irrational fears had to do with Joel Meecum, Nick was going to make the fucker pay.

He retrieved his shirt from the living room and slipped it on along with his boots to check the perimeter of the house. Then, after every window was checked and the back door as well, Nick locked the front door, cleaned up the broken glass, and headed up the stairs to Livy's bedroom. She lay on the bed, back toward him, her legs tucked into her body. Simon—that jealous little SOB—lay at the foot of the bed. His rumbling purr was the only sound in the room and he wondered if Livy had fallen asleep.

"Hey." He settled himself on the bed beside her. "You okay?"

"God, I'm such a chickenshit," she choked out. Nick sensed that she might have been trying to hold back a flood of tears. "You must think I'm an idiot."

He thought a lot of things about Livy. She was sexy, smart, funny. Caring and tough. Never once had Nick considered her an idiot. "You got spooked. Like you said, you live out in the middle of nowhere and you don't have many neighbors. It's important to listen to your instincts. It doesn't make you an idiot or a coward or anything else. It makes you smart."

Livy turned to face him. A bitter smile curved her lips and red rimmed her eyes. "Is that your standard-issue cop pep talk for single women?"

"It's the truth," Nick said. "Don't ever apologize for being afraid. Sometimes, fear is what keeps you alive."

Livy averted her gaze. "I ruined tonight. I'm sorry."

"What did I tell you?" Nick said. "Don't apologize. You didn't ruin anything. Maybe we ought to call it a night, though. It's getting late."

He turned to leave and the plea in her voice snapped out at him like a whip. "Nick, don't go! Please." Nick looked back over his shoulder to find her brow puckered, her lips a thin line. "Would"—she swallowed—"would you maybe stay the night?"

"Sure." Nick couldn't leave her like this any more than he could leave one of his own limbs behind. Livy needed him and he was going to be there to give her whatever she needed. He kicked off his boots, toed off his socks, and shucked his pants and shirt. He kept his underwear on—no matter how much he wanted to be naked with her in that bed, it wasn't what this was about. Livy wanted to be comforted. To feel safe. Livy kept her back to him as she reached into the dresser by the bed and traded her long-sleeved shirt for a T-shirt. She turned down the covers and he crawled into bed beside her, gathering her in his arms.

"You can talk to me, you know," he said as she reached over and turned off the light on the bedside table. "About anything. You can trust me, Livy."

"My dad." Livy's voice pierced the quiet as she snuggled in close to Nick. "He and my mom were never married and he wasn't around much. I guess I've always been a little spooked. I slept with a nightlight until I was seventeen," she added with a rueful laugh. "My mom worked two jobs, sometimes late, and I was home alone a lot."

"That's scary for a kid," Nick replied.

"Yeah." A slow, exhausted sigh escaped from between Livy's lips. She wrapped her arms around Nick's and pressed her back tight against him. "I feel safe with you. Thanks for staying with me."

A knot formed in Nick's throat and he swallowed it down. Had there ever been a man in Livy's life who hadn't let her down? Hadn't frightened or abandoned her? Nick vowed as he held her close that he wasn't going to be one of them. He hoped like hell he'd be able to keep that promise.

Chapter Ten

Nick poured himself a cup of coffee and let out a gust of breath. Livy had trusted him last night. Probably more than she'd trusted anyone in a long goddamned time. And he was about to repay that trust by betraying it. She thought he was a good guy? If she knew why he was really in McCall, Idaho, she'd change her tune pretty damned quick.

Nick had never felt so *dirty*. He'd always pushed the boundaries in the line of duty. Gone the extra mile to make sure that justice was served. Arresting Joel Meecum was about more than a feather in his cap. It was about making sure that the son of a bitch never had the opportunity to harm another person ever again. And that included Livy. He didn't know how she'd ended up being the girlfriend of one of the most notorious criminals in USMS history and he didn't care. Livy's anxiety and fear was enough to tell Nick that whatever Joel had done to her, it had been bad. And that fucker was going to pay for it.

Jesus. Listen to yourself! Nick braced his arms on

the countertop and let his head fall between his shoulders. He didn't know for sure that it was Joel Livy was afraid of. Hell, she was on the run! Every little noise might have scared the shit out of her because she worried that law enforcement was about to knock down her door or throw gas canisters through her window. Nick gave the reason for her fear that *he wanted*. Not because it was the most logical conclusion, but because it made it easier to justify his tender feelings for her. It justified his wanting to protect her.

It justified all of the dirty things he'd said and done to her last night.

Nick let out a gust of breath. He couldn't get the image of her almost naked body out of his mind or the sweet sounds she made when he touched her. Every heated word he'd spoken in her ear had been one hundred percent true. He'd have followed through on every filthy promise he'd made, too, if Simon hadn't intervened in a fit of jealous feline rage. Nothing—not his honor, his sense of justice, his own high standards and morals— would've gotten in his way. He wanted Livy. Wanted her more than any woman he'd ever met. Last night wasn't a onetime deal. It would happen again and Nick knew he wouldn't do anything to stop it.

He needed to get this shit wrapped up before he lost not only his mind, but also the last shred of his dignity and honor. If he was lucky, he'd get a bead on Meecum, make an arrest, and all would be forgiven by his chief deputy. At worst, he'd go home empty-handed and be out of a job. Because Nick realized that there was no way he could do this alone.

He didn't have the resources to investigate Livy. A Google search sure as hell wasn't going to cut it.

After a few deep breaths to calm himself the hell down, Nick grabbed his mug and headed for the kitchen table. He stared at the notes he'd compiled since coming to McCall that were scattered beside Meecum's file. It wasn't calling Morgan that had his heart pounding in his chest and adrenaline coursing through his veins. And it sure as hell wasn't the prospect of facing the deputy chief's anger that tied his stomach into an unyielding knot. Rather, it was what he might find out about Livy that rattled Nick to his foundation. The prospect of learning the truth about her, of shattering the illusion he'd bought into, scared the ever-loving shit out of him.

He spun his phone on the table's surface. Fiddled with his paperwork and gathered his notebooks. Lined up his pens and pencils in a row.

Fuck.

Gut-check time. He couldn't worry about what Livy was or wasn't. He couldn't bother himself with trying to unravel her motives for running when he knew nothing about them. A good investigator got answers by following leads, shaking the bushes, and getting down to business. That's what he had to do now. Put his personal feelings aside and focus on the J-O-B. If he couldn't do that, he wasn't worthy of a U.S. marshal's badge.

He snatched his phone from the table and dialed Morgan's number. His gut churned with acid that burned a path up his throat. He'd accept the consequences of his actions. Whether with Morgan, his chief, or Livy. He just hoped he wouldn't lose everything that meant something to him in the process.

"Are you calling to 'fess up about my file, Brady?"

The guy got to the point, Nick would give him that. "I have a solid lead on Meecum." Morgan knew he had the file; Nick didn't see any reason to verbally confirm it. "But I don't have the resources that I need to follow it." He didn't think it would be so hard to admit he needed help. Nick had always been more comfortable flying solo. As a SWAT sniper, there were moments when there was nothing but him, his rifle, and the voice of the men on the ground in his ear. He'd been a part of the team, but not. The only thing he missed about that job was those moments in his own headspace. If he worked alone, he had no one to blame for his failure but himself. It made the job easier, somehow. The tightly knit team of the USMS took some getting used to. He wondered if he'd ever feel comfortable in the huddle rather than outside of it. The only thing worse than a criminal evading capture was failing someone who counted on him. He swallowed down his pride and said, "I need your help."

"Ho-ly shit. I never thought I'd see the day that Nick Brady asked for help." Nick clamped his jaw down to keep from saying something he'd regret. "Metcalf is going to have your ass over this, you know that, right?"

Nick let out a slow breath. "Only if you tell him."

Morgan waited a beat before he responded, "Why shouldn't I?"

"Because you want Meecum as badly as I do," Nick said. "Because you know as well as I do that the only place that bastard deserves to be is a six-by-six cell. And because you know you'll get half the credit for bringing down one of the top fifteen most wanted."

"Only half of the credit?" Morgan asked.

"You're lucky I'm offering that much."

Another space of silence stretched through the receiver and Nick wondered if Morgan had started to fill out his discharge papers. He cursed under his breath a moment later and Nick punched his fist in celebration. "What do you need from me?"

Nick's elation took a nosedive and plummeted to the soles of his feet. If he let Morgan in on what he'd learned so far, he'd be giving Livy up. That's how someone on the other side of the law thought, though. He wasn't betraying her trust. She hadn't revealed any dark secrets to him. As far as anyone was concerned, she was merely a person of interest in an investigation. If Livy was scared of Meecum, he could protect her. But not until he knew everything there was to know about her. And since there wasn't a snowball's chance in hell that she'd supply the information herself, Nick had to go after the truth the only way he knew how.

"You remember Lonnie Chapman, the informant who said he had information on Meecum's ex?"

"Yeah," Morgan answered slowly. "But since I don't have my file in front of me, I'm not sure what her name was."

Nick ignored the accusation in his tone. He'd get over it. "Kari Hanson," he said.

"Right," Morgan said. "Didn't he say he'd run into her somewhere in Idaho? Going by a new name?"

"Yeah." Nick's gut burned. He would have preferred it was the start of an ulcer than the guilt at revealing Livy's identity to Morgan. "Olivia Gallagher. Livy."

"That lead dead-ended, though. We couldn't find anything on Kari Hanson or Olivia Gallagher or anyone else that fit the description."

True, and Nick still had no idea why. "I don't think Hanson is her real last name. Or she hadn't been going by Hanson for long when she disappeared."

"An alias?"

Nick flipped through his notes. What he knew about Livy wouldn't fill a teaspoon but he hoped it would be enough to find something useful. "I don't think so. Not exactly."

"You're gonna have to spell it out for me, Nick. I'm not a fucking mind reader."

Could Morgan sense his reluctance to give up what he knew about Livy? "I think she might have been going by her mother's maiden name when she met Meecum."

The tiny bits of Livy's life that she'd shared with Nick might have seemed superficial but he knew they'd been deeply personal. She hadn't mentioned her father when she told Nick about her celebration dinner. Just her mom. No one showered her with gifts and she talked about ski racing in a way that made him think she not only loved it, but someone had sacrificed to make sure she could continue to do it. She'd confirmed his suspicions last night when she admitted her parents hadn't been married and that her dad had been scarce.

"I'm pretty sure Kari Hanson's dad wasn't in the picture." No need to let Morgan know just how sure he was. "I think she changed her name because her mother had been her sole source of support."

"That still doesn't get us any closer to identifying her," Morgan said.

"She was a junior division ski racer." The words left Nick's lips with a reluctance that tugged from his chest. "Lake Tahoe area. This would have been six or seven years ago. We should be able to search for competitors with the first name Kari and see if we get a hit."

"It's a long shot," Morgan replied. "But if she was a junior racer six years ago, that wouldn't make her very old now, would it? We put Meecum's ex at about forty-five."

That had been the assumption, but they'd been way off base. "Try twenty-five."

"Jesus," Morgan said with disgust.

Yeah, Nick's sentiment exactly.

"Where are you, Brady?"

That was one thing Nick wasn't willing to tell him. If Morgan knew he was already in McCall and had a *very* solid lead on Kari Hanson, there would be a convergence of marshals on the small town in a matter of hours. It was still too soon for that sort of action. Livy was spooked and Nick had a feeling she was planning to run again. He couldn't let that happen.

"I'm following a lead," he said.

"That's not exactly helpful."

Nick's ears perked to the sound of Livy's car coming down the lane. "Gotta go," he said. "I'll keep you posted. Let me know if you find anything out."

Morgan grumbled on the other end of the line, something about him being an uncooperative SOB, but Nick didn't pay it any mind as he ended the call. The acidic burn churned up in his gut as he stared out the kitchen window at Livy's car. He hoped she'd understand that everything he'd set into motion was just as much to protect her as it was to take down Meecum. Then again, what if all of his good intentions only managed to protect someone who was just as guilty as the bastard he was trying to take down? Nick wasn't sure that was a truth he'd be able to stomach. He said a silent prayer that everything he thought and felt about Livy was right.

Livy glanced through her rearview mirror at Nick's house. She really needed to stop thinking of it that way. It wasn't his house. In a few weeks, it would be empty again and she'd be alone.

A twinge of pain radiated from Livy's knee and she stretched it out as best she could in the cramped interior of her car. She still ached from her epic yard sale on Alpine that had sent her skis and poles flying in the crash. Last night's heated moments with Nick had been on her mind all day and had managed to drive her to the point of distraction. She'd taken the steep run at the end of the day hoping that the thrill of speed and the cold wind in her face would clear her mind. Obviously it was going to take more than a trip down a big-girl run to get Nick off her mind. Either that or she was seriously losing her edge.

A sigh slipped from between her lips as she shifted her focus to the snow falling softly outside the window. She'd expected so much more from her life. Maybe a couple of world titles, an Olympic medal or two. Instead, she lived in a small town in the middle of nowhere and taught tiny little kids when to make their skis like French fries and when to make them like a pizza wedge. She liked the kids. Her job wasn't tedious. But she'd wanted so much *more.* Livy's chest ached with unspent emotion and she brought her hand to her sternum in a futile attempt to rub the pain away. The death of her dream left a nasty scar, even though she'd sacrificed it for a good reason.

The sound of Nick's front door closing drew Livy's attention back to the rearview mirror. She watched as he strolled across the deck and crossed the lane with a slow, rolling gait that caused Livy's breath to hitch. How he could pull it off while wading through the snow was a mystery to her. He was as sleek and powerful as a snow leopard. As though he'd been born to negotiate the drifts with ease.

He would have made a fantastic slalom racer.

Livy's heart rate kicked into high gear. Her own stupid fear and anxiety had interrupted what she was sure would have been a night to remember. Hell, it was already etched permanently in her memory and they'd stopped before they really had the opportunity to get started. A thrill shot through her veins as she recalled the way his bare hands felt on her skin, the heat of his mouth as it moved over hers. His fingers as they circled her nipple, his lips as they'd sealed over her breast. And, *oh God,* the absolutely naughty things he'd whispered in her ear. Livy played them over and over again in her mind and each time she did, a thrill chased through her bloodstream.

A rush of breath left her lungs and heat rose to Livy's cheeks. She got out of the car in the hopes that the winter air would help to cool her raging lust before Nick saw the evidence of it painted on her face. He smiled and raised a hand in greeting and the starch melted from Livy's spine. He made her so hot she was surprised she wasn't standing in a puddle of water right now and not a pile of snow.

"Hey."

Dear God. Did he realize that even a simple word in that deep, edgy voice was enough to cause her sex drive to shift into high gear? She wanted to get him naked right here and now and straddle him in the middle of the snowbank.

"Hey." She tried to keep her voice as calm and cool as Nick but instead, it quavered on the word. *Awesome.* "How was your day?" *Ugh. You're so lame!*

"It's a hell of a lot better now that you're home."

Livy opened her mouth to respond, but Nick leaned in and put his mouth to hers before she could form a coherent thought. The kiss was soft and slow, and far too brief.

Oh, hell. Livy pressed her heels into the soles of her boots as though the simple act would keep her from tackling Nick to the ground. Sharks swimming in chummed waters had better self-control than she did right now. Locking her left knee had been a bad idea, though. It buckled as a flash of pain sliced through her. She'd have to wear a brace to work tomorrow.

"I'm sorry about last night." If she didn't at least try to attempt conversation, Livy would be dragging him into the house by the collar of his sweater. And holy fuck did he ever fill it out.

"What's the matter with your leg?"

He didn't miss anything, did he? Was it because he was a cop that Nick was so observant? Livy wanted to think it was because of his interest in her. "I yard-saled on Alpine today and fucked up my knee."

Nick quirked a brow and a corner of his mouth hinted at amusement. A snowflake drifted from the sky and clung to his long lashes. She fought the urge to brush it away. "Yard-saled?"

"I wiped out. Bad. My skis and poles flew off and ended up about twenty yards up the run from where I landed. My hat and goggles went for a ride, too. I left my gear on the hill. You know, spread out like a yard sale."

His amusement melted under an expression of concern. His brows drew down over his eyes and his lips thinned. "Are you all right?"

Livy's stomach took a similar tumble, a moment of weightlessness before it crashed down. Aside from her mom and her coaches, no one had ever shown much concern for her. It was dangerous to let herself feel anything for Nick. To let him feel anything for her. Three weeks would pass far too quickly and this fairy tale she'd constructed for herself would come to an end.

"I'm fine." She brushed off his concern as though it meant nothing to her. "I'll probably have to wear a brace and ice it for a couple of days, that's all."

Snow had begun to accumulate in Nick's hair. What had started off as a light dusting of snow in the air began to fall more steadily. There was no point in standing out in the cold, getting wet, when they could be inside. Though Livy had to admit that it would be hard not to pick up where they'd left off last night if that were to happen. She should be putting Nick at arm's length, not inviting him closer.

Alone is better than dead.

"You're going to be a snowman if we stand out here much longer. Want to come inside?"

Livy chose to ignore her mantra of the past four years. Just because Joel had dirty cops on his payroll didn't mean all cops were dirty. And besides, Nick worked in Washington. She doubted he'd know or even care about something that happened in Northern California. She deserved to live her life, damn it. Even if it was only for a few weeks.

Nick's gaze heated at the invitation and Livy no longer felt the chill of winter on her skin. Her knees threatened to give out on her again, but it wasn't because of any injury. Unless she considered the irreversible damage Nick would undoubtedly do to her heart if she let this continue.

Athletes learned to live with pain. What was one more hurt?

A quiet moment passed. Nick's gaze swallowed

her until everything melted away but him. He reached out and fiddled with the end of one braid. Indecision made an unwelcome appearance in his expression and Livy's heart pounded. She'd missed her chance last night, hadn't she? The moment was passed.

"Let's go out tonight." He made the suggestion as though he needed a distraction.

"Again?" Aside from her dinner date with Nick, Livy hadn't been out after dark since she moved to McCall. Unless you counted trips to the grocery store as *going out.* "Didn't your credit card get enough of a workout last night?"

Nick gave a low chuckle that sent a pleasant rush of adrenaline through Livy's veins. "I told you I've got cabin fever," he said. "Nothing fancy. We'll grab a bite and see what this town has to offer for nightlife."

She could answer that for him: nothing. "There's a movie theater in Cascade, about twenty miles south. The only other nightlife can be summed up in one hockey rink and a few bars."

Nick smiled. In the back of Livy's mind she heard the *ping!* that should have accompanied the act. Prince Charming with a side of dark intensity. Was there a better combo? "Sounds good to me. Which bar is the best?"

His gaze held hers. Didn't he care that he was standing in a snowstorm in nothing but a sweater? For that matter, did she? Nick had a way of making the world around her disappear. "I have no idea," she said, low. "I've never been to any of them."

The spark in his dark eyes softened. "I think we'd better remedy that, don't you?"

Damn. Was there anything he'd ask of her that she wouldn't do? "Give me an hour to get ready?"

Nick's smile widened and his voice dropped to a husky murmur. "Take your time. We have all night."

Oh boy. Nick coaxed a recklessness in her that she'd thought long gone. Livy was so, so screwed.

Chapter Eleven

"Any of you find that bitch yet?"

Joel eyeballed every sorry son of a bitch seated at the long table. For four fucking years he'd been looking for her. The little twat up and ran at the first sign of trouble, which proved she wasn't quite as dumb as he'd given her credit for. She knew way too much about his operation for him to let her just disappear. If the wrong people got ahold of her before he did, he'd be sent away for good. Either that or he'd wind up in a shallow grave somewhere. That wasn't going to fucking happen.

"Chick's a fuckin' ghost, man." Shorty sat back in his chair, arm slung over the back. "Ain't nobody gonna find her."

"Bullshit. Someone knows where she is. You ain't lookin' hard enough."

"You remember Bill Stuart who used to run with the Lords of Malice up by Idaho?"

All eyes turned to the prospect at the far end of

the table. The kid sat up a little straighter in his seat, suddenly full of confidence.

Joel set his forty on the table, the barrel pointed at the kid who thought he was tough shit. "I don't remember asking you to open your mouth, prospect."

His shit-eating grin faded. Joel didn't have time for these little pricks. So goddamned full of themselves. When he'd been a prospect, the club's officers had taken turns kicking his ass. And that was before they'd torn the shit out of his bike and made him rebuild it from scratch. These cocky motherfuckers had it too damned easy now.

He kept his eyes downcast and said, "I think I might know someone who's seen her, that's all."

Joel scowled. He'd put out feelers for Kari years ago and had come up empty-handed time and again. He found it hard to believe this little shit had a lead on her when none of his other—and much more connected—guys did. Still, he wasn't going to ignore an opportunity to get his hands on her, no matter where the intel was coming from. "You think so, huh? When and where the fuck did Bill Stuart think he saw her?"

"It wasn't Bill," the kid said. "Some guy he used to ride with says he saw her. Back in August. Some little backwoods town in Idaho."

"August."

Joel let the word hang. Six fucking months ago. Kari could have blown out of town by then and that was even if some fucking guy who knew some guy who knew this dipshit kid sitting at his table even knew what he was talking about. Joel wrapped his hand around the grip of his forty and brushed the trigger with his index finger. "What's your name again, son?"

The kid swallowed hard. "Z-zack. Everybody calls me Z-Dog."

Shorty leaned in. "He's been hanging around the clubhouse since last summer. Just barely became a prospect a month or so ago."

Joel sneered. "And that's supposed to mean somethin' to me?" He leveled the gun on *Z-Dog*'s face. Jesus. He ought to shoot him for having such a stupid nickname.

"I'm just sayin', brother." No way was Shorty gonna jump in to save the kid's neck. Not when it might be his that's on the block because of it. "You want to find Kari or not?"

At the far end of the table, Z-Dog looked like he was about to piss his pants. Joel released the hammer and set the gun back down on the table.

"How's this guy know it's her he saw?"

"Tattoo on her wrist," the kid replied. "She was serving drinks at some music festival. Ski area. The guys rode their bikes up there because they knew one of the bands performing."

Joel's interest piqued. "He say what the tattoo looked like?"

"A tree with the branches growing into the roots."

It was the first promising bit of intel they'd gotten in four years. Joel swallowed down the rage that burned in his chest as he thought of the wasted months. If the lead didn't pan out, he'd blow a hole the size of a baseball in the prospect's head.

"Where's the town?"

"McCall, I think. Little place outside of Boise."

Joel regarded the prospect. He should shoot him anyway. Trust was a valuable commodity and there weren't many people he gave his to. Kid could be a fucking cop for all he knew. There'd been too much heat on him for the past four years to jeopardize his freedom now.

"Everybody out." The possibility of the prospect's intel panning out earned him a temporary stay of execution. "Except you." He stabbed his finger at Z-Dog. "And you," he said to Shorty.

The room cleared in a heartbeat. Joel let the silence saturate the room. No one dared make a sound. Every single charter of the Black Death MC had been on the lookout for Kari Hanson for the past four years. She had something that belonged to Joel and he wanted it back. No one had seen her or heard so much as a fucking peep. Like Shorty said, the bitch had gone ghost. He didn't know a damned thing about her aside from the fact that she had a tight ass and a lying, thieving asshole for a father. He'd tried to dig up any information about friends or any other family and came up empty-handed. She could have a taught a criminal or two how to hide like a boss.

Not even the cops had a lead on her. And Joel had enough of them on his payroll to know. Four fucking years he'd been looking over his shoulder, dodging the feds. Worried that his goddamned ledger would end up in the wrong hands. His business associates wouldn't appreciate their names coming across a federal agent's desk. He didn't give a shit about the heat that was on him. No, what Joel feared was being taken out by the Russians or the Cartel because that stupid bitch decided to give in to her conscience.

"How well do you know Bill?" he asked Z-Dog.

"Pretty well. He rode with the Satan's Minions charter from out by Crescent City before he went nomad. Joined the Lords after that I'm pretty sure. I think he's trustworthy."

"You *think*?" Joel leveled his gaze.

"He's solid," Z-Dog amended.

They were on good terms with the Minions and the Lords of Mayhem. Both had run shipments of guns into Arizona and Montana for him a few years back. Joel didn't trust nomads, though. Too fickle. When a man put a patch on his jacket, he should keep his ass loyal and grounded. "Shorty, get ahold of Rich with the Minions and see if you can get any info on this nomad."

Shorty nodded. "And if he checks out?"

Joel wanted that ledger and he wouldn't stop until he got it back. "You and the prospect will go on a road trip."

"Idaho?" Shorty sneered. "Don't they have snow and shit up there this time of year?"

Joel grabbed Shorty by the jacket and hauled him out of his chair. He gave him a rough shake and stood nose to nose with the club's VP. "I don't care if they've got a fucking zombie apocalypse up there. I want my ledger and I want that bitch dead. You understand me?"

Shorty's eyes narrowed but he didn't utter a word. "Yeah, I've got it."

Joel let go of his jacket with a forceful shove. "Good."

Chapter Twelve

Nick couldn't muster even an ounce of guilt over asking Livy out again. The second he laid eyes on her any decent, moral, or even marginally responsible decision-making skills he might have possessed evaporated. He had a little under three weeks left of his month of mandatory leave and Nick knew that with Morgan's help, he could have a solid lead on Meecum's whereabouts before his time was up. Every second with Livy counted because it could be his last. The thought soured his stomach and caused a hollow ache to open up in his chest.

When she found out why he'd come here, she'd hate him. If Morgan found something out that would implicate Livy in a crime, forcing Nick to make an arrest, he would surely hate himself. He'd never harbored any soft emotions for anyone who chose to break the law. You do the crime, you do the time. Period. But ever since he'd met her,

Nick had begun to wonder if his black-and-white outlook on the law was fair. If Livy had done something illegal, it could have been under duress.

Wishful thinking. Whatever her involvement with Joel Meecum and the Black Death MC, Nick knew it was a pipe dream to assume it had been innocent.

But God, he wanted her to be innocent.

Before he could get out of his truck, Livy was headed down the stairs. She pulled open the passenger-side door and climbed in with the aid of the oh-shit bar just above the window. Though she'd tried to cover her wince of pain, Nick hadn't missed it. She must have crashed pretty hard for her knee to still be hurting.

"I didn't realize your knee was as banged up as it is. We don't have to go out."

Her brows knit and she gave him a tight-lipped smile as though trying to gauge his sincerity. "I'm fine. I've had worse injuries."

Nick buckled up and pulled out of Livy's driveway. "Like what?"

"I broke my arm during a race when I was thirteen. Pulled a hammy when I was fifteen. I've twisted knees, ankles, hyperextended my elbow. Bruises, bumps, concussions. When you go ham, you get hurt."

Laughter erupted in Nick's chest. "Go ham?"

"Yeah. Go crazy, go all-out. Balls to the wall. If you want to win, you find your flow state and tell fear to fuck off."

Yard sales, going ham . . . flow state? It was like

Livy spoke a foreign language. He couldn't wait to hear what she cooked up next. "You go ham a lot?"

Livy shrugged. "I did. It's why I won most of my races. It's also why I crashed a lot."

"I've seen some pretty epic crashes on TV. It looks like it hurts to wreck."

"Oh yeah." Livy gave a quiet laugh. "When you're tucked and barreling at super GS gates going sixty-five or seventy miles an hour and catch an edge, the landing hurts like a bitch. Especially when the course is iced."

"Iced?" Jesus, that didn't sound good.

"If the snow's too soft, they'll spray the course with water to ice it down. It helps to keep it from breaking down after so many runs and it makes the snow faster, too."

"You're certifiably crazy. You know that, right?"

Livy laughed. "I think anyone has to be a little crazy to strap a couple of thin composite planks to your feet and point yourself downhill on a four-thousand-foot vertical drop."

Downhill skiers were, in fact, crazy. Nick didn't care about anyone else, though. Just the woman sitting beside him. "You've got that right. But you should be careful up there. I don't want to see anything else on your body broken or hurt."

They ended up at a place called The Sushi Bar for dinner. Livy had bought a few of the rolls they sold to the grocery store and she admitted to wanting to try out the restaurant for a while now. By the time they were done eating, Nick was convinced they'd eaten almost everything the place had to offer. The Sushi Bar actually rivaled the sushi places in Seattle and that was saying something. They ate, drank too much sake, talked about nothing and everything. Nick didn't press Livy for any more personal details. Deep down, he didn't want to. Livy made him want to douse all of his convictions with gasoline and light a match. That part of him that needed to know the truth—was desperate to discover what her history was with Meecum—dulled in the brilliance of her presence. He'd never met a woman like Livy. And the way she made him feel scared the shit out of him.

She rested her arms on the table. He reached out to catch her right wrist in his hand and turned her wrist upward. He resisted the urge to brush his thumb over the black ink of the tattoo and, instead, brought his questioning gaze to hers.

"Tree of life," she said with a nervous laugh. "My coaches used to have me meditate the day before a big race. You envision the tree growing, the branches going back into the ground to become the roots of the tree as it grows again and again into infinity. I got the tattoo as a reminder to stay calm even when things feel like they're out of control."

Nick's brow furrowed. God, he wanted to put his mouth to that mark. Kiss the ink on her skin. "I love it," he replied. "I think we all need a reminder to stay calm every once in a while."

She cleared her throat and straightened in her chair. From the corner of his eye, Nick caught the pleasant flush of color on Livy's cheeks before she turned to look out the window. His gut curled into a ball and he let out a slow breath. *Jesus, what are you doing, man?* He was digging himself a damned big hole, that's what.

"I'm so full I don't think I can move out of my seat," Livy said with a laugh. "You seriously have to quit feeding me."

Nick took in the sight of her, so at ease, her cheeks painted with a blush and her smile wide and shining like the sun. Pleasure and contentment radiated from her and pride swelled in Nick's chest that he'd been the one to make her feel that way.

"I can't," Nick remarked. "Not until we've eaten at every restaurant in town."

Livy's brow arched. "Every restaurant? You sure about that?"

"Every single one," Nick said solemnly.

"You might wish you hadn't laid down that gauntlet."

Nick didn't give a shit about where he ate or what he did. What he really wanted was an excuse to spend as much time with Livy as possible. "I'm not leaving town until I see more than just the view from my kitchen."

"There's not much to see," Livy said with a wry grin. "I bet we can cover it all in about a week."

That might be all the time Nick had left. He pushed the maudlin thought—and the worry that clawed at him—to the back of his mind. There wasn't any use in overthinking the situation until he heard back from Morgan and it was hard telling if the small bit of information he'd managed to get from Livy would do them any good. Christ, part of him actually hoped that Morgan would come up empty-handed.

"Where to next?" Nick could have taken her home, prayed she'd invite him inside again. He didn't want to take the chance that she'd come to her senses and send him on his way after last night's epic fail, though. He'd keep her out until sunrise if he had to.

"There's not much to do but hit up the bars," Livy said with a nervous laugh. Nick recognized a bit of the familiar anxiety begin to creep up on her again. Livy's shoulders inched up toward her ears and her smile didn't quite reach her eyes. "I've never been to any of them."

"Never?" He tried to sound surprised but by now he knew Livy had a done a good job of staying off the radar. He wanted to tell her that she had nothing to worry about. That he'd protect her from *whatever* she was afraid of. But he knew that it was impossible to do so. Especially when he might well be one of the things she was hiding from.

Livy looked away as though embarrassed. "I'm sort of a homebody."

"Do you want to go home?" Nick didn't want to pressure her or cause her any more anxiety. Even if he didn't want the night to end.

"No." She spoke so softly he had to strain to hear the word. "I don't want to go home."

Her vulnerability nearly laid him low. God, he hoped Morgan got skunked in his research of Livy, because Nick knew in his heart that there was no way in hell she was anything but innocent.

* * *

What in the hell are you thinking, Livy?

Every moment spent with Nick made her more
and more reckless. She'd been out more in the
short time since meeting him than she had in all of
the four years that she'd lived here. Joel had eyes
everywhere. Cops, FBI. Criminal connections that
spanned the globe. Nowhere was safe from curious eyes and ears. She wouldn't be surprised if
there was a price on her head. Scratch that. She was
positive there was hefty price on her head. And yet,
she was out enjoying McCall's meager nightlife as
though she didn't have a care in the world.

Nick made her want to reclaim and enjoy the life
she'd put on a shelf when she'd left California,
though. He made her want to laugh and let her
guard down. He made her want to *feel*. And she was
too far gone to his seductive charm to think clearly.
She'd stopped making good decisions the moment
his lips claimed hers the night before.

Livy was simply too far gone to care.

It seemed ridiculous to drive a couple of blocks
from the restaurant to the bar, but with the snow
coming down so heavy—big, white flakes that left
little to no visibility—neither of them was in the
mood to walk. Livy had always been a winter girl.
She liked the cold, loved to wear sweaters and
layers. Thick-soled, heavily insulated boots were so
much better than a pair of flip-flops or heels. But as
she got out of the truck and headed for The Canoe
bar, she wished her outfit wasn't quite so utilitarian.

Especially when she saw how some of the other women were dressed once they went inside.

Livy nearly turned around and walked back out the door. She'd never been overly concerned about her appearance but being with Nick had sparked some ridiculous girly urge to do her hair, put on a fuck-ton of makeup, and pour herself into a sexy outfit that was too uncomfortable for her to really enjoy herself in.

She stopped abruptly and Nick bumped into her back. Rather than pull away, he stood rooted to his spot on the floor. His hands came to rest on her hips and he leaned over her right ear. His breath caressed the outer shell and Livy shuddered. "Come on," he murmured. "It'll be okay. Let me buy you a drink."

Bad idea, bad idea, bad idea. Instinct tugged at the back of Livy's mind and she let out a forceful gust of breath. How could she turn around and leave when Nick's voice was so confident in her ear? So reassuring. And God, his hands on her hips felt good. She tilted her head up to speak over the din of music. "Okay." His crisp, masculine scent hit her and a rush of heat filtered through Livy's body. She wanted to lick him. Just run her tongue from his throat to the lobe of his ear. A groan of pure sexual frustration worked itself up her throat and she swallowed it down. She hadn't been with a man since she'd moved to McCall. Talk about a dry spell. Her night of foreplay with Nick was the closest she'd gotten to anything that even resembled sex. If she didn't find a little satisfaction soon, she might spontaneously combust. He'd shown up in her life out of nowhere and reminded Livy of everything she'd been missing out on. Moving on would be even harder because of him, and still, she couldn't bring herself to put any distance between them.

She refused to think about future heartache now. She didn't want to waste another minute of time with Nick.

They found a table at the back of the bar. Livy shucked her coat and hung it on the chair behind her and once again wished she was wearing something more attractive than a too-big sweater and her clunky boots. Nick's gaze warmed as it roamed over her. A tingle of sensation spread from the center of Livy's chest outward and settled at the tips of her nipples as she called to mind the way it had felt to have his mouth on her.

As they waited for a server, Livy took a quick look around and acquainted herself with the exits. It sucked balls that she felt the need to have an escape route ready to roll in the event a gang of nasty-looking bikers strode through the door. Would Joel be so stupid, though? He'd probably be stealthier than that. He'd send someone who looked like a Sunday school teacher or a harmless-looking old man. Which was why Livy lived like a hermit. She couldn't trust anyone or anything. She trusted Nick, though, didn't she? Which seemed ridiculous since he was the most dangerous man she'd met in a long time.

The intensity that boiled just below the surface of his skin drove her crazy. It excited her, ignited her desires, set her on freaking *fire*. She couldn't help but want him. He drew her to him in a way she was helpless to fight. Her want of him scared her and yet, Livy knew that she wouldn't be satisfied until they'd finished what they'd started last night.

"Have I mentioned how much I love that sweater?" Nick situated his chair so they sat close to each other and he put his mouth to her ear as he spoke. Pleasant chills raced along Livy's flesh. Every touch, every word was electric.

A smile curved Livy's lips and she angled her mouth so that it rested against his cheek. "You do?"

"Oh yeah. I'd like to see you wearing just this sweater, with nothing underneath."

A hot wave of desire crashed over her. Livy started as Nick reached beneath her sweater and laid his palm to her bare torso. His touch crept upward toward her breast. His thumb brushed almost innocently over her nipple and Livy sucked in a breath.

"I've been thinking about these all day," he murmured.

Livy let out a nervous laugh. "My nipples?"

"Tiny, pink, delicious nipples," Nick amended.

His words effectively cranked the heat up by fifty degrees. Livy began to sweat and her clit throbbed. If Nick kept it up, he'd have her worked into a lather long before they made it back to her place.

"Delicious?" She egged him on in the hopes he'd continue to caress her ears with his dark, sensual voice. She couldn't get enough of it.

"I could suck on them for *hours*."

Livy's lower abdomen clenched. "Is that all?"

"Suck, lick, bite. Would you like it if I nibbled and bit them?"

She wasn't embarrassed to admit it. "Yes."

"Hard or soft?"

A few more words from him and she'd be bone-less. "Both."

"What else do you want me to do to you, Livy?"

His thumb brushed across her nipple again. This time, though, the contact wasn't so innocent as he followed up with a pinch through the fabric of her bra. Livy let out a low moan and she was grateful for the loud music and hum of the crowd.

"I thought that taking you out tonight would help me keep a respectable distance," Nick growled close to her ear. "But I can't seem to keep my fucking hands off of you no matter how I try."

Thank God for small favors. "I'm not complaining."

"You haven't told me what you want me to do to you." With every flick of his thumb over her nipple Livy became more aroused. She knew her underwear was already soaked and she couldn't slow her breathing to save her life. "I want to hear it."

"I want you to kiss me," Livy said. She bolstered her courage. She could be as forward as Nick could. "I want you to lick and suck my nipples, my clit. I want your mouth on my pussy so bad I can't stand it. I want you bite me, to put your hands on me." She took a deep breath. "I want you to fuck me."

Their server returned with their drinks and Livy tried to pull away. Nick wouldn't let her, though, and he kept his palm cupped over her breast. Score a point for baggy clothes. The bulk of her sweater allowed him to fondle her in the middle of a crowded bar without anyone realizing it. It was brazen and unapologetic. And fucking *hot*.

A cheerful woman with a bright smile and edgy, short red hair set the bottle of IPA in front of Nick and he reached out and took a pull from the bottle while he stroked Livy's breast under her sweater. His gaze burned and his jaw squared. Livy had never wanted to be home in her bed more in her entire life. Only this time she didn't want to be there alone. She wanted Nick right there with her.

The server lost her grip on Livy's bottle and it toppled over on the table. The beer spilled out and dripped over the table onto Nick's lap. He pulled away with a start and scooted his chair away. Livy wanted to shake their server! Did she not realize that Livy was in the middle of being fondled—*in public*—by a man so perfect he'd made a Greek god weep with envy?

"Oh my God, I'm so sorry!"

Having spilled her fair share of drinks while serving at Brundage's summer music festivals, Livy couldn't be too mad. Nick pushed out his chair and brushed what hadn't soaked into his jeans away.

"Don't worry about it." He turned his attention to Livy. "I'm going to go dry off. I'll be right back." He leaned over her and said for her ears alone, "And when I do, we're picking up where we left off."

Holy shit. Maybe she should ask for a glass of water to spill on herself? Because she had a feeling that Nick wouldn't stop until she smoldered. Livy wasn't afraid, though. She welcomed the flames.

Chapter Thirteen

Like Simon, their server had impeccable timing. Nick grabbed a handful of paper towels and did his best to dry the denim that had soaked up the half a bottle of beer. He couldn't care less about getting a little wet, though. What he'd hated was being interrupted while Livy told him in her sweet and seductive voice about all of the sinful things she wanted him to do to her. He looked down at his jeans where his erection pressed against his fly. The thrill of fondling her in public, of exchanging dirty talk with her in the middle of a crowded room, had excited him to the point that he thought he might bend her over the table and take her right then and there. The game was fun, but he wanted her alone. And naked. It was time to get the hell out of there.

Nick's steps slowed as he emerged from the bathroom. A man stood near their table and attempted to draw Livy into conversation. Anxiety pinched her expression and her brow furrowed as she tried to give the guy the brush-off. The son of a bitch didn't seem to want to take no for an answer. Livy glanced frantically from the front entrance to the back exit as though desperate for an escape. The raw fear she exhibited, the panic etched into every delicate line of her face, was enough to ignite Nick's rage. He couldn't stand for her to be afraid.

He charged toward their table, jaw clenched and hands curled into fists. He caught Livy's eye and the way she visibly relaxed upon seeing him only fueled his need to protect her. "I don't think she wants to talk to you," Nick remarked as he wedged his body between Livy and the guy who looked as though he'd been dragged down fifteen miles of bad road. "I think you should leave."

The bastard looked Nick up and down, a sneer tugging his upper lip. He brought his hand up to rub at the scruff on his jaw and Nick took note of the tattoo that dotted the webbing between his thumb and forefinger. Dressed in worn jeans, a heavy flannel, and black biker boots, he didn't give any outward show that he was affiliated with any gang or motorcycle club but the tat on his hand indicated he'd served a stint in federal prison. He might have served his time, but Nick couldn't be sure that he wasn't more than simply a pushy asshole who couldn't take no for an answer. Either way, it didn't mean Nick would treat the guy as though he weren't a serious threat to Livy.

A slow smile pulled at the bastard's lips and his eyes glittered with an adversarial edge. "I don't think anyone asked for your opinion, asshole."

"You might not have asked for it," Nick said. "But you're sure as hell going to get it. Get lost."

"You gonna make me?" The guy smirked as

though the thought of Nick trying to take him was laughable. "I'd like to see you try."

Nick was sorely tempted. As much as he wanted to bash the snarky fucker's face in, the last thing he needed on his "vacation" was an assault charge. Time to get a grip on his temper before he snapped and did something he'd regret.

Nick leveled his gaze. "You're not worth my time."

He was answered with a derisive snort that made him want to change his mind.

Nick turned his attention to Livy. "Ready to go?"

They hadn't taken more than a sip of their drinks yet but it was apparent from Livy's expression that their night out had come to an end. He'd been trying to avoid a repeat of last night, but it was obvious that Livy was once again spooked. Fear got its claws in her and they weren't letting go. For the hundredth time, Nick couldn't shake the feeling that Livy wasn't so much hiding as she was running scared. *Goddamn it.*

Livy gave a quick nod of her head. He reached his hand out. She took it and her fingers trembled in his grip. Anger burned a path up Nick's throat and he swallowed it down. He could not let his temper get the best of him.

The asshole refused to budge. Instead of stepping to the side, he braced his legs a little wider, folded his arms across his chest. Whether Nick had backed down or not, he had a feeling a challenge had been issued. One he wouldn't be allowed to walk away from. Nick angled his body so that he stood between the other guy and Livy. He'd offer her any small protection he could. She gave him a weak smile that didn't reach her usually brilliant eyes. Instead, they echoed the anxiety that pulled every inch of her taut as she rose to stand. Nick pulled her tight against his chest and turned, keeping his body between the asshole and her.

"Pussy."

Nick bristled. The insult was nothing more than a jab to rile his temper. A little something to help egg him into a fight. He wasn't going to take the bait. Not with the possibility of the deputy chief coming down on his ass if he got himself into trouble working a lead that he absolutely was not supposed to be working. Fighting would only serve to prove to every deputy marshal in the Seattle district office that he was too hotheaded for the job. No way would Nick return to SWAT. He wanted to be a USMS man hunter. Period.

He guided Livy out in front of him at the exact moment the bastard gave him a solid shove. She managed to avoid the brunt of the impact. Unfortunately, Nick wasn't so lucky. He sprawled over a nearby table to the shock of the people sitting at it. Drinks toppled over and a glass shattered as it rolled off the edge and crashed to the floor.

His dignity and professional reputation were one thing; letting some sorry son of a bitch get the better of him was another. With a shove, Nick propelled himself from the table. Livy's gasp of surprise barely registered as he whipped around and clocked the son of bitch in the jaw. He took two stumbling steps backward but appeared otherwise unaffected. His tongue flicked out at the blood that trickled from his lip and he spat to his left. Dude was a brawler, which wasn't unexpected. The big-ass bowie knife he pulled from behind his back was a bit of surprise.

Nick didn't know why he'd anticipated a fair fight. Law-breaking sons of bitches never did follow rules. His assailant held the knife aloft and bar patrons scattered. Either he ended this now, or he waited for the cops to show up and make an already bad situation worse. What he really wanted to do was pull his Glock and flash his badge before slamming the guy face-first onto the beer-soaked table and cuffing him. His gun was back at the house with his badge, though. He had no clout to throw around except his own fighting skills. So the guy had a big knife? Nick didn't give a single shit. He could be lethal without a weapon.

For a long moment, they simply stared at each other. Nick sized up his opponent. Smaller, less bulky, with a beer gut and about fifteen years on him. Nick was younger, faster, taller, stronger. Not to mention he was trained in Krav Maga. Knife or not, he had the upper hand. The bastard smirked as his fingers clenched the knife's grip. He might as well have been holding his dick in his hand as much good as it would do him. Nick had had enough.

He burst in toward the knife with his left forearm at the same moment he jabbed toward the guy's face with his right fist. The speed and suddenness of the attack sent the guy back a step and Nick capitalized on his opponent's imbalance. Nick grabbed him by the wrist and twisted his arm behind him as he forced the son of bitch face-first onto the nearest tabletop. The guy let out a pained shout as Nick plucked the knife from his fist with ease. He spun the handle in his grip as though wielding a baton before he let go of the cocky motherfucker with a shove.

Nick grabbed Livy and tucked her against the left side of his body while he kept the long knife tight against his right thigh. His arm came protectively around her shoulders as he tried to steady the violent tremor that rocked her from head to toe. Their breaths fogged the cold night air as they left the bar and walked out onto the sidewalk. It would have been better had he been able to arrest the bastard. They could have run his prints, determined if he was affiliated with the Black Death. Nick had the guy's knife, but his own prints were all over the damned grip. He'd be surprised if they could lift anything useful from it now.

"Are you okay?" As they came to a stop at the passenger side of his truck, Nick angled his head toward hers and put his mouth to Livy's ear. She didn't answer and Nick's heart kicked against his ribs. "Livy? Answer me. Are you okay?"

"I-I'm all right." The words left her mouth in little more than a whisper. "Jesus fucking Christ, Nick. What were you thinking?"

He'd been thinking that he'd be damned if he let some nasty bully scare her like that. He pulled Livy closer and her arms went around his torso as though by instinct. He tossed the knife into the bed of his truck and dug his keys out of his pocket, his other arm wrapped tight around Livy. Her body relaxed against him and by slow degrees, her quickened breaths began to slow.

He could have stood on the sidewalk all night in the cold, holding her. But they didn't have time to spare. Not when the son of a bitch might come out after them to get his knife back. "Get in the truck." He pulled open the door and helped her in. She stared straight ahead, her expression blank. Nick grabbed the seat belt and reached across her to buckle it in place. As he pulled away, Livy grabbed his hand in hers and squeezed it tight before letting it go.

Nick's stomach sank at the realization that he'd crossed a boundary tonight. Both professional and personal. And damn it, he'd do it again. Livy had turned his world upside down. There wasn't anything he wouldn't do to keep her safe, even risk his own future. He just hoped that in the long run, all of his foolish risks would be worth the sacrifice.

Bile rose in Livy's throat. A violent tremor shook her limbs and her heart pounded in her chest. Adrenaline coursed through her veins, pooled in her quads until she wasn't sure she'd be able to walk on her own steam. She used to feel this way before a race, as she'd wait in the starting gate, poles poised to dig in and get her off to a quick start down the hill. There was nothing thrilling about what she felt right now, however. Livy wanted it to go away. She needed her heart to slow down, for her blood not to pump through her veins. She needed to take a deep enough breath to fill her damn lungs. There wasn't enough oxygen in the world to keep her from feeling as though she were suffocating.

The planet was populated with assholes. McCall was no exception. It was silly to assume that the guy who'd hassled her and threatened Nick had been anything more than another dickhead looking to pick a fight. Fear scratched at the back of Livy's brain, though. The sense of intuition that flashed with red lights and blared with alarms in her subconscious. It wasn't paranoia to assume that Joel had scouts everywhere. Just because the guy hadn't been wearing a patch didn't mean he wasn't affiliated with Joel or the Black Death. Livy's picture was probably being shared with every crime syndicate and motorcycle club from one end of the country to the other. She'd been an idiot to think that moving a couple of states away would protect her. Nowhere was safe. And by letting Nick take her out yet again, she might have screwed herself once and for all.

Not if she moved, though. She needed to get out of this place and keep moving. Like a shark. Just swim and swim because it was the only thing keeping her alive. It was time to leave McCall in her wake. She'd known it for a while and tonight was further proof that she'd stayed too long. She couldn't be allowed to put down roots. Not now, not ever.

Unless you tell Nick what you have and trust him to help you.

Livy banished the thought before it had a chance to solidify in her mind. Trusting Nick had been her problem. She'd opened up to him and no matter how small the details she'd shared, they'd been enough to make her feel vulnerable. Exposed. In just shy of a couple of weeks, Nick made her feel comfortable and safe. She couldn't afford either. Not when she knew that Joel wouldn't stop until he found her.

The five-minute drive back to her house passed in silence. Nick's breath no longer sawed in and out of his chest, and Livy's heart no longer felt as though it would burst out of her damned rib cage at any second. Sleep would be impossible after what had happened tonight and it further weakened her to think that what she really needed was for Nick to hold her, soothe her fears, and provide the illusion that everything would be okay.

Nothing would ever be okay. It hadn't been okay for a long time.

Nick pulled into Livy's driveway and killed the engine. For a few moments, they sat in the dark, gazes cast forward, not a single word uttered between them. Livy started as Nick reached across the center console and took her hand in his. A sob worked its way up her throat and Livy forced it down to the soles of her feet. *Damn it.*

"I'm sorry about tonight." Nick's voice sliced through the quiet, so warm and rich that it caused a swell of emotion to bloom in the pit of Livy's stomach. "I should have been more careful. I should have walked away. I should have . . ." He let out a gust of breath. "Fuck. I don't know. I should have done something different than what I did."

"Come inside." The words were more of a plea

than a suggestion. "I don't want to be alone." She didn't want to be alone ever again.

He turned toward her and Livy was glad she couldn't see his face through the dark. "Are you sure?"

No. She wasn't sure about a damned thing. The only thing she knew with certainty was that she'd never felt as secure as she had last night as she slept in Nick's arms. And if she had to spend tonight alone, she'd crack. Livy swallowed her doubts. "I'm sure."

Nick got out of the truck. The sound of his door closing echoed into the cold quiet. Livy's gaze followed the dark outline of his body as he rounded the front of the truck to the passenger-side door. Her breath caught in her throat when he pulled it open, his large body filling up the available space. He reached over and threaded his fingers through her hair as he drew her close to put his mouth to hers.

Such an innocent kiss shouldn't have brought so much untamed heat. The contact sparked not only on her lips, but also in a pleasant tingle that raced across her arms, over the tight points of her nipples, and down her torso before settling at her clit.

Nick's mouth parted to deepen the kiss and Livy responded. Her sigh became his before he returned her breath to her. She lost herself to the moment, to the press of his firm lips, the hold he had on her that somehow anchored her and freed her at the same time. Too soon, he pulled away. He took her hand in his and helped her from the truck. A tremor rocked through her thighs, the muscles tense and twitching from the adrenaline that remained in her system.

"I've got you, Livy." The words carried much more weight than a simple reassurance. The warm timbre of his voice enveloped her and she leaned into him to bathe herself in the heat of his body as well. She couldn't allow him to be her security blanket and yet she clung to him as though he could shield her from every evil in the world.

As much as it pained her to leave his side, Livy pulled away and took his hand. She led the way across the snowy driveway and up the stairs to the front porch. Nick eased her keys out of her hand and unlocked the deadbolt. She looked up into his face and the intensity of his expression held her rapt.

Nick lowered his mouth to hers until his lips hovered a hair's breadth away. "When we're together, I don't care about anything but you. Nothing else matters. It scares me."

Livy knew exactly how he felt. From the moment they'd met she'd violated her own rules and safeguards. She'd thrown caution to the wind. She'd drawn him closer when she should have pushed him away. Nothing else mattered, not the life she'd made for herself, her own safety, not even the past that she'd tried to bury. Nothing mattered but Nick. "I know. I feel the same way. And it scares me, too."

Relief washed over her the second Nick put his lips to hers. Livy melted against him, gave herself over to the moment, the way his mouth felt as it slanted across hers, the thrust of his tongue. His taste, his masculine scent. The way his arms came around her and held her tight.

He turned the knob and eased open the door. Livy didn't worry, didn't fear anything as he backed into the house and brought her with him. He'd proven tonight that he'd take care of her and for the first time in Livy's life she knew the comfort of someone having her back. God, it felt good.

The sound of the door closing behind them barely registered. Nick reached behind her and the snick of the deadbolt as it engaged was nothing more than white noise in the back of Livy's mind. They stumbled into the tiny foyer and with their mouths still joined, kicked off their boots and shrugged out of their coats. Nick tugged at the button of Livy's jeans and slid them to her thighs. She shimmied them down around her ankles and discarded them somewhere by their boots and coats.

"The bra," Nick murmured against her mouth. "Lose it."

Apparently he'd meant it when he told her he wanted her wearing nothing but the sweater. Livy reached behind her and unhooked the clasp. She pulled her arms out of the straps and tugged her bra out from under the sweater. A growl of approval gathered in Nick's throat as he kissed her more fervently. His tongue met hers in a wild, slippery tangle that conveyed all of the urgency Livy felt and then some.

"Get rid of your underwear."

Livy jerked them down and kicked them off. *Done and done.*

Nick pulled away. He took several steps back and his heated gaze scalded her as it wandered from her feet—still clad in her thick winter socks—up the length of her body. "You look better than I thought you would." His voice went low and husky, a sensual rumble that Livy swore she could feel in her pussy. "I'm going to fuck you while you're wearing that sweater."

God, she hoped so.

"But first, I'm going to do all the things I promised I'd do to you last night. And if Simon interrupts this time"—Nick flashed a sinful smile—"he's spending the night outside."

Livy hoped Simon behaved. Because if he didn't, she'd help Nick kick his furry butt out the door.

Chapter Fourteen

Goddamn. Nick didn't think he'd ever seen a sexier woman. The bulky, large knit sweater skimmed Livy's bare thighs and the gaping neckline slipped off one shoulder. Even the thick wool socks she wore turned him on. He was absolutely going to fuck her while she wore that sweater. He might even make her keep the socks on.

"Let your hair out." The braids were cute but he preferred to see the golden-brown locks free and wild around her shoulders. Livy complied, taking the band from one tasseled end and then the other as she unraveled the braids and combed her fingers through the wavy length.

Stunning.

"I think I'm at a disadvantage." Livy's husky murmur made Nick's cock even harder than it already was.

"Why's that?"

A sweet, seductive smile curved her full lips. "You're wearing a lot more clothes than I am."

Nick flashed a cocky grin before stripping off his shirt.

Livy laughed. "That's better. Together, we make a whole outfit."

Funny, sexy, with a quick wit and a body he wanted to drop to his knees and thank God for. If Livy really was the woman Joel Meecum was looking for, Nick could finally understand why the man would risk his freedom for a second chance at her. A wave of possessive jealousy flared in his chest. Nick never wanted another man except him to ever look at Livy, ever touch her again.

"Now we're even," he said.

Livy nodded. "Fair enough."

The time for playfulness was over. Nick wanted to get to business, down and dirty, and make good on all of the promises he'd spoken low in her ear. He approached Livy slowly as though the slightest movement might cause her to bolt. When less than a foot of space separated them, Nick reached out and gathered the hem of Livy's sweater in his fists. The soft, fluffy fabric slid over her bare skin and for a moment he simply used the bulky length to caress her.

Livy's eyes became hooded. Her breath escaped her lips in shallow pants. Nick brought the sweater over her hips and pushed the fabric up her torso before easing it back down into place. He reached around and cupped her ass through the knit, squeezed the yielding flesh hard enough to elicit a low moan from her parted lips before he eased the sweater over the rounded cheeks and up the curve of her back. His fingers grazed bare skin and Nick sucked in a breath before covering up the very parts of her he couldn't wait to explore. His time with Livy might be short-lived and he was going to make sure he made the most of every single god-damned minute.

"God, I want to touch you. Taste you. Kiss every inch of you." Nick buried his face in Livy's hair and breathed in her clean, fragrant scent. He hadn't realized that snow had a smell until he came to McCall and that's what Livy smelled like.

"What's stopping you?" she murmured with the slightest hint of humor.

Livy liked the game as much as Nick did. Building up the tension with banter and stalling tactics. Prolonging their agony until they couldn't wait another second. Livy gave as good as she got, and Nick planned to give her as much as she could handle.

"Your nipples look fantastic underneath that sweater," Nick remarked.

Livy's mouth quirked into a half smile. "That didn't answer my question."

By the time he finally took her, Nick doubted he'd last more than a couple of minutes. He couldn't remember ever being so worked up. "Show me."

"Show you what?" she asked innocently.

"You know what. Do it."

Livy pulled her bottom lip between her teeth. Slowly, she reached up and eased the gaping neck of her sweater down until it revealed the puckered pink tip of her breast. Nick's cock pulsed in time with his rushing heartbeat and he swallowed down a groan. Livy had the most perfect tits he'd ever seen. They molded perfectly to his palm and filled his mouth without overwhelming him. She eased the sweater back up, hiding her breast from his greedy gaze.

"Let me see it again," Nick said.

"Uh-uh." Livy's teasing tone nearly brought him to his knees. "If you want to see it, come and get it."

Nick never backed down from a challenge. Livy let out a playful squeal as he rushed at her and swept her up in his arms. In such a short amount of time he'd managed to banish her fears and shift her focus. He was more proud of that feat than his entire arrest record. It might've been stupid to make assumptions but there was no way around it. Nick believed that Livy was a victim and that she deserved to be happy. Any contribution he made to that happiness made him feel like crowing.

Their eyes met and Nick kissed her. Slow at first and then with more purpose. Livy's arms came around his neck and he thrust his tongue between her parted lips. She met him with equal fervor and before long they were both breathless. Nick reached up and jerked the neck of Livy's sweater down to reveal the breast she'd dared him to come and see for himself.

He wasn't content to simply look, though. Nick sealed his mouth over her dainty nipple and sucked. Livy's body went liquid in his embrace and a soft sigh graced his ears. He swirled his tongue around the hardened peak, took it gently between his teeth. The pace of Livy's breathing increased. Nick bit down harder and he was rewarded with an impassioned gasp that made his shaft ache and his balls tighten.

God, he wanted her. Wanted her more than anything. His need to make her his far surpassed any obsessive career ambition he'd ever had. For months Nick had thought that nothing could compare to the high he experienced when he arrested a criminal who'd been on the run. He'd been wrong.

The high he experienced with Livy surpassed all of it. She was a drug he couldn't get enough of, an addiction he didn't want to kick. He doubted he'd ever be able to get her out of his system no matter how many times he had her. And nothing, not his job or his own convictions, was going to change that.

He attended to one breast, and then the other. Livy's head lolled back on her shoulder and her hands abandoned his neck to grip his shoulders while her nails bit into the skin. Nick kept one arm around her waist and he reached down with the other and slid it between her thighs. A groan worked its way up his throat as his fingers slipped through the wetness of her pussy, already swollen and dripping for him.

"Livy, you're so wet." As though she needed the confirmation. Her thighs were coated and sticky. Nick spread her arousal over her outer lips and up over the curve of her mons. Her breath hitched and her thighs trembled beneath his fingers. "And you smell good enough to eat."

Livy let out a gust of breath and sucked it right back in. The sound shivered pleasantly down Nick's spine. She cocked a challenging brow. "Isn't that your plan?"

Hell yeah it was.

He guided her to the recliner and urged her to sit. Nick went down on his knees and eased the chair back—not enough for her to lie down, but just far enough to give him access to what he wanted—and eased either leg around the chair's arms. He settled himself between her spread thighs and his breath caught somewhere between his sternum and his lips.

Beautiful.

Nick let out a contented groan as he sealed his mouth over her sex. Just as honey-sweet as he'd imagined. Livy's hips rolled as a low moan filled the quiet. Nick reached beneath her and scooted her closer to the edge of the chair and Livy's legs went wider still to offer him unhindered access to her. He swirled his tongue over her clit before sucking the tight bundle of nerves between his lips. Livy gasped, her back bowed, and her thighs twitched on either side of Nick's cheeks.

"Holy shit, Nick. Don't stop."

A smug smile settled on Nick's lips as he did just that. A tight, desperate whimper escaped her and he dragged his finger from the apex of her sex, down to the opening. He stroked the outer rim and she squirmed. "Does it feel good?"

"Yes," she all but panted. "Which is why I said, don't stop."

Nick chuckled. He leaned forward and blew lightly over her soft, wet flesh. A shudder rocked Livy's body and her hips thrust up to meet his mouth. "If I keep going," he said, "I won't stop until you come."

His words coaxed more of those sweet sounds from Livy's lips. "Promise?"

Nick didn't need to tell Livy he always followed through; he'd show her. He picked up where he'd left off and ran the flat of his tongue from her opening back up to her clit. Livy squirmed in the chair, her breath raced and her thighs twitched. Nick settled back at her clit and flicked out with his tongue in teasing strokes before increasing the pressure with the flat of his tongue and then sucking her bud into his mouth.

With every pass of his tongue, every gentle flick, each pull of suction, Livy's cries became more desperate. Nick reached up and cupped her breast through her sweater. He teased himself as much as he did her with the veiled contact as he used the fabric to brush over her hardened nipples. Her back arched as Nick plucked at the peak before he focused his attention on her other breast.

The slight tremors that rocked Livy's body intensified as Nick increased the pressure of his tongue. Without penetrating, he used the pad of his forefinger to caress the sensitive skin of her opening and when he dragged his teeth over the hood of her clitoris, Livy came apart without preamble.

Her pussy contracted against his mouth. Her thighs shook. Cry after desperate cry echoed out in the silence. Her back arched and her hips bucked. Her fingers came around her knees and she gripped them so tightly that her knuckles turned white. Nick brought her down from the high with gentle passes of his tongue and soft caresses that eased her cries into quiet sobs of pleasure. He swore he could feel the racing of her heart, each and every one of her heavy breaths, in his own chest. And Nick had only chipped the surface of the things he wanted to do to her.

Amazing!

And not just your run-of-the-mill, wow, that-was-a-great-orgasm amazing. What Nick had done to her went far beyond that trivial bullshit. Like, holy-fucking-shit-I-think-I-just-died-and-went-to-heaven amazing!

Livy slumped in the recliner, her legs completely useless, her arms as solid as Jell-O. And not the kind you could pick up with your fingers, either. The kind that required a spoon it was so Jell-O-y. Her heart beat a frantic rhythm in her rib cage and her breath raced. She hadn't even lifted a finger and she felt as though she'd just sprinted a 5k without stopping. True, she was a little out of practice, but she was pretty sure that even if she'd been screwing her way from one end of the state to the other over the past four years, none of those experiences would compare to Nick.

Just, *wow.*

Her fingers wandered over the fabric of what had officially become not only Nick's, but also her favorite sweater in the universe. Nick's heated gaze raked over her body and she shivered. His nostrils flared and his jaw squared as he eased himself up and kissed a path up one thigh to her bare hip and over the sweater before his mouth latched over her breast. He nipped at the hardened peak before bringing his mouth to hers. Livy tasted herself on his lips as he deepened the kiss and it reawakened the flames of her desire that hadn't even had a chance to smolder.

"I think you need to let me return the favor," she said, breathless.

Nick's eyes widened a fraction of an inch and his jaw flexed. Indecision marred his expression and a smug sense of satisfaction crested in Livy's chest. He wanted to control the situation, prove to her that he was a man of his word in all things, and yet, the thought of her putting her mouth on him was enough to lure him from his path.

She wanted to pump her fist in celebration.

Nick liked to talk the talk . . . Livy wondered what would happen if she turned the tables. "I want to put my mouth on you, Nick. I want to suck, lick"— she gazed up at him from lowered lashes—"maybe even bite. I want to taste you." His lips parted and his brows came down over his dark eyes. Livy licked her lips, slowly, to accentuate her point and he let out a forceful gust of breath. "Wouldn't you like to see me on my knees?" She smiled sweetly. "In this sweater?"

Livy's cheeks heated. Something about Nick made her totally unashamed to say things that she'd never usually utter. Sure, she had the vocabulary of a sailor, but not a porn star. Still, Nick had managed to set her on fire with his dirty talk and she wanted to do the same for him.

Nick unfastened his pants so quickly you would

have thought they'd been soaked in gasoline and Livy held a match. Her legs wobbled like a newborn fawn as she stood up from the chair. She gripped onto the waistband of Nick's jeans and tugged them down over his ass the second he got the zipper down. She turned him so their positions were reversed and gently pushed on his shoulders to ease him down into the recliner.

"Socks on or off?" she asked mostly to herself as she pulled his jeans and underwear the rest of the way off and discarded them beside her. "I think on."

Nick smiled and heat bloomed from Livy's chest and spread outward. She ran her palms up the length of his thighs, through the crisp dusting of hair, and her gaze settled on the length of his erection that protruded proudly from his hips. There wasn't anything about Nick that wasn't impressive and Livy realized that no guy she'd ever been with—and there weren't that many—could ever hold a candle to him. Pure. Masculine. Perfection. *Rawr.*

Livy reached out and stroked her palm down the length of his shaft. Nick sucked in a breath that quickened her pulse and she marveled at the velvet smoothness that encased such rigid strength. She brought her lips to the glossy head and kissed him there. She kissed the crown, along his shaft, at his heavy sac and his thighs. Then, she kissed her way back up to where she'd started. Nick's thigh muscles went taut beneath her touch and his breaths were nothing more than well-contained pants. Livy flicked out at a bead of moisture that gathered at the tip and captured his salty-sweet taste on her tongue. Nick gave a low moan that only served to push Livy to go a little further.

She wrapped her lips around his shaft and took him deep into her mouth. There was nothing tame or tentative about it. Livy took as much of him as she could as deeply as she could. Nick's hips bucked at the abrupt motion and he let out a grunt of approval as she pulled away to the smooth glossy head before diving back down again.

"Livy," Nick said between breaths. "Fuck, that's amazing."

She wanted him to feel as good as he'd made her feel and then some. No matter what happened after they parted ways in a couple of weeks, she wanted him to always remember this night. Because she sure as hell would.

Livy hollowed her cheeks as she took Nick deep into her mouth. She sucked hard and then softly, working her mouth over his shaft in a wet glide that stoked her own passion as much as it did Nick's. He let out a low groan as he threaded his fingers through her hair and gave a shallow thrust of his hips. When Livy grazed her teeth along the sensitive skin of the crown, Nick's groan transformed into an impassioned shout that sent a lick of heat up Livy's spine. She teased him for long minutes, nipping and dragging her teeth along his skin before sucking him deep into her mouth.

She took his sac into her palm and massaged the delicate weight in her palm before giving a gentle tug. Nick's back bowed away from the chair and his grip on her hair tightened. "Goddamn, Livy. Do that again."

He didn't have to tell her twice. She fell into an easy rhythm, her mouth and hands working in tandem to drive Nick to the point of no return. She wanted to know what it felt like to have him come against her tongue. To feel and taste every bit of his passion. His muscles grew harder—stone beneath her touch—with every flick of her tongue and his breath sawed in and out of his chest. When his thighs began to tremble in earnest, Livy knew he was there. Just another stroke, maybe two with her mouth and he'd come. . . .

Nick seized Livy by the shoulders and guided her back. His eyes were alight with wildfire and his chest heaved. He gripped the back of her neck and hauled her against him before putting his mouth to hers in a fervent and crushing kiss that left her breathless and shaking.

"I want to be inside you when I come," he breathed against her mouth. "Are you ready for me to fuck you, Livy?"

"Yes." She couldn't manage more than the one word. She'd never been more ready for anything in her entire fucking life. "Hurry."

He scooped up his jeans and dug his wallet out of his back pocket. With shaking fingers he pulled out a short strip of condoms and ripped off one of the packets. "I've only got four of these," he murmured before he nipped at her throat. "Guess I'll have to go to the store in the morning."

"Lofty goals, Officer Brady," Livy purred.

Nick laughed. The sound rumbled through her. "I'm an overachiever."

"I do appreciate hard work."

"Then get ready to be worked over hard."

Laughter bubbled up in Livy's chest. Nick could be sexy as sin one moment and an easygoing goof the next. His intensity and deep, growly voice could easily intimidate or spark a raging fire of passion. She'd never met a more perfect man. Ever. God, she hoped that nothing would break the spell she'd fallen under because if Nick turned out to be anything other than the perfect man she imagined him to be, it would surely break her.

Nick wrapped his arms around Livy and lifted her. He turned and walked the few feet from the recliner to the couch and settled her in his lap as he sat down. She rose up on her knees and cupped his face as she kissed him. The rough grit of his stubble brushed her palms and she let her fingers wander upward to weave through the short strands of his hair. Nick broke their kiss only long enough to rip open the packet in his hand. Livy kept her gaze locked with his as he rolled on the condom and when he finished, she kissed him again as though this would be the last time their lips would ever meet.

For all she knew, it might be.

Nick wrapped his hands around her waist and urged her to come up on her knees. Without breaking their kiss, she reached between them and guided him to her opening. Livy rocked down, slow rolls of her hips that took him an inch or so at a time. Nick groaned into her mouth as his kisses became more desperate and he nipped at her bottom lip. Slow and steady wasn't going to cut it. They both wanted it hard and fast.

At the same moment Nick thrust with his hips, Livy drove hers downward. Mouths pressed together, they both gasped, sharing each other's breath. He stretched her inner walls, filled her completely. Livy experienced only a moment of discomfort before she began to move, slow rolls of her hips that she finished as she came up on her knees and plunged back down.

"*Ungh.*" Nick gripped her hips tighter as the unintelligible sound escaped his lips. He guided her motions, eased her hips up and down over his erection as he used her body to pleasure himself. Livy's head fell back on her shoulders as she rode him, pleasure radiating from her core outward. With every thrust, every roll of her hips, Livy's body coiled tighter. It wouldn't be long before Nick shattered her for the second time tonight.

"Don't stop, Livy. That's it, I want all of you." Nick's urgent command fanned the flames of her desire and she took him as deep as she could. "You feel so good. You're squeezing me so tight. God, you're amazing."

No, it was him who amazed her. His hands abandoned her hips as he gripped the hem of her sweater. He pulled it up over her breasts and buried his face against one swell, taking her nipple into his mouth. Livy drew in a sharp breath as he nibbled and sucked. When he reached up to roll the other nipple between his fingers, she cried out. She'd never felt so good in her entire life. Her muscles became taut and Livy gripped Nick's shoulders as she rode him harder, faster. Took him deeper.

"Ah, God, Livy!" Nick exclaimed as he threw his head back. "Just like that. Don't stop."

"I'm close, Nick," she murmured close to his ear.

"Come for me," he said in that commanding tone that turned her to mush. "Let me feel your pussy squeeze me tight."

His words pushed her over the edge. Livy dug her nails into his shoulders as she came. Her world imploded as deep pulses of sensation spread outward through her body like rings on a pond. Livy sobbed her pleasure as the orgasm ebbed and then crested once again. The sensation was so intense that it stole her breath and she gripped Nick tighter as though it was the only thing keeping her from spiraling out into space.

A moment later, Nick followed her off the edge. He came with a shout as his body went rigid. He pumped furiously into her, his hips coming off the couch. Long moments passed, his breath hot in her ear, his hold firm on her hips and Livy cleaved to him as they both rode out their pleasure and their bodies melted and relaxed against each other.

"So," Livy said on a breath, "was it good for you?"

Nick wrapped his arms around her. His laughter shook them both and Livy had to admit it wasn't an altogether unpleasant sensation with him still inside her. His hands wandered up her back, down her torso, and grazed the swell of her breasts. The husky timbre of his voice sent a shiver over her skin when he said, "I fucking *love* this sweater."

"If you and the sweater need some alone time, I'm sure we can work something out," Livy teased.

Nick pulled away to look at her. The warmth in his dark eyes caused emotion to swell in Livy's chest. She didn't want to fall for Nick. Couldn't. But when he looked at her like that . . . ? *Dear God.*

"Let's go upstairs." He snatched the rest of the condoms from beside him on the couch. "I've got three of these left and I want them gone before the sun rises."

"The sweater?" Livy asked coyly.

"It's coming off," he vowed.

"Okay," Livy said. "But the socks are still up for debate."

"I want you," Nick said, suddenly serious. "Again. Now."

"Let's get upstairs then," she said, low. "Because I'm ready to lose this sweater."

"Just for a while," Nick said. "I might call it off the bench later."

Livy smiled. She could live with that.

Chapter Fifteen

Livy snuggled in beside Nick and he came slowly awake. A chill had settled on the cabin and he burrowed farther under the covers to gather Livy in his arms. Her back molded perfectly to his chest and he curled his legs under hers.

He brought his head up from the pillow to check the time. The bright digital display read five fifteen. They'd only been asleep for a few hours, but Nick doubted he'd be able to go back to sleep. His mind raced as he tried to make some sort of sense out of everything he felt. He'd crossed a line once and for all tonight. There was no going back. He'd always prided himself on his integrity, his dedication to the job, and to justice. When it came to the woman who slept peacefully beside him, though, it seemed Nick had no integrity whatsoever. He'd gladly sacrificed everything he stood for, everything he believed in, for Livy.

And goddamn it, he'd do it all over again given the chance.

His cock stirred at the memory of what they'd

done just a few short hours ago. *Three times.* He grew hard as his hand wandered from Livy's hip over the curve of her waist and up her torso. A slow, contented sigh slipped from between her lips and Nick continued with his unhurried exploration. His fingertips skimmed her ribs and skirted the swell of one breast. Livy's arm reached back and she cupped the back of Nick's neck in her palm. She didn't open her eyes; she simply teased the strands of his hair that skirted his nape with her fingers. A chill raced over Nick's skin as he captured her pert breast in his palm. The roundness filled his hand perfectly. He loved Livy's athletic body. The evidence of her strength that pulled all of her muscles taut. Another slow sigh filled the silence as he teased one nipple to a hardened peak. Her sighs transformed to low moans that heated Nick's blood. He continued with his slow exploration of her body. He teased one breast, and then the other, until Livy's breath came in quick little pants. Nick could have fondled Livy's breasts for hours. He was obsessed with them, wanted to touch, lick, and suck them. He wanted to pluck at her nipples, take them between his teeth. Damn, he wanted to *feast* on her gorgeous, petite breasts.

Nick put his mouth close to Livy's ear. He took her lobe between his teeth before gently sucking. Her gasp of breath was like a shot of adrenaline straight into his heart. He might have fucked up his life, his career, and his integrity. But until the sun came up, he refused to think about his past or his future. For the next few hours, Nick was going to live in the moment.

"I can't get enough of you, Livy," he murmured close to her ear. She arched into his touch and the soft flesh of her ass brushed against his cock. Nick swallowed down a groan. One hand remained cupped over her breast while the other wandered between them toward her neck. He gripped her, his fingers wrapped around her throat and she tilted her head back as though to submit to his commanding touch. "I want to fuck you like this." He rocked his erection into the crease of her ass and she gave a quiet whimper. "I want to hold your leg and open you up. Slide my cock in that tight pussy and fuck you slowly. I'd make it last."

Livy shuddered in his embrace. He kissed her neck, scraped his teeth along the sensitive flesh while he continued to thrust into the crease of her ass. "Oh God, Nick."

Her breathy reply caused his stomach to twist. She liked it when he talked dirty. He tried not to think about who else might have whispered filthy things in her ear. Who might have cupped her luscious breasts or thrust between her silky thighs. If he did, Nick would snap. Instead, he focused on Livy's pleasure and getting her to that place where she was so mindless with need that nothing but finding orgasm mattered.

"I love your breasts." He released his grip on her throat to cup them both in his hands. Her nipples hardened, teasing his palms, and it caused his cock to throb hot and hard.

"They're too small," she said barely above a whisper.

"God, no." There wasn't an inch of her that wasn't absolutely fucking perfect. "I love that they fit my palms. That I can take them almost completely into my mouth. I love your tight little nipples, Livy." He pinched them gently to show her just how much. She sucked in a sharp breath that made his cock twitch. "I love the way you smell, the way you taste. The sounds you make when you come." Nick's hand wandered down the flat of her stomach and past her mons. He slid his middle finger through the swollen lips of her pussy to the wet heat they concealed. "I love the way your clit gets hard and throbs against my finger when I stroke it."

Her nails dug into the back of his neck and her chest heaved with her quickened breaths. Most of all, Nick loved that he could drive her out of her mind with nothing more than a few heated words. "If I touched you, Livy, would you come for me?" Her grip on his neck tightened and she gave a quick nod of her head. Nick put his mouth to her ear. "Say it, Livy. Tell me you'll come if I touch your swollen clit."

"I'll come," she said on a breath. "If you touch my clit, I'll come."

Nick put his mouth to Livy's throat. He kissed, licked, nipped at her flesh while he urged her legs to part. She hooked her top leg over his thigh but kept her back pressed to his bare chest. The softness of her skin was a sweet torture that Nick couldn't get enough of as he slid the pad of his finger over the knot of nerves that protruded from between her slick lips.

Livy let out a low whimper with the first contact. Her hips bucked and her leg tensed as it squeezed his thigh. Nick shifted, so that Livy lay cradled in his free arm. It provided the perfect angle for him to reach around and tease the nipple he'd admitted to being so fond of while he continued to pet her wet pussy with the other. A sense of euphoric power crested over Nick. Livy didn't trust anyone and yet, she let him hold her in his arms, cradle her delicate body as he pleasured her. She'd allowed him to cup her throat in his palm, spread her thighs willingly for him, and mewled with impassioned sighs as he teased her tiny delicate nipples and feathered his fingertip over her clit. Livy had entrusted herself to him. Her body, her pleasure.

Nick was honored to be found worthy of at least some part of Livy's trust. It also made him feel even more like a lousy son of a bitch.

And yet, he did nothing to stop what was happening between them. He was desperate for Livy. Greedy for her. His need surpassed any sense of honor or honesty. They were both players. Liars. Guarded and suspicious. Hiding who they truly were for their own selfish reasons. None of that mattered to Nick, and that's what scared him. He wanted her in spite of all of that. In spite of himself.

He was lost to her.

The upstairs bedroom was cold but Nick didn't want to be buried under the pile of blankets any longer. He kicked them away from their bodies, enjoying the way Livy's nipples puckered even tighter in the chill. Damn, he wanted to suck them. Take those diamond-hard peaks into his mouth and roll them on his tongue. But that would mean changing their positions, and Nick wasn't about to take his hand away from the wet, silken folds of her pussy.

Livy's cries filled the quiet. She tried to writhe in his grasp but Nick held her tight against him. "Nick." The way she said his name, breathy, low, and desperate, caused his cock to throb. "Oh God, Nick. I don't know how much more I can take."

"You can take more," Nick assured her. He circled her clit with the pad of his finger. Careful not to go too fast, or apply too much pressure, he kept her on the edge of orgasm without allowing her to topple off. "I want you to feel good, Livy. When you're ready, I want you to come hard."

"I'm ready now," she panted.

"No." Nick brought his mouth to her throat and she shuddered. "I'll tell you when you're ready," he said against her skin.

Every muscle in Livy's body went taut. There was so much power in her body that Nick found himself in awe. He wanted to turn on the lights, watch the play of muscles that flexed and twitched with each pluck of his finger on her beaded nipple and with every swirl of his finger over her swollen clit. Instead, he settled for the glow of moonlight on her skin that shone through the window—brighter than usual in the winter sky with the white backdrop of snow beyond.

Nick teased Livy's opening before venturing back to her clit. She gasped, her thighs twitched, and her stomach tensed beneath his arm. Once again, he dipped his finger into her heat, deeper this time. Her inner walls contracted around him and he pulled out slowly before inserting two fingers deep inside her.

"Nick. Don't stop."

He alternated between teasing her clit and pumping his fingers inside her. Her shallow breaths transformed to desperate gasps and her whimpering cries became deep, hungry sobs of pleasure that made his sac pull up tight against his thighs. Nick thrust into the crease of Livy's ass and groaned at the sweet release of pressure that the simple act provided. He wouldn't fuck her until she came for him, and like Livy, Nick wasn't sure how much more he could take.

Livy's hips bucked. Her back arched, and her nails dug into the back of his neck where she continued to hold on to him as though the simple act anchored her to the earth. Her wetness slicked her thighs and coated Nick's fingers and palm. The scent of her arousal filled his nostrils and Nick inhaled deeply. "Come for me, Livy. Let me feel you come around my fingers."

Livy had never been so absolutely mindless with want in her entire life. Her body hummed as though conditioned to respond to Nick's touch, his heated commands. He'd kept her on the edge for so long, she wasn't sure she could find release. The intensity of pleasure blinded her, clouded her thoughts, until the world melted away and the only thing left was Nick. His stomach muscles flexed and bunched against her back, his thighs were like redwoods beneath her. His cock was hot and hard, tempered steel as it slid between the cheeks of her ass. Livy had never been so wet before. Her arousal dripped down her thighs, into the crease of her ass. She was a slick, panting, tangled knot of need, passion, and want. And if she didn't come soon, she was going to spontaneously combust.

"Come for me, Livy."

Nick's deep, rumbling voice reached out to her through the darkness. She kept her eyes squeezed shut, focused solely on the way he made her feel and nothing else. Every word spoken coaxed chills to the surface of Livy's skin. Her nipples were so hard they ached and every time Nick plucked at the sensitive flesh, she felt only the slightest relief.

He withdrew his fingers and worked his way back to her clit. Livy gasped and her thighs quivered as he took her clit between his thumb and forefinger. No one had ever touched Livy that way and the intensity of sensation nearly brought tears to her eyes. She moaned, long and loud, the sound echoing in the sparse upstairs bedroom. Nick continued to work her clit between his fingers and Livy's abdomen tightened to the point that the muscles began to spasm. Pressure built inside her, she coiled tight until she felt as though her entire being were encased in a shape the size of a tennis ball. "Nick," she said on a breath. "I'm going to come."

He abandoned her clit and thrust two fingers deep inside her. Livy's back arched and she sobbed her pleasure as her world exploded into myriad pieces. Like snow in a blizzard, the tiny particles that constructed her were tossed in a frenzy as wave after wave of sensation stole over her. Livy rode the crest and came down, only to be thrown high into the air again as another wave of intense pulses contracted her pussy around Nick's fingers. She rode out her pleasure, grinding her hips against his hand until the orgasm calmed and settled.

Every time she thought Nick had reached the pinnacle of what he could make her feel, he surprised her. No man had ever made her feel so cherished, as though nothing mattered more than her pleasure, her comfort, her needs. She was more than addicted to Nick. In that moment, Livy wondered if she'd ever be able to live without him. And the knowledge that they'd soon go their separate ways nearly gutted her.

She couldn't dwell on that right now. If she did, she'd break.

Nick rolled her to her back. There was nothing tentative or gentle about it. Nick pressed her down into the mattress as he situated himself between her thighs. He reached over and grabbed the last of the condoms from the bedside table. His hands shook as he fumbled with the wrapper.

"If I don't get inside you now, I'm going to go out of my mind."

That made two of them. A deep, hollow ache opened up inside of Livy and all she knew was that she needed Nick to fill it and make her whole. "Hurry, Nick." The words left Livy's mouth in an urgent rush. "Oh God, hurry."

He ripped open the packet and reached between them. He rolled it on as he thrust, as though he couldn't wait long enough to put it fully on before he entered her. Their mutual groans of relief filled the silence as Nick seated himself as deep as he could go. Livy's inner walls contracted around his girth and the dark outline of Nick's jaw as it squared let her know that he'd felt every inch of her squeeze him tight.

"Oh Livy," Nick said on a moan. "You're fucking *perfect.*"

Perfect. The word speared her chest. Livy was as far from perfect as you could get. The way Nick said her name, with so much heat and affection, coaxed a lump to her throat. She'd been Olivia Gallagher for so long that she'd almost forgotten she'd ever been anyone else. But right now, she didn't want to be Livy. She wanted to be the woman she'd once been. And it was that woman's name she wanted on Nick's lips.

"Nick," Livy murmured in the dark. "Fuck me."

A satisfied growl echoed in his throat as he began to move above her. Livy wanted to forget everything about her past and the woman she'd used to be. She wanted Nick to take her hard, to banish everything until once again the world melted away and there was only him.

He pulled out nearly to the crown and drove deep. Livy arched up to meet him and a moan formed on her lips. Nick cupped the back of her neck with one hand while the other braced the bulk of his weight beside them. "Look at me, Livy. I want to see your face while I fuck you."

A rush of delicious heat flooded her. The things

he said to her . . . Hot, passionate, commanding, but never crude. Never cruel. Nick sparked an unquenchable fire inside her. How would she ever be able to go back to her life the way it had been after this? After she'd had a taste of what it felt like to feel true passion and abandon.

Nick's breath came hard as he moved over her. His chest heaved, brushing the points of Livy's nipples with each powerful thrust. He filled her completely, stretched her, and still it wasn't enough. "Harder, Nick."

She gripped his shoulders. Her nails dug into his flesh and Nick groaned. He thrust as deep as he could go, grinding against her with each forward shove of his hips. Livy gasped at the sensation. She rolled up to meet him and the delicious friction of her clit as it brushed against Nick's shaft began the slow build that pushed her closer to the precipice of release. She wanted him to fuck her until she had no choice but to leap in a freefall over the edge.

"You feel so good, Livy." Nick's breath was hot in her ear and she shuddered. "So tight. So wet. *Fuck.* I can't get deep enough. Can't go hard enough. I need more."

Livy opened her legs wider as though that would help either of them. She knew exactly how Nick felt and the insatiable need that swept them up had no remedy. Like an endless vacuum it would continue to suck them further and further into this wild whirlwind of want and sensation until they went mad from it. Relationships like this were reckless.

Dangerous. Destructive. Yet, Livy ran headlong into it, more than ready to accept her own ruination.

"Don't stop, Nick. I need it *all*."

Her words seemed only to excite him more. His answering moan was part pleasure, part pain, and one hundred percent desperation. His muscles tensed and Livy might as well have been surrounded by stone. Her hands wandered from his shoulders, over his collarbone and the hills of his pecs. She found his hard, flat nipples with her palms and Nick groaned louder as she teased them for a moment before taking each between her fingers and pinching lightly.

"Again." The word barely made sense but Livy understood the barked command. She pinched again, harder this time, and Nick shuddered. "Fuck!" he barked through a huff of breath. "That feels so good."

Neither one of them was thinking clearly now. Their brains hazed by lust, all they could do was groan, moan, and *feel*. Nick released his grip on the back of her neck to seize her leg. He hoisted it up, resting the bend of her knee in the crook of his arm. It opened her more fully to him and he let out a long, slow sigh that conveyed his relief. His cock was a steel rod encased in slippery satin as it glided in and out of her. Her clit throbbed against his shaft and lower, his sac slapped against her flesh with every powerful thrust. There was nothing sweet or gentle about the way they fucked. It was dirty, messy, and urgent. That didn't mean it was emotionless, though. Livy felt so much that she thought her chest might explode from the excess of emotion.

He pounded into her without mercy. His breath sawed in and out of his chest and ended on low groans that sent a jolt of excitement through Livy's bloodstream. *So close.* Her body once again coiled in on itself, curling and straining until she could do nothing but clamp her jaw shut and ride it out. Nick's pace increased and his frenzied thrusts, the sound of skin meeting skin, and their mingled grunts of breath sent Livy into a sensory overload that pushed her over the edge of release into a spiral of pleasure that left her dizzy and shaken.

The orgasm hit her with the force of an explosion. A sound of surprise burst from her lips as she came. Stars twinkled in her vision and waves of pulsing sensation thrummed from her clit outward through her core in powerful contractions. Nick followed her over the edge with a shout. His body went taut and his thrusts became wild and disjointed. Chills broke out over his skin as he came and Livy caressed from the ridges of his stomach, up his chest, and over his arms.

"Livy," Nick moaned against her sweat-dampened skin as he came. "God, Livy. Oh my God."

She knew exactly how he felt. *Welcome to ruination.*

Chapter Sixteen

"It's her. No fucking doubt."

Joel leaned back in his chair as he regarded Shorty. "You sure?"

He gave a sharp nod of his head.

Joel had been looking for that little bitch for four goddamned years. So far she'd managed to fly under the radar. Could he actually have gotten lucky enough to have found her in some backwoods town in the middle of Idaho? Most of the time, Joel couldn't trust any of these lousy SOBs to do anything without fucking up somehow. He trusted Shorty, though. They'd been riding together from the very beginning. Shorty might not have ever met Kari in person, but he'd seen a picture of her. Shorty should have been able to pick her out of a crowd. If anyone was going to find Kari, it was him.

"What'd she say to you?"

"Not a whole lot. Bitch doesn't get out much, that's for fucking sure. I scoured that damned town looking for her. Was getting ready to pull out the next morning and decided to hit the bar to play some pool and get a drink. She showed up with some tough son of a bitch who fought like a god-damned Navy SEAL."

"Cop?"

Shorty shrugged. "Could be. Maybe ex-military. Hard to tell. He could have been one of those fitness junkies that studies tae kwon do because he thinks it'll get him laid. Doesn't matter how tough he thinks he is, though. A bullet's gonna kill him just the same."

Joel snorted. "You think he knows who she is?"

Another shrug. "He called her Livy. My guess is he's trying to get a little pussy. He thought I was coming on to her and that's when he got pissy."

It took Shorty a week to track her down in a town that wasn't anything more than a blip on the radar. If Joel had to guess, the second she caught wind that someone was asking about her, she'd split. It was a good call for him to play it cool. But how long would Joel have to hang out in the town before he got a glimpse of her? He wasn't about to go back to jail and it had been almost four years since he'd poked his head out of his hole. All because of that stupid fucking twat.

After he got his ledger back, he was going to make her *suffer*.

"How many guys could we get into town without anyone getting suspicious?"

Shorty leaned back in his chair. He scrubbed a hand across his face as he contemplated. "Handful. No patches."

No shit. Like Joel would bite himself in the ass by

flashing his Black Death patch anywhere outside of the clubhouse. "Law enforcement?"

"County and city," Shorty replied. "Nothing big. The sorts of guys who deal with traffic stops and underage parties. I doubt they handle anything too hard-core."

"Good." Big cities had SWAT, staties, FBI, and most annoying, marshals. Joel wanted to stay as far from those man-hunting sons of bitches as possible. "You get a bead on where she lives?"

Shorty smirked. "Think so. After her boyfriend tried to act like a tough guy, they left and I followed them to a cabin about five miles out of town. No neighbors as far as I could tell. Looks like the houses out there don't get a lot of use."

Fucking perfect. No one to hear the bitch scream. "We'll lay low for a week or so. Let things cool off again before we head back." Lucky for Joel, Kari had worked hard to live an isolated life. No one would even miss her when she was gone. As for the boyfriend . . . Like Shorty said, tough guy or not, ain't nobody going to survive a bullet to the head.

"Reach out to Sawyer's crew in SoCal. Let them know that we'll be ready to roll in a few weeks." It wasn't only Joel who'd suffered because of what Kari had done. The entire club felt the pinch. When word got out that someone had swiped his ledger, none of Joel's usual business contacts would touch him. Until they could be assured that their own identities and dealings with the Black Death were still secret, their operations had been effectively shut down. Not for much longer, though.

"Whaddya think she's up to?" Shorty asked.

Joel gave him a questioning glance.

"She didn't go to the cops, she's not using it to get a piece of the action. Far as I can tell, she's just sitting on it. Why?"

"Insurance. She thinks I'll leave her alone as long as she stays hidden."

Shorty snorted. "Stupid."

If there hadn't been enough information—and names—in that ledger to put a fuck-ton of his associates in jail, Joel might have left well enough alone. He had to give her credit where it was due: She wasn't a snitch. That wasn't going to save her life, though. She knew too much and Joel didn't like to be jerked around.

"Tell ya what," Shorty began. "There's a hell of a lot of guys who'll be glad we're going back to work."

Not a damned one of the guys in their charter was interested in going legit. They were good at running guns and drugs for the cartels. It paid better than some fucking nine-to-five at a garage or lumberyard somewhere and it gave them the power and clout they all craved. Joel had been at the top of his game when Kari ran off with his ledger. His pride had taken a serious hit.

She couldn't be allowed to simply walk away. Not when his reputation was on the line.

"What do you want me to tell Sawyer?" Shorty asked. "You know he'll want some assurances."

Short of delivering her head to the SoCal crew in a cardboard box, there wasn't much Joel could offer aside from his word. He wasn't interested in taking her alive. When he found her, the bitch was going to die. Likewise, he wasn't going to fuck himself over by carting her rotting corpse across three states for the benefit of the cartel.

"Tell him the ledger is safe. And that all of the loose ends are about to be tied up. Tell him he'll get photographic proof that she's dead."

"Mendoza might want more than photographic proof." The head of the cartel was a violent son of a bitch who chopped off heads and left the bodies in mass graves. And he was as nervous as a March fucking hare.

"I'll deal with Mendoza." Joel knew for a fact that no one ran the cartel's heroin better than the Black Death. Joel just needed to make sure that he made a very convincing case to the drug lord that his identity was still safe.

"All of this is well and good, brother," Shorty said. "But it don't mean shit if we don't get to Idaho and tie up those loose ends. We need to play this close to the hip. From what I've seen, that bastard with Kari could hold his own. He might not have been anyone to worry about, but what if he is?"

Joel had already considered the possibility. It didn't matter if he was one man or one hundred. A stupid small-town chump looking to impress his old lady, or a highly trained Special Ops SEAL ready to defend her to the death. This might be his only chance to get his ledger back and make sure Kari didn't make any trouble for him in the future. Joel had been hiding from the law for far too long and that ledger was going to buy him a one-way ticket to Mexico and financial security.

"We'll handle it," Joel said after a moment. "Get everything together for the trip. Five of us will roll up there. You, me, Cochran, Teddy, and Bo. The smaller the group, the better. No one else knows, got it?"

"You sure you want to go?" Shorty asked. "It might not be safe."

Maybe not, but Joel wouldn't be satisfied until he saw the whites of her eyes. Or the look of fear on her face as he choked the life out of her. "I'm sure. Get your ass in gear. I want us on the road in four days."

"Can do."

Finally, Joel was going to get what he'd been after for the past four years. And nothing was going to stand in his way of getting it.

Livy dipped a slice of bread in the French toast batter and let it soak for a moment before transferring it to a frying pan. She'd been wearing a perma-grin ever since she woke up in Nick's arms a little over an hour ago. After their latest round of mind-blowing sex, they'd drifted back off to sleep and for the second time in four years, Livy had slept like the dead, never once waking at the slightest sound or to check and make sure the windows were all still locked.

It wasn't lost on her that both of those wonderful nights of sleep had happened while Nick slept beside her. She'd never known that sort of peace. Not even when she was a kid. That knowledge shook Livy to her foundation.

"Do you want one egg or two?" she called toward the living room. It was easier to focus on the *now* rather than all of the things that weighed her down. She chose to bask in the afterglow of the pleasure Nick had given her instead of worry that she'd never find a man who made her feel as safe as he did. The faint smell of wood smoke filled the cabin and Livy smiled. Thanks to Nick's superior fire-building skills, the house would be warm and toasty in no time.

"Three!" Nick called back.

"Three?" she asked with a laugh. Her man was hungry. *Her* man? No. Livy couldn't allow herself to think of Nick like that. He wasn't hers. He'd be going home soon and Livy would be looking for a new town to settle down in. All she could do was enjoy the time she had with him. After all, it would be over far too soon.

"Three!" Nick confirmed. The sound of his footsteps echoed through the house before he poked his head into the kitchen. "Five slices of French toast, and a half a pound of bacon, too." He paused. "Better make that a pound."

He leaned over her and placed a kiss on her neck. Livy shivered from the contact and her nipples hardened. It was absolutely crazy that an innocent kiss could have such a visceral effect on her. But damn, she liked the way he made her feel.

Livy turned to give him a skeptical look. "You seem hungry, Nick. Did you work up an appetite?"

He leaned in and bit down gently on her neck. Livy let out a squeal of delight. "You know I did," he growled next to her ear. His hand reached down to cup one cheek of her ass through the long T-shirt that hung past her thighs. "If there's no bacon, I can think of something else I could eat."

His heated innuendo brought a flush to Livy's cheeks. "I don't know that there's a lot of nutritional value in *that.*"

Nick chuckled. The deep timbre of his voice rippled over Livy's skin. "Believe me, it's *all* I need to keep me going."

He was killing her with the sexy talk. Nick reached for the hem of her T-shirt and dragged it up over her bare ass. He squeezed one cheek and Livy moaned. "You're going to make me burn breakfast," she murmured.

"I don't care," Nick said as he nipped at her throat again. "As long as you take your clothes off, I'll eat burned bacon, black French toast, rock-hard eggs. Better yet, how about you lie down on the table and I'll eat breakfast off your naked body?"

Nick could almost make her come with nothing more than a few naughty words. Any other time the prospect of having someone use her stomach as a serving platter would have turned her off. But when Nick said it in his gruff, dark voice, Livy found herself eager to have him lick the syrup out of her belly button.

Dear God.

Nick didn't pull away. Instead he wrapped his arms around Livy's waist and placed a quick kiss on her head. The domesticity of the moment choked the air from her lungs as she scraped a slice of French toast out of the pan and transferred it to a plate.

"Naked dining has its merits," she said after a quiet moment. "But if I'm going to be laid out on the table as the buffet, I think it's only fair that you're naked too."

"I can make that happen." His hands wandered up her torso to cup her breasts through the thin cotton fabric. "Now, lose the T-shirt."

Jesus, she was tempted. She wasn't interested in a visit from the fire department, however, and Livy had no doubt that once the clothes came off, the last thing on her mind would be the eggs she left frying in the pan.

"Behave or I'll sic Frank Junior on you," Livy warned. "Now, how do you want your eggs?"

"One on each of your ass cheeks," Nick replied.

"You asked for three."

"Save the other one for your puss—"

Livy turned before he could finish his sentence. Her scandalized gasp coaxed a wide smile to Nick's face and all Livy could do was stare. It was downright criminal for a man to be so drop-dead gorgeous. Especially first thing in the morning with less than a few hours' sleep under his belt.

He kissed her, long and hard.

When Nick finally pulled away, Livy was lightheaded and giddy. Drunk from the taste of him, his close proximity, and clean, masculine scent. Their gazes locked for a moment and Livy found it hard to turn away. As though Nick were the moon and Livy were nothing more than the tide that did his bidding.

The sound of her phone ringing from the dining room sent her stomach rocketing up into her throat.

The ringtone was a special one, reserved solely for her mom and they weren't due to talk again for another few weeks. If she was calling now, there must have been an emergency. What was wrong? Was she sick again? Hurt? Livy swallowed. Worse?

"Are you going to answer that?" Nick's brow quirked and a half smile curved his full lips. "Or are you still contemplating my egg request?"

"No. I . . . uh." Livy's heart hammered in her chest and her mouth went dry. "Um." She never let calls from her mom go to voice mail. Not when it would make her worry. But answering when Livy had put such strict guidelines in place to protect her anonymity was dangerous as well. She thought of how safe she'd felt in Nick's arms the way she'd trusted him in dark hours of the night. "It's my mom." The words were difficult to speak. Livy had to push them past her lips. "I need to get that."

Nick's brows drew together over his dark eyes. He let go of Livy and she slipped quickly away as she rushed to the dining room to answer the call. She swiped her finger across the screen as she snatched the phone from the table before it could go to voice mail. She brought it to her ear and cast a cautious glance toward the kitchen as she answered, "Hey, Mom. Everything okay?"

"I know I'm not supposed to call." The sound of her mom's voice brought tears to Livy's eyes. It seemed like forever since she'd heard it and she wanted to sob her relief before she spilled her guts about everything that had happened over the past couple of months, including the man who currently stood in her kitchen, presumably frying eggs.

"But I got a strange phone call and I thought you should know about it."

Livy's earlier fear intensified. Her lungs constricted and she fought for a deep breath. "What do you mean?"

"The other day someone who said he was from USSA called. He said he was writing an article about past junior Olympians. A where-are-they-now sort of thing and wanted to talk to you."

Livy's mouth went dry. "What did you tell him?"

"That he had the wrong number and I had no idea who you were."

Of course she did. Livy's mom had always had her back. "Thanks."

"It could have been legitimate," her mom said. "But I didn't want to take any chances. I just thought you should know about it."

Livy cast a furtive glance toward the kitchen where she presumed Nick was still working on breakfast, none the wiser to her conversation. Still, Livy didn't want to give anything away or say too much. "I'm glad you called."

"Are you okay, honey?" Her mom didn't say what Livy knew she wanted to say. That she should go to the police. Come out of hiding and do something—anything—to reclaim her life. They'd been over, and over, and over it. So many arguments that they'd both simply given up talking about it. Livy didn't know if the choices she made were the right ones, but she was still alive and that had to count for something.

"I'm fine, Mom. Really. Everything's okay. I promise." She didn't bother telling her that she'd decided to move. Her mom didn't know where she was anyway, so it didn't matter. "I need to go, but I'll call you on our scheduled day. I love you."

Her mom let out a slow sigh that seemed to reach through the phone. "I love you, too, sweetie."

"Bye." Livy whispered the word as she ended the call. Unease swirled inside of her. The U.S. Ski and Snowboard Association certainly had her past contact info on file. Livy hadn't been a member for a long time but it was possible they'd write a story about past athletes. Still, it didn't sit right with her and only managed to solidify her determination to put McCall in her wake.

Alone is better than dead.

Oh, who in the hell was she kidding? Alone might as well be dead. Alone was the worst thing in the entire goddamned world.

Chapter Seventeen

Nick sat at his kitchen table and stared at his cell. His blissful morning with Livy yesterday had taken a nosedive after her phone call from her mom. She'd become nervous and withdrawn, and Nick felt as though they'd taken a hundred steps back from the intimacy they'd shared only the night before. Livy's playfulness took a backseat to her worry and conversation had dwindled. They'd ended up eating in silence and spent the rest of the day on the couch watching movies until Livy made an excuse about having an early day and sent Nick away.

Her dismissal had done nothing for his ego but that's not what had stung. It was her continued lack of trust after everything they'd shared that stuck in Nick's craw. He'd hoped that she'd finally open up to him. Allow him to protect her. To come clean about everything and not keep up the pretense. His anger had threatened to get the better of him and more than once Nick had considered going over to call her on her bullshit. But then he'd think of how good she felt in his arms. How willing and responsive she'd been. And how being with her filled his chest with an excess of emotions that damn near sucked the air from his lungs. Nick had kept his ass parked on the couch for the rest of the night and woke up there this morning.

He'd fucked up. Big-time. And he didn't think the damage would be repairable. He wanted to call her out on her bullshit? Who was going to call him out on his? Nick still wasn't sure what he was the most upset about. He'd crossed a professional line and though he wasn't opposed to bending a few rules in the name of making an arrest, last night bent the rules and then broke them over his knee before dousing them with gasoline and setting them on fire. Though he supposed if you asked his deputy chief, he'd say that Nick's inability to follow orders or work with his peers was a clear sign that he was *not* the professional he gave himself credit for being. It wasn't the job that caused his stomach to knot up. It was the way he'd deceived Livy that laid him low.

He stared down at his phone. It had been days since he'd heard from Morgan and he was sure the deputy marshal was working the leads, shaking bushes, and trying to find a way to connect Livy to Kari once and for all. While Livy had spoken with her mom yesterday, Nick had been listening from the kitchen. Livy was careful not to give any of their conversation away. Nick appreciated the way she'd learned to guard herself but it still burned. She'd kept her voice low and her responses short. The conversation ended not long after it began, which gave Nick very little insight into what was going on.

"Fuck." The word left his mouth in an angry bark as he snatched his phone up from the table. He unlocked the screen and dialed Morgan. With every ring, his stomach knotted tighter and his jaw clenched until he felt the enamel grind. On the fifth ring, Morgan answered and Nick bit back a snarky comment about how long it took him to answer. The only person Nick was pissed off with was himself. His foul mood had nothing to do with the other deputy.

"I was just about to call you," Morgan remarked.

Sure. "What's up?"

"You were right about Hanson. She was using her mother's maiden name before she went into hiding. It wasn't an alias."

Nick was both sick and relieved at the information. He'd always known that Livy wasn't the sort of woman who'd have a stack of assumed names and fake IDs ready to use at a moment's notice. No matter what her connection to Meecum was, she wasn't like him. "How did you find her?"

"Through the junior ski-racing circuit like you suggested. We found a racer with the first name Kari who fit her age in the U.S. Ski and Snowboard Association's database. Her given name is Kari Oliva Barnes. She must have changed her name to Hanson after she quit racing."

Nick had gotten the impression that Livy and her mom had been alone. No dad in the picture. Something must have happened to make her want to disassociate herself with his name. What? Would that small piece of her history fill in the blanks as to why she'd hooked up with Meecum in the first place?

"Anything on the dad?"

"We're looking into it," Morgan replied. "I called her mother yesterday. Carolyn Hanson. Told her I was from the ski association and was doing a piece on former racers for their Web site. She was excited at first and then got nervous. Told me I had the wrong number and she didn't know anyone named Kari Barnes. She hung up after that."

That's why Livy's mom had called her yesterday. To warn her that someone was looking for her. Damn it. For all Livy had known it was Meecum who'd found her mother. No wonder she'd been so nervous.

Nick's thoughts screeched to a halt. He'd been thinking of Livy as a victim since the day he'd met her and it needed to stop. She was a suspect. A person of interest who might have been an accessory to some of Meecum's crimes for all he knew. *And you took her to bed and fucked her till the sun rose. Way to distance yourself, asshole.*

"Have you been able to find any connection to Meecum?" Nick wanted Morgan to come up empty-handed. He'd practically prayed for it every day for the past week.

"Not yet." His chest loosened a bit and Nick let out a slow breath. "But I'm still digging. It's not like the Black Death have records of everyone they've ever associated with posted online or some shit. It's going to take a little elbow grease, that's all."

No, they didn't keep those sorts of records, but it would sure as hell be nice.

"We've confirmed that Olivia Gallagher is Kari Hanson. That's a huge step forward," Morgan said. "You've gotten closer to finding Meecum than anyone in the entire USMS has in years of hunting the bastard. It's a good thing you're tenacious, Brady. It's probably going to get us the win."

Maybe. But what would Nick lose in the process? "Let me know if you find anything out."

"Will do. In the meantime, it's probably not a good idea to confront Hanson yet. We don't want her getting spooked and contacting Meecum or leaving town before we can get our hands on him. At this point, I'd say trying to get her to come clean and flipping her is a last resort. We'll only try to use her if we hit a dead end."

Nick had no intention of confronting Livy. Not when his own guilt weighed so heavily on him. "I'll keep an eye on her," he replied. *Like you've been keeping an eye on her?* Nick let out a sigh.

If Morgan picked up on it, he didn't let on. "I'll be in touch."

"Sounds good."

Nick ended the call. He knew that following a lead didn't always produce instant results. It was a long, sometimes frustrating process that tested the patience of even the calmest investigator. There was a time when Nick wanted to bring Joel Meecum in so badly that it made his muscles twitch. Now, he wasn't so sure that he needed to be the one who cuffed him and hauled him in.

Not if it meant losing Livy.

Lose her? Did he even really have her?

She'd occupied his thoughts more often than not over the past week. And after their night together, Nick was convinced that Livy occupied a part of his heart. It wasn't just the sex. They could have lain under the blankets fully clothed and he would have felt the exact same way today. He was sick and fucking tired of the lies and deception that erected a wall between them. Nick wanted to know everything about Livy and not just how she'd wound up tied to one of the most notorious motorcycle gangs in the country.

When she found out why he was really there, she'd turn her back on him. He got the impression that Livy wasn't the sort of woman who forgave easily. If she had been, Joel Meecum wouldn't have put the word out to associates that he was looking for her. At one point, Nick had assumed that Livy was setting up for Joel to meet her. That she'd been out scouting places for them to lie low until the heat died down. Now, though, Nick knew that Joel had done something horrible to Livy. She wasn't running. She was hiding.

And when Nick discovered why, he'd make sure that Meecum paid for everything he'd done to her.

Guilt ate away at Livy. It churned in her gut and burned in her chest. It clawed away at her brain until the dull thud in her skull escalated to near-migraine pain. There weren't enough Excedrin or Tums in the world to banish the pain and discomfort that wreaked havoc on her body, though. The only thing that would fix her was absolution and she wouldn't get that if she didn't open up and trust someone.

Nick?

No matter what he thought to the contrary, Livy knew that he was a good man. Honorable and trust-worthy. But that was part of the problem, wasn't it? Livy wasn't without guilt. If she came clean to him, told him what she knew, showed him what she had and how she got it, would he try to arrest her? Or maybe find someone who could? Would she blame him if he did? She deserved to be held accountable for her actions just like Joel did.

Damn it, Livy was sick and tired of feeling afraid. She didn't want to run anymore. Wasn't interested in hiding. She wanted to live her life how and where she wanted it. She wanted . . . *Nick*. God, she wanted him so badly that she ached. The nights they'd spent together had been beyond amazing. Livy hadn't known that she could feel so deeply. Want so intensely. When he knew the truth, though, Livy was certain he'd be disgusted with her. Wouldn't want anything to do with her. He was a good man and he'd do what good men were sup-posed to do. He'd hold her accountable for her ac-tions and she wouldn't blame him a bit for it.

Nick's hatred would surely kill her faster than any punishment Joel would bring down on her. With every passing day, Livy lost another little piece of herself to Nick. It wouldn't be long before he owned her completely. Heart, body, and soul.

She gazed down at the worn leather ledger on the bed beside her. She never should have taken it. At the time, she'd thought that taking it was the only thing that would keep her alive. Now, she realized that it had done nothing more than secure her death warrant. Nothing could protect her from Joel's wrath. Nowhere was safe. He was the criminal but she was the fugitive. She could continue to run but she couldn't hide. Joel would find her. And when he did, he'd kill her.

Livy opened the book with shaking fingers and flipped through the pages. How many times had she looked through Joel's ledger over the past four years? She'd memorized every business transaction, the names of each and every one of Joel's associates. She could burn the fucking thing right now and still be able to recite every page word for word, number for number. Joel surely realized that. Livy was the biggest threat to not only his safety, but also his livelihood. He'd killed people for less. She knew; she'd been witness to one of his brutal murders.

What if Joel or one of his guys had called her mom the other day posing as a USSA employee? What if he'd put the pieces together of who she really was and went after her mom to get to her? At the time, she'd been convinced that her mom would be safe but now she wasn't so sure. Would Nick protect her mom if Livy asked him to? If he knew the truth, would he help her or would he turn his back on her completely?

She closed the book with a snap and hid it under the floorboards beneath her bed. She wasn't ready to lose Nick. Wasn't ready to feel the sting of his disgust. They only had a couple of weeks left before his vacation was over and he'd be heading back to

Washington. Was it so bad that she wanted to wait it out? She didn't have to make a decision now, did she? Livy could be selfish for two more weeks. Enjoy the life she'd constructed for herself with a man she couldn't get enough of. Then, she'd face the music and come clean.

A weight lifted from Livy's chest. She hadn't realized until now how deeply the burden of her deception affected her. Telling the truth would finally free her from years of worry and fear. It was time. Whether or not Nick would hate her for her admission, she had him to thank for the relief she'd feel when it was all over.

She'd planned to take a shower but instead of hanging a right at the bottom of the stairs, Livy headed for the tiny alcove at the front door. Without even thinking about what she did, she pulled on her boots and slipped her coat on. The door seemed to open on its own and for the first time in four years, Livy didn't grab her keys or triple-check the lock. Instead, she let the door close behind her without locking it as she hustled across the lane that separated her house from Nick's.

Today was her only day off this week. She'd be damned if she spent another minute of it alone. Livy brought her fist up to Nick's door and paused. If she was smart, she'd keep her distance from Nick until she decided to tell him the truth and turn Joel's ledger over to him. Obviously, Livy hadn't been making decisions with her rational brain for quite some time. Her feelings for Nick ran deeper than even she wanted to admit. In two short weeks,

he'd wormed his way not only into her life, but
also her heart. In two more, he might be the one
hauling her off to jail. Was it wrong to allow their
relationship to carry on when she knew it would
only end in disaster?

Probably.

Definitely.

Oh, what the hell.

Livy knocked on the door. Her stomach retreated
into her throat as she waited for Nick to answer and
despite the chill of the air, she broke out into a
sweat. An hour passed in the few seconds she stood
on the damned porch and a nervous tremor vibrated through her limbs that left her weak and
damned near out of breath.

"Fuck."

The word left her mouth at the exact moment
Nick opened the door. Heat rose to Livy's cheeks as
their gazes met. His lips curled into a wide, seductive smile that should have melted her bones. That
she still stood upright seemed like a feat in Nick's
presence. His dark eyes roamed over her, a slow
perusal that made her feel as though she had a hell
of a lot less clothing on.

"God yes," he answered in a husky tone. Livy
smiled, her teeth chattering from the cold as she
tried to keep from throwing herself at him. "Get in
here and get naked." He grabbed her by the arm
and hauled her against him. A mischievous light
sparked in his gaze and he cocked a brow. "On
second thought, leave the boots on."

Livy laughed and before she could protest, he

put his mouth to hers. The kiss was the sort of thing you'd expect after being apart from someone for months or even years. He crushed her to him, slanted his mouth over hers, thrust his tongue in her mouth, and wound his fist through the length of her hair. His kisses robbed her of her breath, dizzied her, and stole any shred of logical thought. The world melted away and Livy's senses were awash with Nick. The clean masculine spice of his scent, the firm press of his lips against hers, and the security of his arms wrapped tightly around her.

Nick hadn't simply wormed his way into her heart in the two short weeks since she'd known him. He'd become her entire world. Livy had learned at a very young age that there were very few people she could truly count on. The rest just let you down. Would Nick end up being like all of the other disappointments in her life or would he stand out from the crowd and be the pillar that held her up and kept her world from crumbling around her?

Nick broke the kiss but didn't pull away. His forehead rested against hers and the only sound in the room was that of their mingled breath and the wind outside. Livy didn't open her eyes. She simply focused on how good it felt to be held in his arms. "Are you trying to heat the entire outside?" she asked a little too breathy. "I think it's going to take more than your baseboard heaters to melt all of McCall's snow."

Nick chuckled. The deep timbre vibrated pleasantly through her and if he hadn't been holding her, Livy wasn't sure her own legs would have supported her. "Who needs baseboards when I have you? You're hot enough to melt the entire North Pole." He tugged on her coat and Livy reached between them to pull down the zipper. "I'll close the door if you promise to take your clothes off."

She'd dropped her coat on the floor and was already dragging her T-shirt up her torso before he finished his sentence. Nick was everything she'd ever wanted in a man: tall, strong, brave, sexy, honorable, honest, funny, easygoing and yet intense when the mood called for it. It wasn't a necessity, but it didn't hurt that he was drop-dead fucking gorgeous. The only thing that would have made him more attractive to her was if he'd had a couple of downhill gold medals around his neck.

As much as it hurt, Livy was more prepared than ever to come clean with him. Nick deserved a woman who was as honest and honorable as he was. And she was going to do everything in her power to make sure she was that woman.

Chapter Eighteen

Another week passed and Nick wished he could do something to stop the clock for at least a decade. Anything to keep him from having to confront Livy. He found himself wishing for one more day. One more night. Another minute with her.

They'd barely slept. Rarely left her bed. When Livy had to go to work, Nick spent the day at her place. He shoveled her porch, cleared the driveway. Did anything he could to keep himself busy so he wouldn't have to think about why he was really there. He even turned the ringer off on his phone and with each passing day he wished he hadn't let Morgan know what he was up to.

Who in the hell was he kidding? Nick knew that even if no one realized what he was doing in McCall, Idaho, he'd still confront Livy. His goddamned pride and sense of justice wouldn't allow him to do anything else. His need to bring Meecum down and make him pay for his crimes demanded it.

"Are the answers to all of the world's mysteries spelled out in spaghetti?"

Nick brought his gaze up to Livy's, his brow furrowed. "What?"

"I know my spaghetti is pretty kick-ass, but I'm just sayin'. I don't think you're going to find the winning lottery numbers there."

He'd been so lost in his thoughts he'd totally zoned out. "You never know. I'm pretty sure one of my noodles looks like a nine."

Livy giggled. The sound warmed him from the inside out and caused Nick's heart to clench. "Well, if you win, you have to promise to share it with me."

Nick gave her a soft smile. "Deal."

A space of silence passed. Livy studied her own plate as though it held the answers to some great mystery. "Did you decide to become a cop because of what happened to your sister?"

He studied her for a moment. Her expression became vulnerable, her hazel eyes wide and almost fearful. "Why did you decide to be a ski racer?"

She answered with a shy grin that set his blood on fire. "You first."

"All right." Nick set his plate aside and took a deep breath. He'd barely cracked the surface of the story during their first dinner date. Not many people knew what had happened to Lindsey, including the guys with the Marshals Service. Before he left Seattle PD, only a few of his SWAT brothers had known about Nick's sister. He hadn't talked about her in a long damned time and it took more effort than he thought it would to push the words past the knot of emotion in his throat.

"Lindsey was assaulted when she was sixteen. I was thirteen when it happened. He cornered her when she was walking home from a friend's house. When Lindsey didn't show up at home by curfew, my parents called the police. They found her unconscious in a park not too far from our house." Nick paused as his throat tightened to the point that he wasn't sure he could manage another word. Livy reached over and placed her hand over his. The depth of emotion in her eyes caused Nick's heart to clench and he let out a slow breath. "She spent six weeks in the hospital and another three years in therapy. The son of a bitch already had a warrant out for sexual assault but he'd been dodging an arrest for months. Lindsey did everything she was supposed to. She cooperated with the detectives, identified the asshole from a previous mugshot. Local PD made an arrest a few weeks later during a traffic stop."

"Nick, I'm so sorry." Livy's whispered words snaked around him, bathed him with warmth.

"He posted bail." Nick pushed the anger that remained with him over the years to the soles of his feet. "Hired a hotshot lawyer that no one could understand how he afforded and his case was dismissed. Something about circumstantial evidence and improper procedure when the police had Lindsey make the ID. He had to have paid off the judge, hell, probably the prosecutor, too. After he was acquitted, the fucker went back to his life as though nothing had happened and my sister's was changed forever. He raped her and nearly beat her to death and he walked. So, yeah. That's why I became a cop. Because I didn't want anyone to go through what my sister went through. I want every last murdering, raping, law-breaking son of a bitch off the streets."

Livy clamped her hand tighter over his and Nick looked down to find his own hand shaking. His entire body tensed to the point that every muscle was rigid and his breath heaved in his chest. Lindsey was married to a great guy and had a couple of kids now. She'd healed and moved on from her attack but she'd admitted once to Nick that there were days that she was still afraid. Still felt as though she had to watch her back. That it scared her to know that such a violent person was out there somewhere and not behind bars where he belonged.

"See? You *are* a good man, Nick."

He snorted. Livy might change her opinion once she knew he'd come to McCall fully intending on arresting her before his vacation was over. His gaze met hers. The truth threatened to spill from his lips but Nick bit the urge back. He was a selfish bastard who wanted every minute he could get with Livy. He'd perpetuate the fantasy for as long as he could. God knew she'd hate him soon enough.

"Don't snort at me." A smile tugged at her lips. "I know you don't want to hear it. You think you're a loose-cannon cop on the edge." Her smile grew and Nick couldn't help but be entranced. Her attempt at levity only endeared her to him more. It didn't matter who she was or what she'd done. Goddamn it, he was falling for her. And it made what he had to do even harder to face.

"A loose-cannon cop on the edge?" His thin-lipped frown gave way to a smile.

"Uh-huh. You want me to think that you're someone you're not, but it's too late. I know who and what you really are, Nick Brady."

I know who you *are, Kari.* With every day spent with her, it mattered less and less. Nick was beginning to believe that he could forgive her anything. And he wasn't the sort who forgave easily, if at all. She'd changed him. And it scared the hell out of him.

"What am I?" he asked, low.

Her seductive smile sent a thrill through his veins. "You're one of a kind."

"A one of a kind, loose-cannon cop on the edge," Nick replied. "Sounds about right."

"Who eats nails for breakfast," Livy added with a giggle.

"With a side of gunpowder."

Livy's giggles evolved into a riot of laughter that drilled through the center of Nick's chest, more beautiful than any sound in the world. "Just to get the point across to anyone who'd cross you."

Nick smiled. "Exactly."

Her laughter subsided and Livy's expression became more serious. Her intense scrutiny made Nick squirm in his seat and he averted his gaze. A hardened criminal with a gun shoved in his face couldn't unnerve him the way that Livy did. He couldn't stand not knowing what she was thinking. "What?"

"I wish I'd met you sooner." Her voice resonated with sadness and it tore a fissure in his heart.

"Why's that?"

"I think if I'd known someone like you existed, I might not have made some bad choices. Maybe I would have believed more."

Nick's brow furrowed. "Believed what?"

"That there are people in this world who aren't selfish assholes interested in furthering their own agendas. That not all of the good men out there are married or gay. Which reminds me—" She fixed him with an appraising stare. "Why hasn't a woman snagged you yet, Nick Brady? How is a guy like you still single?"

She was deflecting again. He'd gotten to know her well enough to realize that Livy used humor as a defense mechanism. If she could laugh something away, she didn't have to think about her hurt. Nick felt it all for her, though. He couldn't explain it, but her emotions seemed to burrow into his skin like a tick where they remained and festered. If he could've, he would've taken the brunt of every hurt she'd ever felt. He couldn't stand for her to be anything other than happy.

"You said it yourself." He could give her levity. For now. "I'm a loose-cannon cop on the edge who eats nails with a side of gunpowder for breakfast. I'm bad news, baby."

Her thin-lipped smile didn't reach her eyes.

"You're anything but bad news. You're the best news I've ever gotten."

Nick's chest ached with an excess of emotion. This woman was sure to be his undoing. "Stop trying to butter me up," he replied with a grin. "It's not going to get you out of telling me why you wanted to be a ski racer."

"I would never try to distract you," she said with a coy blink of her eyes as she traced the bare skin of her collarbone with her fingertip.

Nick swallowed. The heat she threw off was enough to make him break out into a full-body sweat. "Uh-huh," he replied, deadpan. "Spill it. I told you my story, now you have to tell me yours."

Livy should have known that Nick would hold her to her word. Despite her obvious—and overtly flirtatious—attempt to derail him. It had been so long since she'd let anyone get close enough to her that she actually wanted to open up. She'd almost forgotten how wonderful it felt. The prospect of telling Nick everything about her life was infinitely comforting. She trusted him. Wanted him to know everything about her childhood, the isolation of years spent in training, and the endless days of loneliness that she'd feared would never end until the day he waded through the snow to help unbury her car.

"I started skiing when I was four. My mom was working at a ski resort and didn't have anyone to watch me. The resort offered free daycare for employees and ski lessons were part of the package."

"Sort of like what you do now?" Nick asked.

Livy gave him a sad smile. She guessed she'd come full circle. So much for elevating herself past the station of her childhood. "Pretty much. I skied almost every day until I started school. After that, I skied every day after school. My dad wasn't around and my mom decided that rather than let me have a lot of free, idle time to get into trouble, she put me into a Mighty Mite race program."

"How old were you when you first started racing?"

"Six. My mom used to say I looked like a giant helmet on skis barreling down the hill. I guess I was too young to be afraid. My coaches used to get after me because all I wanted to do was tuck and speed toward the finish line. Who cares about technique when you can go fast?"

Nick reached out and captured a lock of her hair between his thumb and finger. He idly stroked the strands while she spoke and pleasant chills blanketed her flesh. "Even as a kid you were going ham, huh?"

Livy laughed. It was so easy to be happy when Nick was around. She tried not to think about what would happen when he found out the truth about her. "Fearlessness is a good thing when you're running gates. But as I got older, the fees got steeper. I had a knack for racing. I won more often than I didn't and so my mom picked up a second job to pay for my coaching and race fees."

The bitterness she'd spent years trying to squash made an unwelcome appearance. "My dad wasn't really in the picture and he never had money to help out. I wanted to quit racing when I hit the juniors but my mom wouldn't let me."

Nick's gaze met hers. The deep brown of his eyes swallowed her whole. "She obviously recognized your talent and didn't want it to go to waste."

"Ski racing is one of the most expensive sports out there," Livy said with a sigh. "Even with a sponsor we couldn't afford it. When I won the giant slalom title at seventeen, the U.S. Olympic team sent a couple of scouts out to talk to my coaches. It was the best day of my life," she said on a hitch of breath. "And one of the worst."

Nick studied her with such deep intensity that Livy had to force herself to look away. "Why the worst?"

A sob lodged itself in Livy's throat. "My mom collapsed during the meeting with the scouts and my coaches. I guess it was a blessing in disguise. If she hadn't passed out, they might not have found the cancer in time."

"Damn." This time, Nick took her hand in his and squeezed. "I'm sorry, Livy."

They were quite the pair, weren't they? Somehow, their histories made them even more perfect for each other than Livy thought. They both loved people who'd suffered. They'd both wanted to do anything in their power to help them. And as a result, their lives had followed a certain path. Nick's for the better while Livy's life certainly hadn't turned out so great so far.

A tear managed to escape one eye. She wiped it away—it was silly to regret things that couldn't be changed—and shrugged. "There are more important things in life than skiing," she said through the thickness in her throat. "My mom taught me about selflessness. I tried to help her as much as she helped me. She's been in remission for almost seven years."

Once again, Nick's intense scrutiny unnerved her. As though he knew more about her than she knew herself and he waited for the time to reveal it to her. "You gave up what you loved for her. You're a testament to selflessness, Livy."

"I didn't do enough." She'd tried and failed. All she'd gotten for her efforts was a life of isolation and fear. "I tracked down my lying, cheating, piece-of-shit dad and tried to get him to help. I told him he owed us for eighteen years' worth of child support and her working two jobs to keep us going. He was all sad apologies at first. Told me he was on the verge of a big payday and as soon as he got it, he'd help us out." Livy's hands clenched into fists. "He strung me along for a while. Convinced me to help him with some stuff that he promised was above-board and turned out to be as crooked as he was. No one has ever let me down as badly as he did."

Nick's fingers wandered to her temple. His touch was feather-light as he skimmed her hairline, over her cheek and across her jaw. Did he know how his touch affected her? Did he realize that his careful handling of her, the way he listened, the way he held her only helped to send her head over heels for him?

"Are you going to let me down too, Nick?" Livy spoke the words so softly she wasn't sure he'd even heard her.

Nick's lips thinned and his jaw squared. "I hope

not, Livy." The vehemence of his words sent a wave of trepidation through her. "God, I hope not."

He took her face between his hands with so much tender care. Livy had never felt so breakable. Nick's lips whispered across hers, a glancing of lip to lip. She wanted to laugh and cry at the same time. Her chest swelled with an excess of emotion that resonated deep in the center of her being. For the past few months she'd felt as though she'd been drowning. Nick had been her lifeline. He'd hate her when he found out the truth and it would ruin her. Because Livy knew without a doubt that she'd fallen in love with him.

Without breaking their kisses, Nick reached over and took her plate from her hands to set it on the coffee table beside his. He released his tender grasp on her face to place his hands on her waist. As though she weighed nothing at all he lifted Livy and settled her in his lap. She turned so she straddled his waist and let her arms wander where they wanted, over his strong, solid shoulders and around his neck.

One week. That's all they had left. And Livy was going to make the most of those seven days.

Nick's tongue flicked out at the seam of her lips. She let out a slow breath that became one with his as she opened up to him. He kissed her deeply, though no less gently. He savored her mouth, the languorous act as lewd and sensual as anything he'd done to her over the course of the past couple of weeks.

"Livy." Nick's hands left her waist to wrap tight around her torso. He abandoned her mouth to kiss along her jaw, down her throat, to the junction where it met her shoulder. His teeth grazed her exposed skin and Livy shuddered. "I need to fuck you."

She trembled with want and Livy's breath quickened at Nick's heated words. Before he could say another word, she'd shucked her sweater—his *favorite* sweater—and reached for the button of his pants. "Then what are you waiting for?"

He pulled away and his wicked smile sent a rush of molten lava through her veins. "Not a damn thing."

Chapter Nineteen

"Brady, we need to talk."

Nick definitely didn't like Morgan's tone. He never should have turned his ringer back on. His stomach knotted so tight he thought it might inch its way right up his goddamned throat. "What's up?"

"I did some digging and I think I found what we needed to link Hanson to Joel Meecum."

Nick's stomach unfurled with the gust of breath that rushed from his lungs. For weeks he'd been trying to convince himself that there was no connection. That Livy couldn't possibly be connected to Meecum in any way, shape, or form. Or even that she was nothing more than a victim, a vulnerable girl who'd been seduced by a lecherous asshole and felt that the only way she could get away from him was to change her name and leave the state.

He'd fallen in love with Livy. Nick wasn't sure he could bear to know the truth about her.

"What did you find?" His heart pounded in his chest as he waited for Morgan to drop the hammer. *Please God, let it be something small like petty theft.* . . .

"Well, we did find out that Hanson had a rough childhood despite the fancy ski medals. It looks like she and her mom were pretty poor from what we managed to dig up. Six or so years ago, her mom was diagnosed with stomach cancer. It's been in remission for a while."

All information Nick already knew. He relaxed a tentative degree.

"Did you know that Kari Hanson's father was murdered?"

And just like that, Nick's heart sank to the soles of his feet. Through the dryness in his throat, he croaked out, "No." How could he have missed something like that? He'd done his homework on Meecum and Kari both, but had never found even a scrap of information on her father. "What do we know about it?"

"Not a whole hell of a lot." Tension radiated from Morgan's voice and it pulled Nick's shoulders taut. "The deeper we dig, the more of a clusterfuck it becomes. Kari's dad, Steve Barnes, has a rap sheet a mile long and several aliases to go along with it. He was a con man and pretty top-notch. He posed as an accountant in several different states under different names, an investment banker a couple of times. From what we can tell, he swindled hundreds of thousands of dollars from people over a period spanning a couple of decades. We don't think Kari was privy to any of it. It looks like her parents were never married and she lived primarily with her mother. I doubt she saw her dad much, if at all."

Jesus. He'd known that Livy's dad was a loser but he never could have imagined just how bad it had been. While she and her mom had been scraping by, making sacrifices, her dad had been hopping from state to state, conning people out of their hard-earned money. What a son of a bitch.

"What do we know about the Barnes murder?" Nick wasn't sure he really wanted to know anything about it.

"He was found beaten to death four years ago in the office he'd been renting in a strip mall in Oakland."

Jesus. It fit the timeline for Livy's disappearance and a wave of anxiety stole over Nick. He reached out and gripped the edge of the table as if it would keep his world from careening out of control. His chest burned, his heart hammered. He didn't want to hear another word and yet, he had to.

"How did we not know any of this?" True, Livy had been going by her mother's maiden name at the time, but it seems they would have found some sort of connection in their investigation.

"The body was identified by a girlfriend." In the background, Nick heard the sound of keys clicking on Morgan's keyboard. "She said his name was Mel Owens and the local PD investigated it as a robbery gone south. Those guys are swamped down there; it doesn't surprise me this got swept under the rug."

The story got more tangled by the second. "What about Meecum? How does he fit in?" Morgan had connected the dots somehow. Nick wanted to know how he thought Livy's dad's murder pointed any fingers at her or Joel.

"Metcalf contacted the chief down there and he sent a couple of deputies to question the girlfriend. She gave them a hard time at first but they shook her down and she caved. She told them that Owens—who was actually Steve Barnes—had been laundering money for a local motorcycle gang and that he'd found a way to skim without them knowing it. He claimed the scam was going to make them rich."

Son of a bitch. Nick blew out a breath but it did nothing to slow the racing tempo of his heart. He didn't need to ask Morgan what club Livy's dad had been working for. They all knew that even though they did business all up and down the West Coast, the Black Death was chartered out of Oakland.

"My guess is Kari introduced Meecum to her dad. They struck a deal and the dad screwed over Meecum, and maybe even Kari. They find out, beat the dad to death, Kari gets spooked and takes off. Joel could have ratted her out. He could have set her up for the whole thing but he doesn't, which means that they're working together, or he wants her to know that he's got her back. He puts the word out that he's looking for her. It makes a hell of a lot of sense."

No. No fucking way. There was no love lost between Livy and her dad but there was no possible way she'd had anything to do with his death. Even less likely was Morgan's assumption that she'd conspired with Meecum to do the deed.

"I don't buy it." Nick might have sounded like a stubborn SOB, but he didn't care. "It's obvious that she had hardly any contact with her dad over the years. They had to have been estranged. There's no way she knew about his scams or planned to rip him off. It's too farfetched."

"Is it?" Morgan's tone hardened. "Think about it, Brady. Kari lives her entire life being resentful of her deadbeat dad who didn't do a goddamned thing for her or her mom growing up. Her mom's beat cancer, but the bills are piling up. She hooks up with Meecum while all of this is going on. He's got money, clout, and muscle and maybe that's what she's looking for. Somewhere down the line, the dad gets involved. Maybe Kari suggested him to Meecum, maybe the dad pressures her for an intro. Either way, Barnes and Meecum form a business relationship but what they don't realize is that Kari's dad is planning to rob Meecum blind. Shit goes south when Meecum finds out and he kills Kari's dad. Kari takes a page from her dad's book and takes off with a new identity and leaves Meecum to clean up the mess. Hell, maybe they planned to kill him all along and they're just waiting for the heat to die down like we'd initially assumed. Kari knows where Joel Meecum is. I'd bet my badge on it."

It was a bet he'd lose. Anger churned hot and thick in Nick's gut. Morgan's assumptions about Livy couldn't be more wrong. The urge to pick a fight with the deputy was almost more than Nick could resist. "How many people know about this?"

A pregnant pause stretched over the line and a burst of adrenaline dumped into Nick's bloodstream. "So far, you and me and Metcalf. And of course the guys down in the Northern California office but they're going to let us run point since we did the leg work and there isn't a state on the West Coast Meecum isn't wanted in. The deputy chief is ready to roll on this, Brady. He wants to assemble a task force. All he's waiting on is for you to fill in the blank on Hanson's location."

Absolutely not. The last thing he wanted was for an army of U.S. marshals to converge on Livy's cabin, guns drawn. If Morgan considered her a murder suspect, they wouldn't go easy on her. Nick would be forced to watch as she was hauled out of her house, shoved to the ground, and cuffed. His stomach heaved at the thought and he swallowed down the fear that threatened to choke him.

"Not yet," he said.

"What are you talking about?" Morgan barked. "Why the hell not?"

"Like you said, we need to play this close to the hip." Nick needed to make a compelling argument for *not* sending a team of armed marshals to Livy's door. "It took us years to get this close to Meecum. I have a feeling she's getting ready to run again. We don't want to spook her."

"All the more reason to send a team in now, don't you think?"

"She's evaded not only us, but Meecum for four years, Morgan. Do you think that's just dumb luck?"

"No," Morgan said with a sneer in his voice. "I think it's a very clever daughter following in her father's footsteps."

If Morgan had been standing in front of him right now, Nick would have been hard-pressed not to coldcock him. He knew dick about Livy.

And you do?

The niggling voice of doubt scratched at the back of Nick's brain. Could she have possibly conned him? Could her innocent eyes, soft body, and seemingly fierce loyalty have lulled him into a false sense of security? She knew he was a cop. Could she have played him all along?

No. Damn it, Nick refused to believe that Livy was anything other than who she was. She might not have given him the entire truth, but she'd bared her soul to him. She wasn't a cold-blooded murderer. Livy wasn't on the run, she was running. And he'd be damned if he let Morgan and a squad of the USMS's most stalwart man hunters show up on her front porch and haul her off to a cell somewhere.

"Give me three days," Nick said. "Let me do this my way. I'll confront her, let her know we're on to her and give her the chance to come clean. She trusts me, Morgan. Let's try to avoid a potential disaster."

"Sounds like you've been a hell of a lot busier than you've let on," Morgan replied with disdain. "I can maybe buy you two days. But this isn't your show anymore. It isn't even mine. Metcalf is calling the shots from here on out. You might not be concerned about your job, but I am. We need to get the ball rolling and have people in place in case she doesn't trust you like you think she does. We can't take any chances. This might be our one and only opportunity to get our hands on Meecum."

Nick had no other choice but to agree to Morgan's terms. Even if Nick didn't see the situation the way everyone else did, Morgan was going to do what he thought was right. "Fine. Get the ball rolling on your end. I'll take care of Livy."

"Kari," Morgan corrected. "I don't know what's been going on during your *vacation*, but you need to get your head out of this fantasy she's constructed. You need to get back in the game."

What if Nick didn't want out of the fantasy? "I'll take care of Kari," he said. "Keep in touch."

"Will do," Morgan said before he ended the call.

Fuck. Nick set his phone down on the counter. His palms were slicked with sweat and his heart pounded in his chest. Of all of the things he'd done since becoming a cop, this would be by far the hardest. When he confronted Livy, he knew it would break both of them. Maybe permanently.

"Are you sure you won't reconsider, Livy?" Stacy, the ski instruction supervisor asked. "Good ski instructors are hard to find and the kids love you."

Stacy's sad expression caused Livy's heart to clench. She didn't *want* to leave. She liked it in McCall. Liked her job, the town, the lake, not to mention some of the best powder she'd ever skied in her life. She liked living somewhere with four seasons and plenty of space. But this life was a lie. And Livy had decided once and for all that she was tired of living a lie. She wanted to be a better person. For herself. For Nick. It was time to fix everything she'd broken and whether it would put her in danger or not, Livy was prepared to face the music.

"I wish I could stay, Stacy. I feel like I need to be with my mom, you know?" Even though the cancer was in remission, Livy wasn't lying to her boss. She was through with deception. She'd talked to her mom sixteen times in four years. She couldn't isolate herself from the only family she had. Livy didn't want any more regrets. Being with Nick had shown her that she was wasting her life by hiding in fear of what might happen and she was sick and tired of being afraid.

"I understand. We're going to miss you, though. And if you decide to come back, you'll always have a job here."

"I appreciate that. Thanks." Leaving was so much harder when everyone was so damned nice. Livy had so many regrets from the past few years. One of them being that she'd been too guarded to make lasting friendships with some of the people she worked with.

Livy left Stacy's office with a heavy heart. She would have liked to have given at least a week's notice before leaving, but when she told Nick the truth about who she really was and what she'd done, there was a pretty good chance he'd arrest her on the spot. She'd rather Stacy had a day's notice that she wasn't coming back to work than no notice at all.

Every footstep walked through the snow toward her car was a slog. Lead weights wouldn't have weighed more than her boots as each reluctant step took her closer to the beginning of the end. As much as she didn't want whatever this was to end with Nick, it was going to happen. Even if she'd decided not to tell him the truth, he was leaving. Admitting to someone that you loved them didn't magically make everything perfect. In fact, those three little words usually made things more complicated. They sure as hell would as far as she and Nick were concerned. A fugitive in love with a cop. Could she get any more cliché?

By the time she pulled up to her house, Livy was shaking. Sweat beaded her brow and her heart raced as though she'd just sped down an icy downhill run at eighty miles per hour in a low tuck. Her mouth had gone bone dry and her brain buzzed with so many thoughts she couldn't narrow them down to a single one. She hadn't even confronted Nick yet and she felt as though she might pass out. God, she'd worried that he would let her down? She was about to drop him from a fifty-foot cliff. *Splat!*

Livy killed the engine, but she didn't get out of the car. Who would take care of Simon if she was arrested? He was a fat, spoiled, inside cat that'd never make it on the outside. Bitter laughter rose in her chest and came out in a splutter. She was worried about Simon making it? What about her? She'd never so much as gotten a speeding ticket. Now she was contemplating the possibility of jail time. *Dear God.* Her head smacked against the steering wheel as another crippling wave of anxiety hit her. Would she have to pee in front of a hundred other women? She could barely use the bathroom when Simon stuck his paw under the door.

"Hey! You okay?"

The sound of Nick's voice sent a super jolt of shock through Livy's body. She bolted upright with a squeal and her hands came down on the horn in the process. Nick jumped back at the sudden sound, his own expression as pinched and worried as she felt.

"Son of a bitch!" she exclaimed on a sharp exhale. "You scared the shit out of me, Nick!"

His brows came down over his dark eyes. The days were getting longer as February was drawing to a close and there was still enough of the gray twilight remaining to allow Livy to take in every beautiful detail of Nick's face.

Goddamn, he was gorgeous.

And for a couple of weeks he'd been hers. Next to skiing and her mom, Nick was the best thing that had ever happened to her. Livy didn't want to lose him, but she had no choice. It was time to come clean.

"Someone's jumpy," Nick said as Livy got out of the car. His expression, though relaxed, sent a shiver of trepidation through her body. He didn't seem to have the energy he usually did, as though he'd been dealt a hard blow. Maybe this was how he looked after a particularly bad day on the job. Which made her wonder what had happened today. "Did those rug rats give you grief today?"

"What?" Livy's brow furrowed. "Oh, no. My day wasn't too bad." Aside from the total collapse of her life and current happiness. "How was your day?"

Nick cupped the back of his neck. He appeared at ease but Livy knew him well enough now to sense the tension that he tried to hide. "Good. I lounged around and binge-watched *Hill Street Blues* on Netflix."

"That's a little dated," Livy said with a laugh. "Eighties cop dramas do it for you, huh?"

"No." Nick's gaze smoldered and Livy's intentions were incinerated by the heat. "Former junior Olympic ski racers do it for me."

Livy also knew Nick well enough to realize that within the next few minutes they'd both be naked and in bed. He reached out, took her hand in his, and led her up the snowy steps to her front door. Her confession could wait until the morning, couldn't it?

"It feels like you've been gone for *weeks*," Nick murmured in her ear as Livy unlocked the front door. A round of delicious chills broke out over her skin. "I'm glad you're home."

So was she. Even a few minutes away from Nick felt like hours. Today had lasted at least a year. "So, what do you want to do tonight?"

He kissed her neck and then the corner of her mouth. "I don't care as long as it involves you being naked and on my cock."

He got her with the dirty talk *every time*. She didn't think she'd ever not want Nick.

One last night with him. A few more hours where she could live Livy Gallagher's life. "I think that can be arranged."

Livy would be sure to make their last night together count.

Chapter Twenty

Joel's lip curled. "This place is a snow-covered shithole."

Shorty snickered. "The touristy types seem to like it."

Joel cut him a look and said, "Yeah, well, they can keep it. I'm freezing my fucking ass off." People actually enjoyed this shit? He wanted out of this cold-as-fuck town as soon as goddamned possible. Joel lit a cigarette and the smoke mingled with the steam that rose from his breath. The steel toes of his boots had turned them into refrigerators and his flannel shirt and plain denim jacket weren't doing shit to keep the chill of the wind away.

Kari Hanson had made herself a ghost. Joel wanted her to stay that way. You'd think there'd be tons of places to stash a body in the middle of fucking nowhere, but with all of the goddamned snow he doubted he'd find anywhere to dig a hole. His best bet would be to bury her body in a snowbank somewhere. It'd likely be a few months before anyone found her and even then, he'd like to see anybody try to connect him to the murder.

First, though, he had to get his fucking ledger back. Then he'd make the bitch pay for taking it from him.

They'd blown into town late in the afternoon. He wanted to wait until dark, rip the bitch out of her bed by the hair. Make sure she was good'n scared before he laid his fist into her. Ambushes were Joel's favorite means of attack. Catching his enemy off guard filled him with a perverse sense of satisfaction and power. He might not be in this fucking mess right now if he'd ambushed Owens at his home in the middle of the night. Instead, he'd let his temper get the best of him and beat the son of a bitch to a bloody pulp right there at his desk. If he'd kept his head cool, he would have checked the closet beside the office. He would have known that little bitch had hidden herself inside with his ledger. And he wouldn't be standing in the middle of this tiny as fuck town, freezing his balls off, and wishing he'd kept his head on straight.

Joel took a long drag off the cigarette and blew out the smoke in a rush before tossing it to the ground beside him. A woman sidled past him on the sidewalk. She glanced down at the discarded butt and back at him, her lip curling in distaste.

"The fuck you lookin' at?" he barked.

Her gaze slid quickly to the ground and she picked up her pace as she raced down the sidewalk and ducked into a real estate office.

God, this place was fucking uptight. Joel cracked

his neck from side to side and turned toward Shorty. "You sure no one's going to notice us at her place?"

So far, Joel had felt the eyes of every curious asshole in the entire town on him. Small towns were full of busybodies and gossips who couldn't wait to rat out their neighbor for whatever reason. Then again, towns like this were exactly the sorts of places where people's loyalties could easily be bought. If he didn't have the FBI and marshals up his ass, he could probably do well in a place like this. If he could stomach the motherfucking snow, that is.

"It's tucked back in the woods," Shorty said. "Down by the lake. The other houses on the lane are closed up for the winter as far as I can tell. I watched the place for two days and the only traffic in or out was Kari and her old man."

"He could be a problem." Joel knew the type: pussy-whipped with a hero complex.

"Unless he's got an arsenal and ten hands, he won't be," Shorty said with a snort.

"So, what're we doin' for the next few hours?" Z-dog asked.

Joel scowled at the prospect who couldn't seem to keep his mouth shut.

Shorty had suggested they bring that idiot Z-Dog along—let him roll with the big boys as a reward for bringing in the intel on Kari. But with every idiotic word out of the kid's mouth, Joel was starting to reconsider. The kid was wild and unfocused. The second shit went down, Joel suspected he would crumble. Joel wasn't interested in hiding more than one body tonight—maybe two if Kari's old man was around—and he'd be damned if he let some prospect disrupt his plan to get his ledger and his life back.

"We're not doing a goddamned thing." Joel turned a caustic eye toward the kid and his shoulders slumped. "We're going to stay nice and invisible. You understand me, son?"

He gave a slow nod. "Can we at least be invisible at the bar?" He jerked his chin across the street. "Get a beer while we wait?"

The last thing Joel needed was his crew to be shitfaced or passed out on a table before they got to Kari. But the bar was a better option for them than hanging out at the cutesy fucking café to their left. At least they'd blend in at the bar. "You can get a beer," Joel said. Z-Dog turned to leave and he grabbed the kid by the scruff of his neck and spun him around. "But you mind yourself, son. If you fuck up my chances of doing what I came here to do, I'll bury your ass in a ditch somewhere between here and California. You understand me?"

Z-Dog's muddy brown eyes went wide. "I get it. Jesus, I just want a beer."

Joel let him go with a shove. Fucking prospects didn't have any damned respect anymore.

Shorty and the other three guys they'd brought along fell into step behind Joel. He was so close to tying up his loose ends once and for all. He'd be damned if he let anything or *anyone* screw it up now.

* * *

Nick molded his chest to Livy's back. Her body bathed his in heat as she nestled closer. Over the course of a few short weeks he'd lost himself so completely to her that he wasn't sure he'd ever find his way back. He'd jeopardized his career, his reputation, everything he stood for and he'd do it all again for just another day with her. Another night. Another minute.

He'd meant to confront her when she got home from work. He'd planned to tell her who he really was and why he was there. But his own damned fear at how she'd react silenced him. His own damned fear about hearing the truth from her lips—not her deception or Morgan's suspicions—had curtailed all of his plans. One look into her beautiful hazel eyes and nothing else had mattered but getting every last scrap of clothing off her and getting her into bed.

Now that the haze of lust had cleared from his brain, a stone of guilt and regret settled in Nick's gut. He could protect Livy. Help her if she'd let him. He didn't believe for a second that the woman he'd grown to love so quickly could have had any part in her father's death. *Jesus.* The realization hit Nick with the force of a battering ram. He was in love with her. Whether she was Kari Hanson or Oliva Gallagher, or anyone else, it didn't matter. Nick knew she had a good heart and an even better soul. Whatever sins she'd committed, he could forgive her. At least, he hoped he could.

But he wouldn't know until he confronted her and got the truth out in the open once and for all.

Morgan and a team of deputies would be here in under forty-eight hours. He didn't want Livy to find out who he was when Morgan crashed through her door. He needed her to hear it from him before shit went down. He needed her to know that no matter what happened after tonight, he'd be there for her. Even if it meant his badge.

Nick wrapped his arms tight around her. She hadn't fallen asleep yet. Chills danced over his skin as she traced a light pattern up and over his forearm with the silky soft pads of her fingertips. He held her as though worried she might slip away from him After what he was about to say to her, he was pretty damned sure she would.

He opened his mouth to speak. Closed it. Let out a measured breath that did nothing to slow the frantic beat of his heart. His tongue stuck to the roof of his mouth. Goddamn it, he didn't want what this was between them to end.

"I know who you are, Kari." The words slipped from between Nick's lips in a whisper.

Livy's body went rigid in his embrace and her breath quickened. Her fingers stopped drawing a pattern on his skin. The flush of heat from her body intensified and he kept his arms around her as he felt her begin to pull away.

"I haven't worked with SWAT for a while." Nick put his mouth close to her ear as he spoke. Her delicate crisp winter scent filled his nostrils and his chest swelled with emotion. "I'm a deputy U.S. marshal. I can help you. But you have to tell me where Joel is."

Livy's breath stalled and Nick's heart lodged itself in his throat. He'd taken down violent criminals without a scrap of backup. Been shot at more times than he could count. Single-handedly wrestled down guys who were hell-bent on killing him and none of it scared him as much as Livy's still silence did.

"Help us," he said. "You can trust me, Livy. Let me help you."

Silence answered him. Would she deny the truth and make this harder on the both of them? He waited, gave her the time she might need to process everything he'd said to her. No more secrets. No lies. It was time for them to lay everything out on the table. Nick knew it was for the best. He hoped that Livy did too.

"You think I know where Joel is?" Her quiet voice filled the silence, full of disdain. "Jesus, Nick. Exactly who in the hell do you think I am?"

"We know you were in a relationship with him, Livy. Joel's been looking for you for a long time. Whatever he coerced you to do, whatever he was to you doesn't matter now. Help us put him away and I'll do whatever is in my power to help you."

Livy gripped his arms and shoved them away from her body. She trembled, not with fear, but with anger as she pushed herself up from the bed and turned to face him. "You son of a bitch!" Nick sat up on the bed as Livy searched the floor for her clothes. She pulled on her sweater—the sweater he loved—and a pair of leggings.

"Livy."

"Don't call me that!" she spat. "Don't ever call

me that again. If you know so goddamned much about me why bother with the pretense? Is this standard operating procedure for a deputy U.S. marshal, Nick? Get to know the suspect, take her to bed, and then question her post-orgasm? I've got to say, your interrogation tactics are *stellar*."

Nick scrubbed a hand over his face and let out a gust of breath. He'd handled this all wrong and he was about to pay the price for it. "I didn't mean for any of this to happen the way it did, but there's nothing either of us can do about that now. Liv—Kari, this has become a multi-district operation. Hell, maybe even multi-agency by this point. My chief is sending deputies down from Boise to arrest you. I managed to buy us another twenty-four hours but before they get here, I need to know the truth. I need to know how much involvement you had in your father's murder. You've got to be straight with me or there won't be anything I can do to make this easier on you."

"You know, Nick," Livy said. "Your amazing powers of deduction are proving why I didn't think I could trust the cops in the first place. You guys just make assumptions and run with them. Jesus! I thought you knew me better than this! You think I was Joel's *girlfriend?* The man is a pile of human garbage!"

"I know about your dad, Livy. If you were in any way involved—"

"You think I killed my dad?" With each word her voice escalated. Simon let out a warning growl that echoed his owner's mood before he hopped down from his spot on the bed where he'd been curled up. Her rueful laugh filled the silence. "This just gets better and better, doesn't it? You think I'm a murderer and you're okay with that? After all of your honorable, take-the-bad-guy-down bullshit you just hop into bed with me as though your high standards and morals don't mean shit? I suppose I should be flattered that you thought I was hot enough to set all of that aside." She let out a derisive snort. "Guess I wasn't the only one lying about who and what I really was. Vacation my ass. You've been staking me out!"

The barb stung but she was absolutely right. Nick had tossed all of his convictions to the side the minute he'd laid eyes on her. But not simply because she was a hot piece of ass that he couldn't wait to toss. "You have no idea what I think or feel, Livy."

"I said, don't ever call me Livy again."

"It's your name," Nick countered. "Kari Oliva Hanson. Or Kari Olivia Barnes Hanson. I know you took your mom's name and I know that your dad was an even bigger piece of shit than you let on."

"So you think that justifies my killing him?" she asked with incredulity. "Wow Nick, you really are taking the moral high ground, aren't you?"

He chose to ignore her sarcasm. She was trying to rile him, to goad him into a fight and he wasn't going to let her do it.

"I'm not trying to justify anything," Nick said. "All I want is the truth."

"You're not interested in the truth," Livy said with disdain. "If you were, you wouldn't have pretended to be someone you're not."

"Which is what?" He tried not to let her words get to him, but it was damned tough not to.

"A decent guy who doesn't have an agenda."

Nick opened his mouth to protest but he couldn't deny it. He'd absolutely had an agenda. Denying it would make him look like an even bigger asshole. He wasn't going to sit by and allow Livy to think that he'd used her, though. "That was before."

"Before what?"

Nick raked his hands through his hair. "Before *you*."

"Give me a fucking break, Nick."

His temper flared. He understood her anger with him over his deception, but hadn't she been dishonest as well? Nick had simply done his job in coming here to try to get a bead on Meecum. Livy was the one who was about to be arrested as an accessory to murder. He was sick and tired of defending his honor to her, trying to justify what he'd done when it was Livy who was in the wrong here. She'd turned the tables on him and he'd let her. Not anymore.

"I am giving you a fucking break, Livy. Otherwise, I'd have cuffed you by now."

Harsh? Maybe. But it needed to be said. Nick had given her a lot of leeway and so far, Livy hadn't done anything to assuage his suspicions or doubts. He didn't want Morgan to be right, damn it. But Livy had done little to deny her involvement with Joel or her father's death. The guilty always professed their innocence. He'd heard the same spiel too many times to count. Or did she simply realize she'd been caught and didn't see the point? Either way, her continued silence on the matter drove him crazy.

Livy held out her hands. "Don't let me stop you. Arrest me."

If he didn't think she'd take off, he'd get his damned cuffs from his cabin and slap them on her just to make a point. "I need you to start talking, Livy. Or you're going to give me no choice but to arrest you."

"Does it matter what I say?" Her eyes narrowed and she wrapped her arms around her torso as though the simple act were the only thing keeping her whole. "You've already passed judgment on me. You already think you know what happened. Whatever I say, you're going to assume it's a lie."

God she was stubborn. And frustrating the shit out of him. If she were any other suspect, he would have read Livy her rights by now. He flung his legs over the side of the bed and reached for his jeans. Sitting under the sheet, naked, wasn't going to help him to gain the upper hand.

"That's bullshit and you know it." Nick scooped up his jeans. He stuffed one leg and then the other inside and stood as he pulled them over his bare ass. "I know you're scared, Livy. I know you're worried. Let me protect you."

"Let you arrest me. Isn't that what you mean?"

Nick felt like throwing something. "If you don't stop acting like a spoiled kid, then yeah. I'll happily arrest you if that's what it takes to keep you safe. You've done a damned good job of keeping yourself hidden for the past four years but if I can find you, that means Meecum can find you."

Livy's expression changed from anger to stark fear. "Exactly," she said more to herself than Nick. "Which is why I've got to get out of here."

"That's not going to happen," he replied. "You're not running again. I won't let you."

Chapter Twenty-One

Nick was right. She couldn't run.

He was also right that if he'd found her, so could Joel. She'd known it was time to pull up camp when Nick first came to town. She should have trusted her instincts rather than let him get under her skin with his Prince Charming smile and sexy talk. Nick had been her fatal flaw and that scared the ever-loving shit out of her.

Livy let out a bitter bark of laughter. "I can't believe what an idiot I am. A cop lands right next door and I start to think of it as some sort of blessing! And you were so charming, so good at putting me at ease. I thought I could trust you, Nick! Hell, I was ready to spill my guts to you. You were working an angle the entire time."

Nick's expression darkened. "What in the hell is that supposed to mean?"

The hurt Livy tried to squash rose up inside of her like a tide. "You know damn well what that means! You fucked me into a false sense of security so that you could pull the rug out from under me when I was good and vulnerable." His jaw squared and he took a lunging step toward her. Livy didn't cringe away. She was sick and tired of being afraid. Instead, she stepped right up to him. "Deny it, Nick. I dare you to."

"You're goddamned right I'm going to deny it." Livy had always known that Nick had a dark edge. She saw that darkness now in the anger that shadowed his handsome features. "What happened between us has absolutely *nothing* to do with this investigation."

"Is anything you told me true?" She couldn't keep the tremor from her voice. His betrayal burned in her chest. "Did you make up that story about your sister? To make me think that you were sympathetic? To make me think that I could trust you?"

His gaze further darkened. "A guy just like Joel Meecum attacked my sister when she was a fucking *kid.*"

She let out a sad chuff of breath. "And you slept with me even though you thought I was the ex-girlfriend of a man who'd do something like that. Looks like you really will do anything to get your man."

He flinched as though she'd slapped him. Maybe it was a low blow but Livy was too angry to care. Too hurt to care. So damned devastated by the truth to give a single shit about the words she flung around.

Livy slumped down on the small wicker chair beside the bed. All of the indignant fire drained out of her in an instant. She'd gone too far, accusing him of making up the story about his sister. The depth of hurt in his eyes was proof enough of the truth. She'd been angry with Nick for deceiving her but who was she to judge? She'd been lying about who she was for a long damned time. It was the way he'd wormed his way into her heart that laid her low. To know that he'd gotten close to her in the name of serving justice stung. Livy had thought—had hoped—that Nick wanted her for her. That she meant something to him because of the person she was, not what she could do for him. All of her plans yesterday to come clean and turn herself in had been waylaid by her feelings for Nick. She'd worried about how his feelings for her would change once he knew the truth. She loved him. And all she was to him was a gold star on his arrest record.

That didn't change the fact that she was ready for all of this to be over. Livy had let her own stupid heart get in the way of confessing the truth to him. The truth *hurt*. It was time to tear off the Band-Aid.

"I was never in a relationship with Joel Meecum." She did nothing to curb her indignant tone. Livy cleared the emotion that clogged her throat. She couldn't meet his gaze and so she kept her own locked on the wood floors. "I didn't even know who he was until about five years ago. My mom's hospital bills were out of control and neither one of us had the money to pay them all. I went looking for my dad for some stupid reason." The vice of bitter emotion squeezed her chest. Livy drew in a shuddering breath as she gave a rueful shake of her head. "I guess I thought he'd feel bad for leaving us high and dry. That his guilt would force him to help my mom since he'd never done a damn thing to help me. What I didn't realize about him was that he didn't give a shit about anyone but himself and in the end, that selfishness got him killed."

"Livy."

She held up her hand to silence Nick. "Don't. If you don't let me get this out now, I'm never going to be able to do it." Livy felt the weight of his stare but she refused to look at him. If she did, she'd break down for sure. "I found him in Oakland, which really stung since he couldn't even be bothered to drive the three measly hours to Tahoe to see me. He was working as an accountant, and he offered me a job as his secretary. Can you believe that shit? Not a dime of child support in eighteen years and the jerk offers me a job. You know what's worse? I took it. I'd been skiing my entire life. It's not like the job prospects were pouring in. I worked for him for three months before I realized what he was up to—what I'd been helping him to do. He was laundering money for gangs, drug dealers. . . ." Her voice quavered and she forced it to steady. "Motorcycle clubs. Apparently it was the best scam he'd ever run. They didn't notice a few dollars here or there gone on top of his fees," she said. "Not when they were sometimes cycling hundreds of thousands of dollars through him."

Livy's limbs shook with unspent adrenaline. Already she felt lighter getting some of this off her shoulders, but it wasn't enough. It didn't matter anymore how Nick felt about her or why he'd done what he'd done. She needed to do this for herself. For her own peace of mind and conscience.

Nick's voice stretched out between them, warm

and solid. "So he was embezzling the money he was supposed to be laundering?"

Livy nodded though she still couldn't look at him. "I wouldn't have known about it at all but I overheard him bragging about it to his girlfriend one day. I confronted him and he promised to help pay Mom's medical bills if I agreed to keep my mouth shut." It was a shame that had blighted Livy's soul. That she'd trade her own integrity for a shallow promise and dirty money. "I'm not proud of myself for it, but I didn't think we had any other options. Of course, giving my dad a free pass didn't change anything. He kept stringing me along. Told me that if I stayed another week, and then another, he'd wire the money to my mom. I worked at his shithole office every day for an entire summer, watching thugs, murderers, and criminals cycle their dirty money through his dummy corporations, waiting for him to finally step up and take care of us. That's how I met Joel.

"My dad had been laundering and stashing money for him for a couple of years. He was also the person my dad was skimming the most from." Livy let out a bitter laugh. "I guess he thought a stupid biker wouldn't catch on to what he was doing. That he wouldn't watch his money as closely as the drug dealers did."

"Joel Meecum isn't stupid," Nick replied. "If he was, we would have found him a long time ago."

That was the truth. "I knew if Joel ever found out what my dad was up to, he was as good as dead and I realized too late that he was never going to give me or my mom any money. He was scamming me like he scammed everyone else. I went to his office to tell him I was leaving and when I got there, my dad was packing up his shit as fast as he could get it into boxes."

Livy finally met Nick's gaze. She couldn't tell if the anger that furrowed his brow was directed at her or simply the story she told him. At this point, did it matter?

"I didn't even get the chance to ask him what was going on when we heard the motorcycles pull up." She sighed. "I guess it was lucky for me that Harleys with straight pipes are loud. My dad shoved a ledger into my hand and forced me into a closet. I hid behind a stack of boxes and listened to Joel beat my father to death."

The tears that she'd refused to allow herself to shed spilled over Livy's cheeks. She hated her dad for leaving her and her mom. For failing to take care of them. For making their lives so much harder than they'd had to be. But she'd never wished him dead no matter how much she hated him. And she'd never had to endure anything as frightening and gruesome as the long minutes she'd hidden in that closet and been forced to listen to her dad die.

"Jesus." Nick's single word pierced the quiet.

That pretty much summed it up. "I think I waited in the closet for three hours or longer before I figured it was safe to come out." Livy swiped at the tears that cascaded over her cheeks. "There was blood everywhere. My dad was on the floor, dead. I took the ledger and I ran."

"Joel must have come back later for his ledger," Nick said more to himself than Livy. "That's why he's looking for you."

"No. I screwed up," she said through her tears. "I figured he'd come after me next if he couldn't find it so I left him a message telling him I had it. I thought I could use it as leverage. I told him that if anything ever happened to me, I'd turn it over to the cops. He knew I wouldn't, though. I couldn't trust anyone so I took his stupid book and I ran."

"This ledger," Nick said, "it's got financial records in it?"

"Yeah. I know it back to front. I can tell you the names of every single person he's ever done business with. What they muled, traded, sold, or smuggled and for how much."

"God, Livy. No wonder he put the word out that you were an ex-girlfriend. If any of his business associates had known why he was really looking for you, they would have killed him before they went after you."

She'd never thought of that. *Good Lord.* It was a miracle she'd survived so long without someone finding her. "I learned a thing or two in the few months I'd been hanging out with my dad. A friend of his made me a fake ID and set me up with a new Social Security number. And as far as my dad was concerned, there was nothing to connect him to me. His entire life, he'd never told anyone he had a daughter. The only person who'd ever met me besides his friend Bruce who did my new ID was his girlfriend, and Joel and he didn't tell them I was his daughter. How's that for a daddy-daughter moment? I'd been using my mom's name since I was seventeen so I knew no one would connect me to my dad but I changed my last name to Gallagher to protect my mom."

"Why didn't you go to the police, Livy?" The anger in Nick's voice gave way to concern and it sliced through her. "Running only makes you look guilty."

She knew that but at the time she hadn't trusted anyone. "My dad told me that Joel had police, FBI, and customs agents on his payroll. I couldn't go to anyone local and I was too afraid to reach out to anyone out of state. I had no idea how far his reach was. He's in business with people from *everywhere*, Nick." Her voice dropped to a whisper. "Who could I trust?"

"*Me.*" The forcefulness of the word caused her to look up. His gaze bore through her, the intensity of his dark eyes and the emotion there left her feeling too full of emotion and shaken. "You can trust me, Livy."

The glow of headlights shone through the upstairs window. A fresh wave of fear crashed over Livy and pulled her into its undertow. Her breath stalled in her chest and no matter what she did, she couldn't draw in enough air to fill her lungs. Black spots swam in her vision and she swayed on her feet. Two in the morning wasn't exactly a prime time for company. Nick had found her. Easily. Who else had managed to figure out where she'd hidden herself?

"Don't move." Nick held his arm out as he eased

his body toward the window. He kept his back flat against the wall as he peeked through the partially closed curtains to the driveway below.

Don't move? Livy didn't think she could take a single step if she tried. Paralyzed with fear, she had no choice but to wait for Nick's assessment of what was going on in her driveway and pray for the best. Maybe some drunk idiot had gotten lost on his way home. She'd deal with a shit-faced asshole and face the consequences of turning him in for a DUI any day of the week over a visit from Joel Meecum and his band of violent thugs.

"Livy?" Nick's careful tone sent a renewed spike of fear through her bloodstream. "Does this place have a basement?"

"N-no," she stuttered. "There's an old food cellar under the laundry room, though. It's not much bigger than a closet. I've never used it."

"You're going to use it," Nick said. "We need to get downstairs. Now."

"Why?" Violent tremors shook her and Livy remained planted to her spot on the floor. Nick spun and grabbed her by the elbow. He hauled her against him and rushed down the stairs, all the while helping her along. "What's going on, Nick? Who's here?"

"I'm not sure." They hit the bottom of the stairs. The house was cloaked in darkness but Nick urged Livy to hustle through the kitchen hunched over and below the windows. "I counted five bodies total." Once in the laundry room, Nick eased Livy behind him. "Where's the cellar?"

Livy pointed to the floor. "There's a trapdoor under that rug."

Nick swept the rug aside. He lifted the door and urged Livy down inside. "Don't come out until I give you the okay, do you understand me?" She stood there, gaping, unable to acknowledge the fact that he was about to stuff her into the cellar while he ran off and possibly risked his life. "Livy. Do you understand?"

"I understand." Her teeth chattered with every word. It was a wonder she got anything past her lips.

"Good." Nick reached for the trapdoor and lowered it over her head. Livy slid down the last three stairs, her legs no longer able to support her weight. "Now, be quiet and don't move."

Holy shit, this was bad. Livy didn't need confirmation to know that Joel had found her. They were both as good as dead.

Nick closed the trapdoor over Livy and shut her in the cellar before spreading the rug back over the floor. Barefoot, unarmed, and without backup to face five possibly armed men, his situation wasn't exactly ideal. Especially when he wasn't sure what direction the ambush would be coming from.

Meecum had evaded capture for so long because he was a smart son of a bitch. Livy's dad had underestimated him and it had gotten him killed. Nick wasn't about to make that mistake. He knew exactly who he was up against and what the man was capable of. If Livy had Meecum's ledger, you could bet the asshole wouldn't stop until he had it in his hands and she was dead. Nick was bound and determined to make sure he didn't get so much as a finger on her.

The sound of muted voices carried through the thin outer walls of the old cabin. Whoever was out there thought they were stealthy, but they'd obviously never ambushed a quiet rural lane before. There were no city sounds or streetlights to mask their approach. Even if he and Livy had been asleep when Meecum's guys rolled up, they would have woken.

On any other night, no one could have gotten into the house without making a hell of a lot of noise. Livy never left or went to bed without making sure every door and window was locked. Nick had distracted her last night, however. He'd closed the front door behind him and they'd made their way up the stairs. As far as he knew, it was still unlocked. *Damn it.* So far all Nick had managed to do was leave Livy more vulnerable. His actions hadn't helped her. If anything, he'd provided the necessary distraction for Meecum to sneak right into her house and take her. Some fucking great cop he'd turned out to be. Everything Livy had accused him of stung with bits and pieces of truth. He'd lost his focus. Let the job—his investigation—take a backseat to his feelings. He'd let her down. But damn it, he was going to make up for it.

The easy access into the house might have been a disaster if they were still asleep, but now Nick could use it to his advantage. Ambush the ambushers. He didn't have a gun, but he could be pretty goddamned dangerous without one. Careful not to make a sound, he padded to the front door. He kept his back flush to the wall and let the dark interior of the house mask his presence. Nick's gut tightened with anticipation and not a little anxiety. He wished that Livy wasn't so close but he was confident that as long as she stayed quiet, Meecum's guys would never know she was right below their feet. Nothing mattered more to Nick than keeping her safe. He was going to make sure that she never feared Joel Meecum or any of his associates ever again.

The snow that dusted the front porch steps muted their approach, but Nick knew that it was only a matter of seconds before his skills would be put to the test. He centered his focus and slowed his breathing. His heart beat a mad rhythm in his chest that he swore battered his rib cage. Adrenaline pooled in his limbs, causing his muscles to burn. Nick's teeth clenched and his nostrils flared. His hands tried to ball into fists but he forced them to remain loose despite the self-preservation instinct that made him want to swing out rather than grab at the first body through the door.

The knob turned and Nick's gut twisted into a knot.

He held his breath. He was more than simply outnumbered and this would be his only opportunity to get a leg up in what was guaranteed to be a violent, deadly fight. He never should have waited so long to wrap this up. He shouldn't have put Morgan off. He should have confronted Livy and gotten her the hell out of here. Because there was

no way everyone involved would walk away from
this one. He just hoped that he and Livy survived
this.

Fuck.

Nick willed his nagging thoughts to silence as the
first body eased through the doorway. The door
didn't even squeak to betray their entrance but the
groan of the aged wood floors gave them away.
Visibility wasn't ideal but Nick made out the dark
outline of an outstretched arm and, from his hand,
a monster revolver cast its shadow.

Nick lunged forward and grabbed the guy's wrist
with his left hand while he swung out with his right.
Stunned, it didn't take much for Nick to twist the
guy's arm behind his back and wrangle the revolver
from his grasp. The entire maneuver only took a
couple of seconds to execute right before all hell
broke loose. Angry shouts preceded the flash and
bang of gunfire. Nick's ears rang and spots swam in
his already hampered vision. The chaos of wild
shouts and shuffling bodies was a distraction he
couldn't afford. He needed to neutralize the situation at the front of the house before the rest of
Meecum's guys barged in through the back. Nick's
only advantage at this point was the deadbolt on
the back door. But if they couldn't get in that way,
he didn't doubt they'd circle around to help their
comrades at the front.

Brothers till the end.

He brought the gun he'd managed to wrangle
from the first guy around with a wide sweep of his
arm. The butt caught thug number one square in
the jaw and he went down like a stone. Another

wild round of shots rang out and Nick hit the deck but not before he felt the air from a passing bullet whiz past his face. A fresh wave of adrenaline dumped into his bloodstream and he kicked out with his legs to knock thug number two off his feet.

Boom! Boom! Boom!

Apparently the lock on the back door wasn't much of a deterrent for Meecum's crew. Rather than run around to the front of the house, it sounded like they were trying to come through the door with a battering ram. Nick prayed that Livy had done what he'd told her and stayed in the cellar. The shift of Nick's focus won his attackers a moment to regroup. His breath left his chest in a *whoof!* of air as a large body crashed down on top of him. Hands groped through the dark for the gun he still clutched in his hand and Nick swung out blindly with his left fist. The blow glanced off a shoulder, maybe the guy's chest. It was too hard to tell in the dark. He kicked and shoved, putting enough space between their bodies for Nick to bring his knee up and catch his assailant in the soft part of his gut.

With a muffled grunt, Nick managed to throw the heavy body from his. He was still at a disadvantage, whether he had a gun in his hand or not. The sound of the jamb splintering at the back door reached his ears and Nick's nerves jacked up to totally fucked-up proportions. One of Meecum's guys was unconscious but that still left four against one. He was a master marksman, but even so, he sure as hell wasn't that good.

A light flipped on in the kitchen. A second later

another flipped on in the dining room. The sudden brightness caused Nick to shield his eyes and he looked up to find the same ratty SOB he'd roughed up at the bar for hassling Livy staring down the barrel of his gun at him.

The bastard turned his attention to the guy Nick had tripped. "Get Z-Dog up off the floor and the two of you get upstairs. Turn everything upside down, you hear me? Joel wants Kari alive."

"I'm a deputy U.S. marshal," Nick growled. "Think carefully about what you're about to do."

The guy pulled back the hammer. "I don't need to think about a goddamned thing."

Chapter Twenty-Two

The inky blackness that permeated Livy's vision to the brink of pain was almost tangible, sensory even in its obscurity. It made her think of licorice and she wrinkled her nose in distaste. She could almost smell it, taste it, as the pungent flavor filled her throat and nostrils. Banishing the illusion from her mind, she forced herself to fight the effect of sensory deprivation. She should have mentioned to Nick before he shoved her down into the hole that the lightbulb had burned out a few months ago and since she never used the cellar, she hadn't bothered to change it.

Shit.

Cold seeped through the thin fabric of her sweater and leggings. Goose bumps rose to the surface of Livy's skin and she tried to rub them away as she remained perched on the steep wooden stairs. No way in hell was she going any farther. God only knew what was down there. Mice. Spiders. She shuddered as the sensation of tiny insects crawled over her flesh. She was going to kill Nick for stuffing her down here. Kill. Him.

The disorientation of not being able to see her own hand in front of her face caused panic to well up in Livy's chest. She commanded herself to stay calm and her trembling subsided as her breathing slowed. How long was he planning on keeping her here, blind and confused? Not knowing what in the hell was going on up there or whether or not he was safe.

"Nick." The barely whispered word was as good as a shout in the empty dark. "Goddamn it, you'd better not die."

The quiet was almost as bad as the darkness. Livy strained to hear even the faintest sign of Nick moving around above her but the concrete walls of the cellar insulated her from any outside sound. He was one man against who knew how many others and if Joel had sent them, you could bet your ass they were armed to the teeth. They'd tear the house to the foundation in their quest to find not only the ledger but also Livy.

God, she hoped Simon was okay.

Joel was just the sort of guy who'd go out of his way to kick a defenseless cat. Not that he'd have the balls to come out of hiding and take care of business himself. No, Livy was sure that he'd sent members of the MC to track her down and get his stupid book. She never should have gotten mixed up with her dad. Never should have run.

Coulda, woulda, shoulda. None of it mattered now. Livy was in serious danger. Nick was in serious danger. Rather than worrying about how she

could have avoided it in the first place, she needed
to figure out how to get them out of it now.

Livy didn't have her cell to call for help. Nick
didn't have a gun. Hell, he didn't even have shoes
on! Hiding out in the damned cellar wasn't going
to do either of them an ounce of good. He couldn't
take Joel's guys on single-handedly. He needed
help and Livy wasn't going to sit down here like a
coward while he put his life on the line for her.

She reached for the trapdoor at the exact
moment a succession of loud cracks rent the quiet.
The sound startled her and Livy lost her balance. A
grunt of pain escaped her lips as she slipped and
toppled down the stairs. Each bounce sent a jolt of
pain through her body. Her ass made contact with
the unyielding concrete floor and tears sprang to
her eyes. Thank God she'd been halfway down the
stairs already before she fell. Four or five steps was
an easy trip compared to ten or twenty. Still, her
body felt as though she'd been tumbled through
the dryer for an hour along with a bag full of bricks.

When the fog from her brain cleared, her confu-
sion was replaced with fear. The gunshots sent
spears of icy dread through Livy's chest and her
stomach twined into a tight tangle that made her
sick. What if he'd been hit? What if Nick lay bleeding out on her floor? Livy's concern wouldn't allow
for her to stay down in this impenetrable darkness
like a total chickenshit. She'd hidden for too long
and she wasn't going to do it any longer. Nick
needed her and she'd be damned if he died up
there alone.

If she could just get to her phone, she could call

911. It might not be much, but at least she'd know that help was on the way. Her phone was on the kitchen counter. Maybe. Or had she left it on the dining room table? Hell, she used the damn thing so seldom, it wasn't a surprise that she might not know its exact location. Still, she had to try to do something. Even if that meant taking a quick dash into her kitchen to call in the cavalry.

Far above her, Livy heard the muted thud of footsteps stomping up the stairs to the second story. If Joel's guys had headed up there to look for her—and the ledger—it would buy her a few minutes to get Nick, maybe get her hands on her cell, and get them the hell out of there. He was a deputy freaking U.S. marshal, for Christ's sake. He had to have a gun stashed somewhere at his place. If she could just get them across the lane to his cabin, they'd at least have what they needed to make a stand until the cops showed up.

If she got her ass in gear, they might have a fighting chance.

Livy braced her palms on the cold concrete floor and tried to push herself up. Every muscle screamed with pain and she was pretty sure she'd be sporting some nasty bruises in a few hours. She groped in the darkness for anything she could use as a crutch and said a silent, hopeful prayer that she wouldn't grab on to anything too disgusting. Her hand found something solid and she wrapped her fingers around what might have been a broom handle. She let her grip slide down the worn wood and found that the shape flattened and grew wide at the base. An oar, maybe? She supposed it didn't matter as long as it helped her get her ass up off the floor.

Every second it took her to get moving was a second wasted. Livy hobbled up the stairs, each step carefully placed so she wouldn't lose her footing in the pitch black and fall again. The oar did a good job of supporting her and maybe it would make a decent weapon if she could manage to swing it. The damned thing was long and awkward but if she put enough force behind the blow, she could probably knock someone off their feet. Maybe even knock them out completely.

She felt her way up to near the top of the stairs. Her hand met the trapdoor and she fumbled around as she searched for the latch. When her fingers found the cool metal of the D-shaped ring, Livy gave it a half turn and she heard the latch give way. Slowly, she lifted the trapdoor and peeked out from under the rug that draped over it.

The cellar had been so dark that the glow of the light in the kitchen nearly blinded her. She squinted against the brightness and did a preliminary search for feet anywhere in the laundry room or kitchen. As assured as she could be that the coast was clear, Livy eased the door up higher. It whispered open without a sound and she said a silent prayer of thanks as she just as silently crept out of the cellar, pulling the oar out with her.

The oar was a hell of a lot more rotted than she'd first thought. The top was broken off, leaving a jagged end of splintered wood. Well, if she couldn't effectively knock someone out with the piece of driftwood in her hand, maybe she could use it to stab instead.

"I'm a deputy U.S. marshal." Nick's voice carried to Livy from the living room and he didn't sound happy. "Think carefully about what you're about to do."

A distinctive click filled the silence. "I don't need to think about a goddamned thing."

Oh shit. Livy held the oar high in her grip and a twinge of pain raced along her shoulder. From behind her, a sound like someone was trying to drive a pickup through her back door startled her into action. She ignored the pain that flared through her muscles and rushed through the kitchen for the living room. Without even thinking she took a wide swing with the oar and knocked it into the arm of a man who had a large pistol pointed at Nick's face. He pulled the trigger and the shot went wide. So quickly that Livy couldn't process it, Nick brought his arm up, gun in hand, and fired.

A scream pierced the air as the man toppled over. Livy looked around, shocked, before she realized the sound had escaped her own throat. Nick turned to face her, his expression that of barely concealed anger. His brows drew down sharply over his eyes and his lips thinned.

"I told you *not* to leave the cellar, Livy."

She stood rooted to her spot on the floor, stunned. Nick had just shot someone. With a gun. In her living room. Visions of her dad slumped over and bleeding invaded her mind and a wave of anxiety crested over her. Her breath sped in her chest, her stomach launched itself up into her throat, and spots swam in her vision. Livy swayed on her feet as she became light-headed and she would have toppled over if Nick hadn't gotten up to steady her. The pungent odor of gunpowder hit her nostrils and she stifled a gag.

"Oh my God, is he dead?" The man had been about to kill Nick. Whether or not he was still breathing shouldn't have mattered.

The sound of urgent footfalls headed toward the top of the stairs above them and both Livy and Nick raised their heads to the sound. "Get out of here, Livy, now." He pushed her toward the front door and she took a stumbling step. "Run to my place, my phone's on the counter. Dial nine-one-one and tell them a deputy needs assistance and shots are being fired." He gave her one last push and she reached out for the door. "Go!"

Any remaining rational thought had left her brain the minute she watched that man fall to the floor. Livy was operating on autopilot now. It was survive or die.

Nick shoved Livy out the door just as two of Meecum's guys came flying down the stairs. He brought the gun up and waited. Shooting someone in self-defense was one thing, cold-blooded murder another. Nick stood by his convictions. He wouldn't fire unless fired upon. If his life wasn't in immediate danger, these two would get the opportunity to have their day in court. He still wasn't sure how he was going to arrest four men when he was only one cop with one set of cuffs. The details could be worked out later, after Livy called for backup and he knew the situation would soon be under control.

"Police! U.S. marshal!" he called out. Right before both men opened fire.

Marshals were trained to identify themselves as police due to the fact that most people didn't believe that the U.S. Marshals Service existed outside of westerns. Either way, his declaration didn't stop Meecum's guys from trying to drill a bullet or two into his dome. Nick dove beneath the kitchen table. Bits of wood flooring flew up around him and chunks of the table scattered around him. He shielded his head—as though that would do him a whole hell of a lot of good—and scooted until his back was to the wall and his right shoulder rested against the rear leg of the table.

With his elbow braced on the floor, he used his left palm to steady the heavy revolver. The lighting was dim and the dust stirred up by the barrage of bullets wasn't doing shit for the visibility, but Nick sighted as best he could and aimed for the closest man's shoulder. He gently squeezed the trigger. The report of the shot was like a cannon, which only helped to renew the ringing in his eardrums. His aim was true, though, and the bastard toppled down the stairs with a shout and crumpled to the floor as he rolled from side to side, clutching the hole Nick had made to the upper left quadrant of his chest. He'd probably missed the guy's heart by four or five inches but it was still a wound that could be fatal without immediate care. Nick didn't want him dead, but he did want him out of commission.

Maybe he'd finally managed to tip the odds in his favor.

God, he hoped Livy had made it to his house all right.

His worry for her nearly stole his focus. The way she'd reacted to seeing the man he'd shot laid him low. She probably didn't realize that she'd been so deeply affected by what had happened in her dad's office so many years ago. That shit stuck with you. Nick knew that. He had his own not-so-great experiences to prove it.

Another rally of shots peppered the wall above him and the floor beneath him. Nick flinched with every shot and he tucked his head between his shoulders as he waited for the asshole to run out of ammo and take a break to reload. Nick was all about quality versus quantity. He didn't need to let his bullets fly like a scene out of *Scarface* to have the impact he wanted.

His next target was farther up the stairs than the first guy, which posed a problem. Nick sighted the revolver and aimed for the guy's thigh. The slats in the bannister might deflect the bullet but he squeezed off the shot anyway. Wood splintered and the bullet hit its mark. Black Death alum number two went down hard on the stairs and skidded down on his ass until the wall stayed his progress. They were down, but not out. It was enough of an opportunity for Nick to get the hell out of there and find Livy.

Nick scurried out from beneath the table. Sounds came to him as though he were underwater. He hoped the hearing loss was only temporary but for now it meant that he needed to be even more on his toes. With one of his senses dulled, he was vulnerable. Meecum's men didn't share Nick's sense of honor. They shot to kill. If he didn't keep his guard up, one of them was bound to put him in the ground.

He pushed himself up from the floor with a grunt. The inside of Livy's cabin looked like a war zone, the walls peppered with bullet holes, the floors as well. Splinters of her dining room table lay around him and the stuffing from her couch and one recliner littered the living room. Glass pebbles from the framed photos that hung on the wall glinted on the floor. The bastards hadn't even managed to spare her fireplace. Chunks of broken brick lay on the hearth and floor. Either these guys were shitty shots, or they were determined to destroy everything in their path. Probably both.

Nick headed for the front door. Darkness permeated his vision; the sun wouldn't begin to rise for another couple of hours yet. His gaze searched out any sign of light—or life—from his cabin but its still, dark facade didn't fill him with hope that Livy had made it across the lane. Fear rose in his throat. It choked the air from his lungs and caused his limbs to quake. He might have sent her straight toward danger. Right into the arms of the men who wanted her dead.

He kept the gun at the ready, his eyes scanning the darkness as best he could for any sign of attack as he eased across the porch and down the front steps. His breath fogged in the frigid morning air and his bare toes and feet went from a tingle to a burn as the cold penetrated his skin. It had to be fifteen degrees or colder outside. Maybe even below zero. With no shoes or socks, and no shirt, it wouldn't take long for Nick to become hypothermic. His house was a mere thirty yards away but as he crept to the bottom of the stairs and across the cleared flagstone walkway, it might as well have been thirty miles.

Nick wasn't going to be worth a damn to either of them if he didn't get some goddamned clothes on. He paused at the edge of the house—still no sign of Livy—and cursed under his breath. His anxiety jacked up another notch and his teeth began to chatter despite his clenched jaw. Where in the hell was she? If any of Meecum's scumbag guys laid even a finger on her, Nick would throw all of his convictions to the wayside. Screw his honor. His badge. Nothing mattered more to him than Livy. He'd make them all pay.

He raced across the lane and hopped up on the steps of his cabin. The snow soaked through the cuffs of his jeans to chill his legs and Nick's free hand formed into a useless claw as he pawed at the doorknob. It was a wonder he could still hold the gun without dropping it. Hell, at this point his hand was probably frozen around the grip. The latch finally gave way and he stumbled inside, going to his knees on the plush carpeting just past the entryway. He used the door to leverage himself upright and stumbled through the dark for the mudroom.

"Livy?" He spoke in hushed tones, not sure what he might find. The house was dark and eerily silent. Nick's boots were at Livy's house but he managed to find a pair of sneakers tucked beneath the bench. He slipped them on, cringing at the shock of pain that raced along the tops of his feet, and grabbed a sweatshirt from a hook next to the washing machine. He was far from warm, but it was a start.

"Livy?" Nick spoke louder this time. He ventured from the mudroom to the kitchen. His cell phone sat on the counter, untouched. "Fuck." Anxiety pooled in his muscles and Nick stretched his neck from side to side in an effort to ease some of the tension that settled there. She was outside somewhere. She'd never made it to the house. *Goddamn it.* A sense of urgency rose up inside of Nick. She'd been outside longer than he had and though she wore a sweater and pants, she'd been barefoot too.

His fingers were stiff as he snatched his cell from the counter and unlocked the screen. He opened the phone app and dialed 9-1-1. Nick looked to the heavens when the dispatcher answered, "Nine-one-one, what's your emergency?"

"This is Deputy U.S. Marshal Nick Brady. I'm on Cottonwood Drive off of Warren Wagon Road. There is a possible fugitive on the loose and five armed assailants. Three have been shot and two are still unaccounted for with a possible hostage. I need backup ASAP."

Without waiting for a response from the dispatcher, Nick ended the call. He wasn't interested in coordinating anything, he needed to get back outside and find Livy before Meecum's men did. Already, it might be too late.

Chapter Twenty-Three

Livy watched as Nick sprinted from her house, across the lane, and up onto his porch. She tried to scream, but the hand held tightly over her mouth muffled any sound she might have been able to produce. A muscular arm held her in an iron grip and squeezed the air from her lungs until spots swam in her vision. She struggled to take a deep breath, her nostrils flared and burned from the cold in the air.

"You so much as grunt, I won't think twice about drilling a bullet into your pretty skull."

The cold of the gun barrel poking into her temple drove the point home and Livy stilled. Nick's front door slammed and it might as well have been the lid to her own coffin.

"Take care of him," Joel said to a guy standing beside him. "Kari and I are going to have a talk."

No! She tried to scream again and Joel shoved the barrel against her head with enough force to coax tears to her eyes. She needed to warn Nick. To do something to make him get the hell out of there. There was no way she was getting out of this alive, but he didn't have to die. *God, please don't let him die.*

Violent tremors shook Livy's body as Joel dragged her down the lane toward one of the cabins that was closed for the winter. Her feet had gone completely numb about ten minutes ago and her fingers weren't faring much better. Joel was an idiot if he thought he'd be able to break into one of the several fortresses that lined the lane without triggering an alarm. Did he seriously think a million-dollar summer home wouldn't be well protected? Of course, Livy wasn't about to warn him. She hoped he triggered a motion sensor and the cops showed up and rained bullets down on him. She wouldn't even mind being caught in the crossfire as long as it meant the murdering son of a bitch was wiped from the face of the earth.

Livy tripped as Joel continued to drag her and he hoisted her upright with a harsh jerk of his arm that left her ribs bruised. She couldn't feel her feet, for Christ's sake. She'd like to see him try to take a step without falling on frostbitten feet. Livy swore, if she lost one of her toes over this, she was going to kill the bastard herself.

The entire lane wasn't more than a few hundred yards but it felt so much longer. Joel passed up the cabins closest to Livy's house and dragged her to the end of her lane and then over to the next. *Damn it.* Joel was definitely smarter than Livy had hoped he was. Closest to the main road sat one of the only other houses in the area besides hers and Nick's that didn't look like it had a million-dollar price tag. Didn't mean the place wasn't equipped with ADT, though. At least, Livy hoped.

They waded through the two-plus feet of snow as Joel dragged her up onto the front porch. The house was dark, the driveway hadn't been plowed and the deck hadn't been shoveled. Obviously shut up for the winter. Livy's leggings were soaked through and the numbness in her feet began to spread up her calves and into her thighs. If she didn't warm up soon, she wouldn't have to worry about Joel killing her. The cold would get it done.

"You make even a whimper, I'll beat you within an inch of your life, girl."

Joel took his hand away from Livy's mouth. She filled her lungs with air, fully prepared to defy him when she called to mind the memory of her dad, lying in a bloodied heap on the floor and beaten so badly he was unrecognizable. A sob lodged itself in Livy's throat and the tremors that shook her body now had nothing to do with the cold. The stark realization that she was in fact going to die tonight hit her with the force of an avalanche. She wasn't ready. She'd barely lived her life. She was in *love*, damn it! Maybe for the first time ever! It wasn't fair!

The sound of glass shattering distracted Livy from her personal pity party. Hope soared in her chest as she waited for the wail of an alarm and then crashed to the ground on broken wings as she heard only silence. Why should she think her luck would change now?

Joel reached through the door where he broke out the pane and unlocked it. He pushed it open and sent a pile of snow into the house in the process.

The snow wouldn't be half as hard to clean up as her blood that would soon be splattered all over the living room, she supposed. Joel shoved her inside and Livy tried to force any more morbid thoughts from her mind. She might have been up shit creek without a paddle, but on the plus side, maybe now that she was inside the feeling would return to her legs and feet.

A little optimism couldn't hurt, right?

Joel grabbed her by the neck of her sweater— Nick's *favorite* sweater—and hauled her upright before throwing her back down on a long couch in the living room. The breath rushed from Livy's lungs with the hard landing and she turned to glare her hatred at the man who loomed above her.

"You're going to regret it if you rip my sweater."

Joel leaned down, his lip curled into a sneer. "You got bigger problems than a goddamned sweater, girlie. You're lucky I didn't break your neck the second I got my hands on you."

Livy bucked her chin in the air. "You're not going to do shit to me until you get what you came here for."

The show of bravado took more out of her than she expected. Livy was outgoing, sometimes crass, and she tried to be funny whenever she got the chance. She had an epic potty mouth. But none of that equated to bravery. She might have appeared tough, but inside, she was falling apart.

Joel leaned down until his nose almost met Livy's. His breath reeked of beer and stale ciga-rettes and she swallowed down a gag. "You're right about one thing. You have something that belongs to me, and I want it back."

The only thing keeping her alive right now was Joel's ledger. Did he seriously think she'd give it up so easily? "I don't have it," Livy said. "You know that guy you think you're going to get rid of so easily? He's a U.S. marshal. He knows who I am and he knows what I have."

Joel cursed under his breath. He reached out and grabbed a handful of Livy's hair. A cry of pain escaped her lips as he twisted and pulled. She felt the strands give way and she leaned in toward him to try to slacken his hold. He continued to twist until tears pooled in Livy's eyes and he released his grip with a rough shove.

"That son of a bitch is gonna die, same as you are."

"That's what you think." Fear lent Livy's voice a quaver but she willed it to still. "Nick is one of their top fugitive hunters. He's taken down more men than any other marshal in history." Okay, so she had no idea if any of that was true, but he'd found her, hadn't he? "He doesn't even need a gun to be deadly." She'd seen that with her own eyes. "You're fucked, Joel."

The back of his hand whipped across Livy's face with a *crack*! Her tears flowed in earnest as white-hot pain exploded along her jaw and cheekbone. She spoke through her tears this time, in spite of them, and infused her tone with venom. "I memorized your ledger front to back. The marshals know every single person you've ever done business with. You can't run far enough to get away from what's coming for you."

He hit her again, this time on the other side of her face. Livy cried out—there was only so much she could take—and she tried to breathe through the searing pain that set her face on fire. On the plus side, it distracted her from her frostbitten feet. *Optimism!* But it wasn't enough to quell the fear that shook her to her very core. Despite the fact she was begging for it, Livy didn't want to die. She didn't want Nick to die. Joel . . . ? He could die painfully and violently for all she cared. But honestly, what she truly wanted was for him to rot in a jail cell. Isolated. Alone. Just like she'd been for the past four years.

"That better be a fucking lie," Joel snarled next to her ear. "Because if it's not, I'm going to give you to the cartel and let them deal with you. The things they'll do to you will make you wish I'd killed you."

Livy swallowed against the lump that formed in her throat. "Either way, you'll be dead. That's all I care about."

"Where's my goddamned ledger, Kari?" Joel gripped her by the wrist and gave it a sharp quarter turn that forced her to twist her entire body to keep it from snapping. "I want it. *Now.* And you'd better fucking give it to me."

She met his gaze in the dark interior of the cabin and sneered. "Go to hell."

He jerked her up to her feet. The pain she'd felt from his fist connecting with her face was nothing compared to the razor-sharp pins and needles in her feet. They'd finally begun to regain some feeling and it was about as pleasant as walking on broken glass. Livy's legs gave out from under her and Joel yanked her upright once again, forcing her to stand.

"Where the fuck is it? And don't jerk me around or I'll beat that cocksucker marshal boyfriend of yours to death while I make you watch. Understand?"

Livy could take all of the threats Joel wanted to throw at her and then some. But the second he mentioned Nick, she lost it. Rage, hot and thick, boiled up in her throat. Livy's hands balled into fists and she filled her lungs with air. "If you lay a finger on him, you'll regret it!"

"Who's gonna make me regret it?" Joel asked. "You? Fuck, you hid in the fucking closet while I beat that thieving son of a bitch Owens to death. You didn't seem too concerned about saving his ass, did you?"

Maybe her dad had gotten what he deserved. Joel's words stung, though. She hadn't known her dad and when she finally got the chance to know him she realized that she'd been better off not having him in her life. Still, she'd never wanted anything truly bad to happen to him. And in the end, he'd shoved her into that closet. Tried to protect her. And that counted for something.

"That thieving son of a bitch," Livy spat, "was my *dad*."

Joel's eyes narrowed. "You're an even colder-hearted bitch than I gave you credit for, Kari. You just let your old man die while you hid. You gonna do that to your boyfriend, too? Throw him under the bus while you save your own skin?"

"Your ledger is in my cabin. I hid it under the

floorboards in my bedroom. Not that getting it back is going to keep you safe from *anything*."

"Let's go get it then," Joel growled as he grabbed her roughly by the wrist. "And don't try anything or you *and* your boyfriend will pay for it."

Livy's heart thundered in her chest. Her mouth went dry and she thought she might throw up. Her legs ached, the cold seeped through her leggings and sweater to turn her skin to ice. Her feet ached as though someone had driven spikes into them and her hands weren't faring much better. Her face felt swollen and it pulsed in time with her heartbeat; little shocks of pain to remind her of Joel's capacity for violence. She couldn't remember a time in her entire life that she'd endured so much abuse. Had hurt so much. She'd endure all of it and more, though, if it meant she could buy Nick a little bit of time. Maybe give him an opportunity for a fair fight with Joel's last remaining guy. With any luck he'd get out of there in one piece. And she hoped that he wouldn't play the hero.

Like her dad, she was getting exactly what she deserved.

Nick stuffed his cuffs in the back pocket of his jeans before he grabbed his badge and slung the lanyard around his neck. He retrieved his Glock from the closet and checked the clip. He wasn't about to possibly confront local law enforcement, armed and without a badge to identify himself by. That was a damned good way to get his ass shot. He was looking to stay alive tonight. So far, so good.

His gut churned with nervous energy and his brain buzzed as he emptied the remaining bullets from the cylinder he'd taken off the guy who'd barged into Livy's cabin. With one dead and two seriously wounded, Nick had managed to level the playing field somewhat. But there were still two of Joel's guys out there who were unaccounted for and he had no idea where Livy was. He needed to hope for the best and expect the worst. And be prepared for anything.

Anything barreled through his front door in a blaze of gunfire.

Nick dove for the floor as the first spray of bullets struck the counter bar that separated the living room from the kitchen. A gunfight in the dark and the middle of winter was absolutely his least favorite scenario for the way this had all gone down. Each new complication, each shot fired, only kept Nick from finding Livy. And it pissed him the hell off.

A muzzle flash accompanied each shot and it didn't do much to help Nick see in the dark. It did, however, give him something to aim at. The idiot currently unloading his clip into Nick's kitchen didn't seem to realize that all he was doing was wasting ammo. Guess he figured he'd get lucky with his blind shots and take Nick out before he had a chance to retaliate.

"Police!" Nick shouted. Hey, it was worth another try. Maybe one of Meecum's guys had an ounce of self-preservation instinct. "U.S. marshal!"

Nope. The stupid son of a bitch didn't even pause.

His assailant couldn't have had more than fifteen rounds in his clip and as Nick counted them off, he waited for the opportunity to act. When the sound of gunfire echoed into silence and he heard the distinctive *click* that signaled an empty clip, Nick lunged from the cover of the kitchen counter ready to take his shot.

Only to find the bastard had taken cover.

Fucking great.

"Local law enforcement is on their way!" Nick called out. "If you surrender now, it'll be easier for you. Put your hands up and step into plain sight."

The sound of a clip sliding into place answered him. *So much for diplomacy.* Not that Nick had ever considered himself much of a diplomat. He could hide behind the counter and they could do this song and dance all over again, but he wasn't interested in wasting another goddamned second. Livy was out there and could be hurt or worse. God, he hoped not worse. He'd be damned if anything or anyone got in the way of him finding her.

The thought that something horrible might have happened to Livy chilled his blood in a way that the winter cold never could. Fear unlike anything he'd ever felt gripped his heart with icy talons that wouldn't let go. He had to find her, assure himself that she was safe before he went out of his damned mind with worry.

He squinted through the darkness as though that would help him to see. Nick knew all he was going to manage was a few wild shots. He'd settle for accidentally winging the bastard at this point. Nick pushed himself up from the floor, gun at the ready. He swung the weapon to his left, toward the hallway that led to the bedroom. His finger caressed the trigger as he waited. . . .

A shadow to his right drew Nick's attention and he swung his arm around, aimed at the open doorway, and squeezed off two successive shots. Steam rose from the body, illuminated by the bright snow outside, before it collapsed in the doorway and then landed on the floor. Nick's arm dropped and he let out a shuddering breath as he braced a hand on the kitchen counter. It didn't matter how many times he discharged his firearm, it never got easier. It never failed to rattle him.

Nick didn't have time to be rattled or anything else. He charged through the front door, leaping over the body that blocked his path. Snow and sneakers weren't the ideal combination and he nearly fell on his ass as he slid down the icy front steps of his porch.

Slow down. Assess your surroundings. Use your damned head.

Nick's steps slowed as he hit the driveway. Visibility wasn't great, but he could make out a trough in the middle of the tire tracks that marred the new snow that had fallen overnight. He took off toward the tracks and followed them down the lane. Nick's heart hammered in his rib cage despite his measured pace. His heavy breaths fogged the early morning air and he fought to keep his focus on what he could see and hear, *not* the distressing images his overactive imagination wanted to conjure.

The tracks stopped at the end of the lane and cut

across a small lot. Nick clutched the grip of his Glock as he waded through the deep snow and onto the next lane. From there, his pace quickened as he noticed the trail ended at a small cabin fifty yards away. The front door of the cabin was wide open, the interior dark. Nick took a stumbling step forward as the breath stalled in his chest. If anything had happened to Livy, someone would pay with their life.

Nick brought his gun up as he approached the front porch. Livy stepped out the front door at the same moment, her eyes wide with fear. Behind her, with a gun pressed to her temple, was the man Nick had spent months tracking down.

That the bastard would risk coming out of hiding only proved that the ledger Livy had in her possession had enough shit in it to put some heavy hitters away. It also proved that Joel had come in person because he didn't trust anyone to clean up the mess but himself.

"Back away!" Meecum shouted. "Unless you want her brains scattered all over the snow."

Nick held his hands up in the air and made a show of taking his finger off the trigger as he backed away from the porch. "Take it easy," he said. "No one has to get hurt."

Meecum snorted. "I'd say it's a little late for promises like that, don't you?"

True, the rest of Meecum's guys were either bleeding or dead.

"Lose the piece."

"I can't do that." The second Nick discarded his gun, he was dead.

"You want her to die?" Meecum asked.

Nick glanced at Livy. The eastern sky started to show the first signs of dawn and it cast her face in shades of gray that gave her an ashen pallor. Nick swallowed down the lump of emotion that rose in his throat. If Meecum shot her, he might as well shoot Nick, too, because he knew there was no way he'd ever be able to live without her.

"I think we both know that you can't let her walk away from this."

Livy flashed him a look that was half resignation, half fear. He hadn't said anything that she didn't already know. What he wanted to tell her was that he'd throw himself in front of a bullet before he ever let anything happen to her.

"We're goin' for a walk," Meecum said. "If you try anything, I'll make her watch while I drill a bullet in your head. Understand?"

Nick kept his arms up. "I hear you."

Livy visibly trembled as Meecum guided her down the stairs. As they passed him, Nick realized that it wasn't dawn's light that gave her skin a death-like hue. She was practically blue from the cold. Her face was swollen—one eye almost completely shut—and bruises marred both of her delicate cheeks. A wave of rage washed over Nick. If the local cops didn't show up soon, he didn't think he could keep himself on the straight and narrow and arrest Meecum like he knew he should.

Nick felt Livy's pain in every step taken back to

her house. Meecum had come for his ledger; Livy had obviously agreed to give it to him. By the time they walked the few hundred yards back to Livy's house, her teeth chattered. Meecum came to a stop at the bottom of Livy's stairs and he pulled her to a halt beside him.

"That's close enough!" Meecum barked. "You're making me twitchy, Deputy." Nick sure fucking hoped so. "We're going inside and you're staying right fucking here. Understand?"

Right. Like Meecum would let him hang around on the porch while Livy got his ledger. Nick knew that Meecum would shoot him the first chance he got. Nick didn't think he could protect himself and Livy. If it came to a shootout, he had to hope he was the faster man on the trigger.

From the corner of his eye, Nick noticed Livy inch away from Meecum. He hooked his finger around the trigger of his Glock, ready to squeeze off a shot. A clump of heavy snow fell from the tree near Livy's driveway. Meecum started and turned toward the sound at the exact moment Livy turned and reached for her snow shovel that stood propped against the deck. She swung it in a wide arc and caught Meecum in the face. He staggered backward and his revolver discharged.

"Livy, get down!"

She fell to the ground at the same moment Nick threw himself at Meecum. Snow flew up around them as they struggled. Meecum caught him in the gut with a wild swing and Nick doubled over. The pain barely registered in the wake of his adrenaline rush, though, and Nick countered with an uppercut that caught the bastard at the edge of his jaw. Nick used Meecum's momentary disorientation to his advantage. He kicked out and caught him in the knee, sending him to the ground with a grunt. He followed up with a left hook that put Meecum down once and for all.

Nick didn't waste another second. He dropped his Glock, threw himself fully on top of Meecum, and laid his knee into the son of a bitch's back. With a jerk, he hauled one arm and then the other behind the bastard and held them in his left hand as he fished his cuffs from the front pocket of his sweatshirt. He secured them around Meecum's wrists, sure to make them extra tight, as he read Miranda to one of the U.S. Marshals Office's top fifteen most wanted fugitives.

"Joel Meecum," Nick said with satisfaction. "You're under arrest. You have the right to remain silent . . ."

He repeated the words that he'd spoken a hundred times in the course of his career, but his focus was on Livy. Her face was swollen and bleeding, she shivered violently as she leaned on the shovel for support. Tears streamed down her cheeks as she took in lungsful of shuddering breaths that filled the air above her with steam. In the distance, the sounds of sirens grew louder and for the first time in what felt like hours, Nick let out a sigh of relief. He'd thought that cuffing Meecum would be one of the most profound moments of his career—hell—his *life*. But as his eyes drank in the woman who'd managed to steal his heart, he realized that there were much more important things in life than taking down the bad guy.

Nick loved Livy. No matter what. And he wasn't ever going to let her go.

Chapter Twenty-Four

Livy slumped against the front porch steps and then into the snow as she watched Nick cuff Joel Meecum. She was past the point of feeling cold—of feeling anything, really—and her eyes drifted shut despite the adrenaline that coursed through her veins. God, she was tired. It might have been bad timing, but a nap wouldn't hurt, would it?

"Livy?" Nick's voice sounded as though it came from miles away and not just beside her. "Hey! Livy, talk to me."

"Later," she mumbled. "After I wake up."

Her eyes cracked for the barest moment. Nick loomed over her, his expression pinched with concern. His mouth moved but no sound seemed to come out. Weird, because from the looks of it, he was shouting at her. A slow smile curved Livy's mouth. Nick was the most breathtaking man she'd ever laid eyes on. "I love you, Nick," she said before she drifted into a dark and dreamless sleep. "I'm sorry I didn't tell you sooner."

* * *

Warm, humid air expanded Livy's lungs. Good God. Had she fallen asleep and woken up in the freaking rain forest? She pawed at her face, at the plastic cup that covered her mouth. She had a feeling there was a fantastic story behind how she wound up in the jungle with a cup on her face. Her thoughts began to clear and Livy realized that there couldn't possibly be a fantastic story because that would require having an actual life. Livy didn't have friends to party with. She didn't live anywhere near the jungle. Her life was about the snow and cold and days of never-ending loneliness and isolation. Well, sort of. A pair of dark, intense eyes came to mind and Livy smiled. Nick. The godlike man of her dreams. Adonis with a badge and sidearm.

Livy sucked in a sharp breath of warm air. Her eyes flew open and she choked on the exhale. Bright light nearly blinded her as an unfamiliar room came into focus. She clawed at her face, at the mask that covered her nose and mouth. Something connected to the back of her left hand that gave a tug and she looked over to see an IV tube taped there.

Alarms beeped and blared in the recesses of her mind as her heart rate kicked into overdrive. Panic infused her veins and her head swam. What in the hell was going on? Where was Nick? The last thing she remembered he had Joel on the ground and . . .

"Hey." A deep, comforting voice caressed her ears. "Hey." Firmer this time. "Livy, try to calm down.

You're okay. You're in the hospital." Nick's gorgeous face filled her vision and she wanted to cry with relief. "Do you understand me? I need you to settle down."

Settle down? Unanswered questions peppered Livy's brain. They both could have died! She didn't know if she could ever settle down again.

Livy started to talk but it was tough with her face all covered up. She reached for the mask once again and Nick's expression became stern as he reached out and took her wrists in his hands. "Hold on. Do me a favor and quit trying to rip out your IV and I'll help you with your mask. Deal?"

Livy nodded.

"Okay, first things first. Lie back."

She let herself fall back against the hard hospital pillows. She inhaled another deep breath of warm air before letting it out slowly. Once she was settled down, Nick reached over her and gently removed the mask from her face.

"Why am I breathing in rain-forest air?" Livy asked. She rubbed at her cheeks where the elastic had rested and instantly regretted it. Tears sprang to her eyes from the pain that radiated from both of her cheeks and down through her jaw. "Ow." She groaned. "Ow, ow, ow."

Nick's brow furrowed. He reached out and smoothed her hair back. "You're hypothermic," he said. "You lost consciousness and your heart rate was dangerously slow. We had to get you warmed up." His wan smile and furrowed brow conveyed his worry and anxiety tugged at Livy's chest. "Warm blankets, warm air, IV fluids, the whole nine yards."

Livy tried to push herself up farther on the bed and she realized heavy, warm blankets weighed down her torso. Why not her legs? Her arms? Her eyes went wide and the sounds on the machines attached to her perked up once again. "Did I lose my toes?" God, she wasn't sure she could feel them. Livy tried to sit up, to tear off the blankets, but Nick urged her to stay put. "My feet?" How bad was it? She didn't know if she could handle it if she could never ski again. "Don't sugarcoat it, Nick. Give it to me straight."

He answered her with a nervous chuckle. "You didn't lose any toes or feet. It's dangerous not to warm you up from the middle outward. That's all. You have mild frostbite on your toes and your fingers were almost there but you're going to be okay. No amputations. I promise."

"You swear?"

Nick lifted two fingers. "Scout's honor."

Relief swamped her. The tears she'd tried to quell escaped and rolled down her cheeks. "Do I look horrible?" Joel had really done a number on her. She doubted she'd be winning any beauty pageants in the near future.

Nick's jaw squared. "There's only one other time in my life I've wanted to hurt someone that badly." His voice quavered and he took a slow breath through flared nostrils. "When I saw what he did to you—"

Livy reached out and took his hand in hers. "But it's over, right? You arrested him?"

Nick gave a sharp nod of his head as he averted his gaze. He wasn't telling her everything. Not that Livy was surprised. She knew she wouldn't walk away from this scot-free.

"It's not over, though." Sadness cut through her, deep and sharp. "Is it?"

Nick opened his mouth to speak at the same moment the door swung open. A uniformed sheriff's deputy walked in and a guy in jeans and a striped button-up followed him. Nick's gaze darkened. "You can talk to her later when she's feeling better."

Livy gave him a searching gaze. Her heart rate kicked up. "I feel fine."

Nick quirked a challenging brow. She sensed he'd wanted her to give a different answer.

"We just need a minute," the plainclothes guy said to Nick.

Who in the hell was he? He wore a badge on a lanyard around his neck. Another marshal maybe? The machine that monitored Livy's vitals beeped with her increased pulse.

"Later," Nick said from between clenched teeth.

"No," Livy said softly. There was no point in putting it off. Worrying and wondering about her fate would only prolong the torture. She'd been prepared to face the consequences. Might as well rip the off the Band-Aid. "It's okay, Nick. I want to talk to them."

The county sheriff remained silent. The guy Livy

assumed might be another marshal cut Nick a look. "You can wait outside, Deputy. This won't take long."

Nick turned to face Livy, his jaw set stubbornly. "I'm right outside," he said. "I'm not going *anywhere.*"

Livy gave him what she hoped was a reassuring smile. He reached out, took her hand in his, and gave it a light squeeze. When he let go, cold seeped into Livy's skin and she shuddered. He didn't even exchange a glance with the other men in the room as he stalked toward the door and left.

A quiet moment followed and Livy wished she hadn't been so damned confident about being left alone with these guys. Intimidating didn't even begin to describe the man who'd taken point. He regarded Livy as though already working some sort of lie detector mojo on her. Well, she hated to disappoint him but she was through with telling lies.

"I'm Deputy U.S. Marshal Ethan Morgan." His crisp, all-business tone didn't do much to put Livy at ease. "I think we'd better have a talk about what happened last night, Livy. As well as what happened four years ago at your father's office."

If he knew about her dad, Nick had obviously filled everyone in. Which meant that Deputy Morgan wanted her to corroborate Nick's story. He could try to catch her in a lie, but Livy had nothing but the truth to offer. "Sure." Her mouth went dry and she tried to muster up enough saliva to talk. "But for the record, my name isn't Livy. It's Kari. Kari Barnes."

Deputy Morgan's expression softened. Score a point for her! "Okay, Kari. Let's start at your dad's office, four years ago, and go from there. Sound good?"

She let out a slow sigh that loosened the tension in her chest. Another shock of cold caused her to shiver and she pulled the heated blanket up closer to her chin. She could do this. She could get through this. No matter what happened from here on out, she'd be okay. There was definitely something to that saying about the truth setting you free. All she'd given Morgan so far was her real name and already she felt lighter. "Can I get some water, please?"

Morgan gave a shallow nod of his head. The sheriff's deputy stepped up to the rolling tray beside her bed and poured a little water into a plastic cup. She took it from him with shaking hands and sipped. It wasn't the cold that caused the quaking in her limbs. Nothing was scarier than dropping the facade, it seemed.

Kari. The name didn't even ring with familiarity anymore. She didn't want to be Kari. Didn't want to be that woman who'd seen her father die and, instead of helping to bring his murderer to justice, had run away.

Deputy Morgan waited patiently, but his gaze was focused and hard. He was used to dealing with people on the other side of the law and she was no different. Guilty until proven innocent, it seemed. Her stomach twisted into a knot as she reminded herself that even Nick had assumed she was guilty.

"Kari?" Deputy Morgan took a seat beside the bed. "Are you ready?"

He came across as a little less intimidating at eye

level. His lips didn't so much as twitch, though. No hint of humor accented his hard features. Morgan was there for answers, and he wasn't leaving until he got them. He activated the voice record function on his phone and set it on the tray table beside her. Livy watched as the seconds ticked away, recording nothing but silence.

The faster she spilled her guts, the faster Nick would be allowed back into the room. They still had a lot to hash out, the least of it being her confession of love before she'd passed out face-first in a snowbank.

She'd put out one fire at a time. Hell, she'd already been beaten, nearly frozen to death, and almost shot. It couldn't possibly get worse, could it?

"A little over four years ago, I went looking for my dad," she began. Deputy Morgan leaned forward in his chair, his attention focused solely on her. She took another sip of water. What she really wanted was a steaming mug of hot cocoa. "When I tracked him down, he was working as an accountant. After a few months, I found out that he'd been laundering money for a bunch of drug dealers, gangsters, and a couple of motorcycle gangs. That's how I know Joel Meecum. . . ."

An hour passed while Livy relived the worst four years of her entire life. She didn't shed a single tear, though. Her voice didn't so much as quaver. Every word spoken was one hundred percent the truth. The only part she omitted was the extent of her relationship with Nick. As far as she was concerned what had happened between them was nobody's damned business but theirs.

"There's nothing else?" Deputy Morgan asked. "Any detail you might have forgotten?"

"No." Livy didn't think she could ever forget the details of her dad's death or how it came about. "That's all of it."

"And you still have this ledger?"

That leather-bound book had ruined her life. "I do." And she couldn't wait to get rid of it.

Deputy Morgan studied her. "Care to tell me where it is?"

No one had mentioned an arrest but Livy knew that it was too soon for him to slap the cuffs on her. It could be days—weeks—before they decided whether or not to press charges against her. If she gave them the ledger now, would it compromise any chance she had at freedom? Nick already knew it was hidden beneath the floorboards in her bedroom. He could turn it over to Deputy Morgan at any time. "Nick knows where it is," she said quietly.

He gave her a shallow nod before retrieving his phone from the table and disabling the voice recording. "Thank you, Kari," he said as he stood. "I'll be in touch soon."

With his cryptic parting words, Deputy Morgan left the room with the county sheriff in his wake.

Anxious nerves churned in Livy's gut as she was left alone with her thoughts. Another chill shook her and she brought the mask to her face to breathe in more of the warm air they'd been pumping her full of. *Hypothermia. Jesus.*

A swath of light cut across the floor as the door to her room glided open once again. Nick's shadowed form came into focus and Livy took another deep breath of warm, humid air before she tucked the mask beside her once again. Bruised, frozen, and exhausted, it wasn't exactly how she wanted him to see her. Especially when they still had so much to hash out.

His dark gaze devoured her and Livy's stomach shot up into her throat. Even as hurt as she still was by his assumption that she'd been Joel's partner, Livy couldn't help but admire him. Nick was certainly one of a kind.

Chapter Twenty-Five

"How you holding up?" He approached the bed cautiously, as though afraid he'd spook her.

"I feel horrible," Livy said after a moment. "I hurt everywhere. My face feels like it's been run against a cheese shredder and I'm so cold I don't think I'll ever get warm." That bothered Livy more than she wanted to admit. She liked the cold. Lived for winter sports. What if her frostbite and hypothermia had some psychological effect on her and she was forced to move to Florida where it was summer 365 days a year?

"It's okay to go slow, Livy," Nick said. "You've been through a lot."

The events of the previous night flashed through Livy's mind once again in a wild blur. Her fight with Nick, the accusations he'd made, still stung. As did the fact that he'd slept with her, cradled her in his arms, while holding on to his preconceived notions about her. Even after all of that, she'd told him she loved him. She really was a glutton for punishment, wasn't she?

"Just another day in the life of Joel Meecum's ex-girlfriend, right?" She hadn't meant to throw Nick's accusation back in his face, but her emotions got the better of her. "I probably got what I deserved."

Nick let his head fall between his shoulders and cupped the back of his neck. He looked tired. Exhausted, really. "Don't say that. Nobody deserves to go through what you went through. I'm sorry, Livy. I'm so damned sorry for the things I said last night. For not giving you the benefit of the doubt. I knew. I knew that wasn't who you were. What you were capable of. I never should have made those assumptions about you. I don't know what the hell I was thinking. I'm so sorry, Livy. So damned sorry. I wish I could take it all back."

Emotion swelled in Livy's chest. His apology warmed her, but she wasn't exactly without guilt, either. They'd both made some boneheaded mistakes. And whereas Nick's had spanned the course of a week or two, Livy's had spanned years.

"I shouldn't have lied to you, Nick. Especially after . . ." She averted her gaze, unwilling to meet the open intensity in his. She cleared her throat. "After everything that happened between us. I should have trusted you. I'm sorry."

"Jesus, Livy," Nick said on a breath. "There's *nothing* for you to be sorry for. Do you understand? Don't apologize. For anything."

He took a couple of tentative steps until he stood

next to the bed. Livy brought her eyes up and her attention landed on the badge that hung from a chain on his neck. The five-pointed star reminded her of Captain America's shield. Pretty fitting, actually. Nick was certainly a superhero. If he hadn't been there last night, she would have died. She'd been so stupid to think she could go it alone. No one was an island, especially her. She meant what she'd said. She should have trusted him sooner with the truth. Nick wasn't simply a good man. He was the best man Livy had ever known. He'd followed through on his promise to her. He hadn't let her down.

Livy lifted her right arm. "After the conversation I just had with Deputy Morgan, I'm surprised I'm not cuffed to the bed."

Nick's gaze darkened. They both knew there would be repercussions for her actions. "It's not as bad as you think." The gentleness of his voice did more to warm her than the pile of heated blankets currently trapping her to the bed. "You fled the scene of a crime. You technically obstructed justice. Hardly anything that'll land you in a super-max."

Livy cringed. She was so ashamed of her decisions, especially now that Nick knew the truth. "What about my dad?" she asked. "Do you think they all still believe I helped Joel kill him?"

Nick took her hand in his. The temperature of his skin was surface-of-the-sun hot against her *almost* frostbitten skin but she refused to pull away.

His touch was the most comforting thing she'd ever experienced.

"I know you had nothing to do with it," Nick replied. "I'm sure Morgan does too. Now that everything is in the open, I doubt anyone is going to recommend that charges be pressed against you."

"What about the obstruction and fleeing the scene? They can't let that slide." Livy looked away, embarrassed. "I was a fugitive for four years."

Nick gave a gentle laugh that caused Livy's stomach to do a backflip. "Meecum was a fugitive. You were a scared woman who made a decision to hide in order to protect herself."

"Still, I have to be held accountable. Right?"

"You forget that you have a pretty big bargaining chip, Livy."

"I do? What?"

"You have the ledger."

She did have the ledger. But was it enough for her to be forgiven? Turning over the ledger would certainly help, but it wouldn't end there. "Joel doesn't just go to jail and that's the end of it, though. There has to be a trial." She inhaled a deep breath and the dry, cool air caused her lungs to ache. "I'll have to testify."

Nick's eyes darkened and his expression became grim. "Yeah. You will."

She'd thought her life had been lonely and full of fear before? It was only going to get worse from here. Livy knew what happened to people like her. Joel would try to have her killed before the trial. And to remain safe, she'd have to go back into hiding.

"I don't know if I can keep doing this, Nick," Livy whispered. "I'm not sure I have it in me."

Another new identity? Another city? Another life? She couldn't do it again. Couldn't isolate herself. Hell, she didn't know if she could live another hour, let alone a day, without the man standing beside her bed. "Do you want to know what the worst part of all of this is, Nick?"

He gave her a questioning look.

Livy swallowed against the emotion that rose in her throat. Damn it, she didn't want to cry because she needed to get this out. "I hated it when I had to come clean with being Kari because that's not who I wanted to be. I don't ever want to be her again. Livy is so much better."

Nick studied her with his deep, expressive eyes. His hand twitched as though he'd thought to reach out for her but changed his mind. "Why is Livy better?" he asked, low.

She took a deep breath and a fresh round of icy chills danced over her skin, but whether from the hypothermia or her own fear, she didn't know. "Because Livy had you."

It had taken an hour for Nick to stop shaking after Livy passed out in the snow. Another hour of worry while they warmed her up and stabilized her heart rate. His stomach felt as though it had no lining left and exhaustion pulled at his limbs. After making sure the local sheriff's deputies knew exactly what sort of criminals they were taking to the county jail, Nick had met Morgan at the tiny city airport and filled him in on what had happened so he could bump up the timetable and get a few more deputy marshals to McCall to transfer Meecum and the surviving members of his crew ASAP. He'd filled him in on the situation with Livy and hoped that he'd done enough to convince his colleague that she shouldn't be taken into custody. Then, Nick had waited. Waited beside Livy's bed, his heart shredded in his chest, as he faced the realization that he was so fucking in love with her that he didn't think he could live another second without her.

So much for keeping this investigation professional.

He might be new to the job, but Nick wasn't without connections. He'd do whatever in the hell was within his power to help her. Livy was a victim. Period. He'd plead her case to anyone who would listen until they were all convinced as well.

"You've been through a lot." Nick felt like a broken record. The words he wanted to say stuck at the back of his throat and refused to come out. "But I promise you it's all going to be uphill from here."

Livy wouldn't meet his gaze. She'd told him she loved him before she passed out. Reaffirmed it in so many words just now. She'd bared herself to him and Nick was beating around the bush like a pussy. Livy was the strongest person he'd ever met and she deserved more than what his chickenshit ass was giving her right now.

"I don't care what name you want to go by," Nick

said. "I didn't fall in love with a name. I fell in love with *you*."

As Livy brought her face up to look at him, her bright hazel eyes shone with emotion. "You love me?"

"I am *so* in love with you." Nick bent over her and stroked his fingers gently over her temple. "I love every single thing about you."

Tears pooled in her eyes. "You don't know anything about me."

"I know what matters. I know that you're funny, sexy . . . loyal. I know that you make great spaghetti and love winter. You're kind. Caring. You tie me into knots and make my heart beat so fast I feel like it's going to burst out of my chest. There isn't a minute of the day that I'm not thinking about how beautiful you are, how smart. How determined. And you can swing a shovel like a boss."

"The credit goes to Frank Junior," Livy said with a wry smile. "He's a legit crime fighter."

Nick laughed. She was one of a kind and he wasn't ever going to let her go. "I love you, Livy. I love you so much it hurts."

"Love isn't supposed to hurt," she whispered.

"It hurts in a good way," Nick replied. "In a way that makes me feel alive."

"For years I've told myself that alone was better than dead," Livy said. "That the pain of loneliness was worth protecting myself."

"Do you still believe that?"

She reached up and cupped Nick's cheek with her right palm. Her thumb brushed over his skin. Her touch held on to the chill and a wave of worry rolled over him. If anything ever happened to her, it would kill him. He'd spend the rest of his life making sure that no one ever hurt her, ever let her down again.

"I stopped believing that the day you pushed my car out of a snowdrift," she replied. "I love you, Nick."

"You love me?" Hearing those words from her again only made Nick want to hear them more. A daily—no hourly—affirmation that he couldn't get enough of. "I thought maybe when you said it earlier, it was the hypothermia talking."

"No way. I knew exactly what I was talking about. You're the best man I've even known, Nick."

His chest ached with an excess of emotion. He hadn't been kidding when he said he loved her so much it hurt.

"What now?" Livy's tone once again became serious. She clutched the blankets around her as a slight shiver possessed her.

Hell if he knew. Nick was as uncertain of the future as Livy. Metcalf wasn't going to let him off with a slap on the wrist, plus there was the added complication of being involved with a witness in an open investigation. Those weren't even the worst of Nick's worries, however. There would be a possibility that Livy would be placed in WITSEC.

"Now, we worry about you getting back to one hundred percent. After that, you'll tell your story." Anxiety pinched Livy's expression and Nick added, "I'll be there with you. Every step of the way."

"You can't stay here with me." Livy's voice cracked

with emotion. "You have to go back to your life, Nick. I can't be the reason you're held back—or worse."

"I've got a week left of my mandatory vacation," Nick remarked. "I'm not going *anywhere*."

"What happens when the week is over?" Livy murmured. "We can't go back to living the lie no matter how much we both want to."

Nick wasn't interested in living a lie. "Do you have any other deep, dark secrets you're keeping?"

Livy frowned. "No."

"Then I don't see a problem here."

"How about the fact that you could lose your job?" Livy asked. "I don't know a lot about the Marshals Service, but I'm willing to bet that taking a suspect—or a witness—to bed isn't rewarded with a pat on the back and an 'atta-boy!'"

Nick knew what she was trying to do and he wouldn't let her. "You're not pushing me away. I don't care what you say. I want you. I'm not scared."

"You want Livy," she whispered.

"I want Livy, Kari, or whatever the hell else you want to call yourself." Nick braced his arm on the opposite railing and met her look for look. "And you want me, too."

"It doesn't matter what I want," she said. "You said it yourself, I'll have to spill my guts to cops and marshals for days. After that, I'll have to testify in Joel's trial. I know what you guys are famous for: witness protection. I'll be back in hiding the second I'm done telling my story. I won't make you wait around for me while I'm hiding out. It wouldn't be fair to either of us."

"There are ways around that." She could talk until she was blue in the face, it didn't matter.

"I want to live near a ski area," she said. "Not a small hill like Stevens Pass. I want world-class. I wouldn't expect you to give up the job and life you've made for yourself because I'm selfish and stubborn."

"The last thing you are is selfish," Nick remarked. "But you might be the most stubborn woman I've ever met. I don't give a single shit where I live. As for my job, this might shock you, but there are offices in districts all over the country. I can work anywhere and still do what I want to do. You want to work near a world-class ski resort? Say the word. I'll pack up my shit and move. Because nothing"—he leaned in until their lips nearly touched—"*nothing* means more to me than you. Arresting Meecum was supposed to be the big feather in my cap. A win that would enable me to write my own ticket. And do you know what I felt when I cuffed him? Nothing but rage that he'd hurt you. I didn't care about the win. All I care about is you."

"I want Frank Junior to live with us," she whispered. "Can you handle sharing me with him?"

God, he loved her quirkiness. Nick smiled. "I'm a man who's secure in his masculinity. Frank Junior doesn't threaten me. Besides, I owe him one."

Livy's smile grew from sheepish to blindingly brilliant.

She'd been through so much and not only tonight. Nick realized that she was afraid to trust. Afraid to let go. She'd been hurt over and again. She pushed Nick away because she was used to being left. Aside from her mother, she'd always been alone. "I'm not leaving you, Livy," he said. "I told you I wouldn't let you down and I meant it. I'm not going *anywhere.*" Nick would make sure that she didn't have to go through anything else alone. He'd be there for her no matter what. Whatever happened after tonight, they'd deal with it together.

"I love you, Livy." Nick couldn't say it enough. Would never get tired of telling her.

Her eyes pooled with tears and joy lit her face. "I love you, too."

He kissed her gently. When he pulled away Livy's expression shone with mischief and a smile tugged at her lips.

"What?"

"You do realize that I'm going to have to teach you to ski, right? By the time I'm through with you, you'll be shredding pow with the pros."

Nick quirked a brow. His own silly smile couldn't be quelled. Goddamn. He loved her so much. "Pow? Is that like going ham?"

Livy's lighthearted laughter was the sweetest music to his ears. "No," she said. "But you'll catch on."

"You'll have to go easy on me," he replied. "I know I told you I skied when I was a kid but the truth is, I quit after the first run because I was tired of falling."

"That's because you never had me as a teacher," Livy said with pride. "We'll start with pizza wedges and French fries, and go from there."

"I don't understand a word you're saying, but I can take whatever you throw at me."

Livy's expression became serious. "Are you sure, Nick? Are you sure you're ready for this? For me?"

She'd been alone for so long. Had lived her life with so little love. Nick would spend every day of the rest of his life making sure she knew how much he cared. How much he loved her. He put his mouth to hers, a gentle kiss that ended far too quickly. When he pulled away, Nick smiled.

"Try me."

Love the U.S. Marshals?
Keep an eye out for

LOCKED AND LOADED,

the latest in Mandy Baxter's series,
available in Fall, 2016
from Zebra Books.